World Wonders

Silas Memoir, no. 1

James Perrone

Dedication and Legal

With thanks to my beta readers and editors:

Matthew Sikes, Michael D'Ambrosio, and Anthony Emerson

You all gave me the courage to both finish and put this out there. Thanks.

Prologue: A Late Night Out

Craig Masters simultaneously loved and hated his job. As a dentist that catered to the average nine-to-fiver, he got awesome pay and benefits. Enough to provide him with a comfortable life and have enough disposable income that he could indulge. And so, he did, in things like going out every weekend with his friends, drinking to the wee hours of the morning. Or a pricey '74 Mustang that he worked on in the winter and showed it off in the summer.

It also meant that he worked Evenings, Saturdays, and Sundays most weeks and his "weekends" were actually Tuesday and Wednesdays. Craig blamed that for his abysmal dating life and, if he was being perfectly honest, why he spent so much time drinking. Nothing else really to do on a Monday night besides watch football and drink.

Which is how Craig found himself staggering out of a bar in the Little Village around 5:30 am on a Tuesday in August. The sky was just beginning to lighten in anticipation of the morning sun, but the clouds were still thick enough to provide a light drizzle. Even though sunrise was a good half-hour away, the pre-dawn glow and streetlights burned his eyes. Already, he could hear the city coming alive with the early risers and commuters. A trickle of people here and there moved through his vision, but he paid them little attention. For now, his struggle was walking straight. His hand traced the wall, pushing on it every so often to stop him from slamming into it. He was making good progress when he ran into a dumpster, causing it to echo hollowly.

His addled mind didn't register the pain, which was a notable blessing. However, it also didn't have a solution to navigating the metal bin without collapsing. While he tried to pull through the fog of alcohol and to activate his problem-solving skills, he realized he was breathing heavily. "That's odd," he thought. All attempts to transverse the garbage bin stopped as what few brain cells were working attempted to figure out that conundrum.

"You smell delicious," rumbled a voice behind him.

Craig turned, and miraculously didn't fall over. The man standing there was dressed in a flannel shirt had an odd look on his face. Craig was staring at his impressive beard and then looked up to see his eyes. "Oh, he's the one breathing heavily," his brain finally realized. There was something else wrong with the situation, but he hadn't put his finger on it yet. He stalled for time, as eloquently as he could.

"Mrgg???"

Pure beauty there.

"I said, you smell delicious. Like beer battered cod, you've been marinating in alcohol all night. If you taste half as good as you smell, I'm in for a treat."

Fear started seeping through the alcohol buzz as what the bearded man was talking about started to creep in. "I'm not food," Craig thought, without any real comprehension of why that was disturbing. Still, he decided to leave the odd man behind and get away from the vague discomfort he felt.

Apparently, the odd man took offense at that and suddenly Craig was flying through the air. He cleared the dumpster and crashed into the brick wall, face first. Adrenaline started pumping, and the haze started to clear. The vague discomfort turned into realized fear. This man was threatening to eat him and was strong enough to toss him like a rag doll. The fear took control and decided the best course of action was running.

Unfortunately, that plan was stopped by the dumpster flying over Craig's head and landing with a thud ahead of him, blocking the alley. Craig scrambled forward and tried to push against the dumpster to no avail. He couldn't get it to move. Climbing was the only option, but by the time Craig had committed to that, the man had closed the distance with methodical and heavy footsteps and grabbed Craig's shoulder from behind. Craig tried to squirm out and flee, but the hand just grabbed and squeezed. There was an odd pressure, like only his shoulder was underwater, and then he felt his collar bone crumple. The pain nearly knocked Craig out and all thoughts of running were replaced with the screams of, "OH FUCK MY SHOULDER! YOU BROKE MY FUCKING SHOULDER!"

The man smiled and whispered, in a sickenly honied voice that possibly was meant to be soothing, but just caused Craig to shudder, which in turn caused spikes of pain to radiate from his crushed shoulder, "Shhh, it'll be okay." Craig could only whimper.

Out of the corner of his eye, Craig saw the man's right-hand reach forward, nails first. The nails settled on his chest unevenly causing minor discomfort as they started twisting back and forth, digging into his chest. Methodically, the hand twisted. Craig's shirt, and then his skin, tore away at the relentless grind of the nails, blood welling up from the gouges, soaking his shirt and causing the nails to glisten in the pre-dawn glow. Craig whimpered in pain and tried to squirm again, but only succeeding in causing the pulp that was his shoulder to grind against the crushing grip and send a crippling wave of pain that nearly caused him to black out.

The man's sickenly honied voice was in his ear suddenly, dragging Craig back from sweet unconsciousness, "I do like it when you struggle. Scream for me?"

The man accompanied the request by shoving his hands, nails first, through what little skin remained and into the muscles beneath. There was but a moment where Craig's rib cage resisted before they popped aside. Twice in ten seconds his metric for pain had been redefined. Craig screamed wordlessly until eventually he passed out and saw no more.

Chapter 1: Home Again

As I dropped my keys the third time, I had to restrain myself from just blowing the apartment door off its hinges. I just spent the past 96 hours in Keane County Alabama doing a massive divisional training and update of all the MCD[1] Marshals.

For most, that was informational about the newest strains of lycanthropy that had popped up in New Mexico, how to use the new ARCHIVIST system, some nominal time on the firing range, and reviewing tactical hand signals. For Government EEPs[2] like myself and McCoy, it *also* meant running through our metahuman abilities and pushing our limits to keep our records in the ARCHIVIST system current for reasons ranging from 'Useful for understanding and assigning deputies' and "Building an action plan in case someone ever went rogue." And limit pushing included minimal sleep on a hard, military style cot, which I hated with a passion most wouldn't understand.[3]

As bad of an idea as sleeping on a cot was for my back, being up and moving generally resulted in more work and tests, so I at least pretended that I could sleep on the torture device that was their too-broken-for-the-military cot. As I stooped to pick up my keys, the mess of knots that had

---

[1] Officially: Metahuman Control Division. Unofficially, Mayan Calendar Dipshits. We're a colorful bunch.

[2] Officially: Empowered and Employed Persons. Unofficially, the things that makes Homeland security go "EEP!"

[3] The cots were one of the most prominent reasons I actually studied for the ASVAB when I got into the military. A lifetime of camping and living on military bases had already turned me off the idea. Doing well on the ASVAB was what allowed me to be in the military without needing to sleep on a cot. Perks of speaking other languages.

previously been my back fought the motion, reaffirming that my choice to not be an infantry man was the right one. Regardless, four nights on a hellish cot, two midnight flights, and pushing all my physical and mental abilities to their limits had taken their toll.

I finally fumbled my key into the lock, turned it, and watched the door slide open. After the shock of having access to my apartment wore off, I stumbled in, took off my shoes, and started staggering to bed. I cursed when I realized the door was open and unlocked, and gas I turned around to fix the problem. My shoulder winced as I extended my right arm to close the door. Eckles had burned me in a training exercise and the new skin I had grown back came in tight, like it always did. It'd be a few days before I had full motion again, but it sure beat the months anyone else would spend in the hospital. Wincing at my painful reminder, I closed the door and continued the shuffle to the bedroom. I was so tired that by the time I got to my room, I had only managed to get my shirt off. My pants button had proved to be difficult.

Tired and weary, I decided that I could just sleep in my pants. That particular struggle just wasn't worth it, and just fell into bed face first. My pillow caught my face, and I fell in love immediately. It was soft and comforting, unlike anything I had seen in my past few days. I cuddled the pillow like a long-distance girlfriend I hadn't seen in months. I considered showing my appreciation in more physical ways, but I was too exhausted to do so. For now, I would settle for sticking my head to it for the foreseeable future until we had melded together. And then tomorrow, I would reconsider. Kissing such a wonderful and supporting device only seemed appropriate. But for now, sweet cuddles and facetime with my pillow. It was going to be glorious and….

And my phone was ringing.

I resisted the urge to smash it into a fine powder and congratulated myself on my impressive show of restraint. All I needed to do was turn it off and execute my plans for an all-night, rapidly expanding into all day now, cuddle fest with my pillow. I picked my phone up to turn it off but paused when I saw who was calling.

Fucking Slate.

Against my own self-preservation and sanity, I answered the call from my boss.

"I just got home Slate and it's my travel day off. Can't I just sleep?" I stated in something just this side of a whine. I imagined Slate's stone jaw face in something of a scowl. He always scowled. "I've read your file Tennant. Your powers mean you don't need to sleep. Hence, I'm calling you to cover since everyone else in the office is busy."[4]

I put my face into my feather-filled lover and muffled a scream. He was right. I didn't need to sleep. My current record was somewhere around two months without even any adverse effects besides a slight uptick in my weight and caloric intake.

However, not needing and not wanting were completely different things. Ever since the Mayan Event, sleep for me was something like four times as effective than it was for the average man. A two-hour nap got me as much energy and

---

[4] What he really meant was, "You're the only one of the three people who went to Keane County who'd actually take the phone call and who I can leverage into coming in on your day off." McCoy was probably at the bottom of a very large bottle and no one knew what Carlson did on his days off. Probably something I didn't want to know about.

refreshment as a full night's rest did for most people. Between the impressive knot and the freshly regenerated skin, I needed the recovery. Not that my boss would care about such personal appeals like that, having long ago traded the stick in his ass for steel rebar. Which meant I needed a different approach. I racked my brain, searching for any excuse to stay home.

Wait, I had just been at a mandatory training and the federal government hated paying overtime. "Sir, I'm scheduled to have the next three days off so I'm not straining the budg ..."

"Tennant, we have a corpse whose heart has been ripped out of its chest and you are literally the only person I can count on to actually make it there in a reasonable timeframe. So, stop pretending you're worried about the budget and get to 24th and Kedzie over in the Little Village. Cops are holding the scene for you."
There was the barest of pauses where I might've been able to rebut, but there was no point. I was already awake and the same pesky conscience that had me answering the phone wouldn't let me sleep with something that awful running around.

Taking my silence as acceptance, he continued, "Call me when you have something." I went to reply, but my affirmation was cut off by the click of him disconnecting.

Groaning, and knowing that I would hate myself, I dragged myself out of bed and staggered to the closet grabbing a fresh pair of socks and undershirt. I worked my way into those and snagged a fresh button down from my closet. Unfortunately, my standard motion of whipping the shirt on made the fresh skin on my arm to spasm as it was stretched farther than it was ready which then made me drop the shirt in pain. Gingerly, I bent to grab the dress shirt, back complaining the entire way.

Shirt in hand and cursing, I grabbed my holster and stomped towards the door, finishing dressing as I went.

This was going to be a long fucking day.

Chapter 2: Boots on the Ground

Slate had said that the victim had their heart had been ripped out. What he failed to mention was how the blood pooled had been splayed across the ground and the alley walls making a macabre Jackson Pollock. Or how the chest cavity had been pried open, rib shards decorating the ragged puncture wound which reminded me too much of Aliens for my own comfort. Or how the natural tendency for a corpse to void their bowels had blended with the Chicago back alley smell to make a horrid blend that made most violent crime scenes smell like a scented candle.

I wanted to barf, but I was too tired to deal with the fallout of my vomit being on a homicide victim, so I stuffed that urge back down and forced my brain into logic mode.

I stopped thinking of the body as a person and started thinking of it as a corpse. There wasn't a pried open chest cavity, the corpse had a puncture wound that was uneven, suggesting a ripping motion. And with the lack of obvious lacerations around the wound, claws and knives seemed increasingly unlikely. Still, forensics would need to confirm.

As my brain settled on the depersonalizing facts and observations, the mental patterns changed. Since it was a corpse, things were done to it not a him which made them far less nauseating, and my urge to vomit faded. Carefully, I continued to catalogue facts.

I looked back at the cavity, noting that there were jagged breaks on the few arteries. A ripping motion seemed most likely which suggested some amount of enhanced strength, though once again I'd have to wait for forensics to tell me how much.

Which took me to the elephant in the room, or more accurately missing from the room. The absent heart. Someone had gone full Temple of Doom on this body.[5] I glanced around. Even with the copious splatters and the large pool of blood, it would stand to reason that the heart would still have some blood in it. If our perp had walked off with the heart or stashed it nearby, there'd be some kind of trail. I glanced around, eyeing the dented dumpster that I had passed on my way in. It was unlikely that someone willing to go through the effort of ripping a heart out just to dump it. I'd have someone else toss the alley, just to be safe but doubted the search would go anywhere. Still, better safe than sorry. My eyes fell to the bloody hole and my brain whispered, "And we thought Indiana Jones had it bad."

Mistake.

Relating the corpse to a character personalized it again. I quickly looked away from the body, fighting the rising urge to vomit, forcing myself back into the rational and depersonalized mindset. No, it was worse than Harrison Ford ever had it. They had pulled out chunks of the ribcage and the better part of a pectoral to get to the heart. I looked around the scene. There were plenty of bone fragments, but no signs of the muscle. I added it to the list of things to be found in the toss. Spiraling outward, my eyes settled deformed mess of blood that was the right shoulder. I took a second to center myself, dug deep, and woke up a sleeping part of my brain.

---

[5] I decided that holding my hand up and going "KA-LI-MA!, while good for my mental state, would not only be in bad taste, but possibly be something that Slate would deem worthy of discussing at a disciplinary hearing. And people said I would never grow up.

For most people empowered by the Mayan event, they got one power. Or one narrow band of powers that they could use in a variety of clever ways. Quinn Eckles, for instance could just spew out large swaths of fire whenever she wanted to. However, she'd also figured out how to suck the heat out of an area to make it super cold, or pump more into make it super-hot. Her personal favorite had very little to do with fire and everything to do with the rate at which her powers burned calories. Woman regularly got shuffled out of all you can eat buffets and *still* fit into her skinny jeans. Although, I got the impression that she would be just as comfortable at the weight her caloric intake would normally result in, she relished being able to inspire envy in every woman she met with both what she could eat and how little she had to work out to keep her figure.[6]

Back on point, most people got one. I won the lottery, so to speak, and got two.[7] My primary power is regeneration, resulting in a natural healing rate somewhere around twenty-five times faster than the average human. The second-degree burns Eckles gave me over the weekend were already fully healed instead of the three weeks it takes most

---

[6] Lindsey Niccols, one of the local medical examiners, was particularly frustrated by the unfairness of the situation and had the mistake of complaining about it in front of Quinn. Quinn, like the very best friends, had responded by ordering an extra large order of loaded nachos. For herself. There were days where I wondered if they were friends only the sheer virtue they hadn't managed to kill each other yet. Still, they both regularly showed up to conferences where we all hung out together.

[7] The most gifts granted to a single person anyone had heard about was a man by the name of Jacob Devalic who had publicly demonstrated five unique gifts in a bid to make metahumans more accepted. He's currently so far off the grid that some people aren't even sure he's alive or on the planet anymore. My money was some secret government lab.

people. Plus, no scar. This also meant that I didn't need to sleep as the things that trigger tiredness and repairs that require sleep are also apparently healed. I don't quite understand how that works, but the metahuman doctors with the Marshals tell me it's about as normal as any of this is.

The secondary power I developed was telekinesis. It took me a while to realize it and it's still rather tiring, but damn useful. Don't like a door, I can blow it off its hinges with enough thought and effort. Don't want to pick something up from the floor, just grab it, provided you're awake enough to think straight. Want to investigate a wound but don't want to touch the body or otherwise disturb the scene? Reach out with telekinetic fingers which are far more delicate than my physical hands could ever manage.

And that's what I did. I took a deep breath and reached out. The shoulder felt much like a moldy fruit. All squish and no resistance. Whatever had grabbed this corpse had pulverized the shoulder in doing so. Explained the lack of self-defense wounds. Too much pain and strength to fight against. The chest cavity had indents under the pooled blood that felt like knuckles, reaffirming the scooping and strength. And, the pocket still had what felt like a phone and wallet, which meant the murderer didn't care about money overly much and John Doe wouldn't be anonymous much longer. I pulled my feelers back in and came back to the world. Strong, unconcerned with material possessions, and, if the missing muscle was any indication, carnivorous.

My first thought was werewolf, but that was almost immediately shut down. Firstly, most werewolves don't hunt in the city like this.[8] Too many smells tend to offend the

---

[8] Outside of the Walkers. But they tended to keep to the Southside and as far as anyone I knew could prove, had never actually eaten

nose. Secondly, no claw marks. Thirdly, most werewolves eat more than just the heart. Despite all the blood, the body was just too intact. Plus, we'd probably see teeth marks somewhere from the eating. And fourth, and probably most damning, the new moon was last night. Historically, not the highest point of werewolf attacks.[9] I bit my lip, ran through my mental catalogue of spooky things that we had talked about at training or had popped up in the past five years again. No matches sprung to mind. Whatever this was, it wasn't something I or the US Marshals had run into.[10]

I took a few pictures with my phone and then walked over to the officer in charge. He was a younger male by the name of Mallory. Slightly short and with brown hair. "Officer."

He practically jumped and turned around. Bad set of nerves here. "Marshal Tennant. Sir. What can I do for you?"

I bit back a smile. One, it wasn't professional and two, it would only ruin the poor guy's day. "Only a Deputy, Officer.

---

anyone, tending to get their protein requirements from large amounts of steak. One of the perks of having second-gens instead of firsts in the city.

[9] The highest number of werewolf attacks were a day or two before the formally recognized full moon, not on it. Each moon phase lasted for around three days, generally one before and one after the one that shows up on your desk calendar. Every werewolf without the experience-granted restraint to hold themselves back shifted, leading to high occurrence rates of werewolf attacks. The following two nights only featured those with barely enough control to make it through the first night and those with an appetite that was unsatiated by one night of hunting. Or those who we didn't notice amongst the more impulsive attacks.

[10] I spent a lot of time in the ARCHIVIST catalogues by the simple virtue of not wanting to get blindsided by something I could've been prepared for. As they say in the military, "Proper preparation prevents poor performance."

Regardless, you said there was a witness. Can you give me a report on what she saw?"

The officer grimly shook his head, "Afraid I can't sir. Dispatcher received the call and said she only got through 'Thing eating someone' before there was a grunt and the line went dead. She was slumped against the wall when I came here. No blood, but a hell of a dent in the wall. She's already been shipped off to Saint Anthony's."

I nodded knowingly, but inwardly frustrated. Knowing that the attacker fled when the cops were called was useful information. It suggested someone who didn't want to deal with the cops, be it fear or the practical advantages of anonymity. Useful, but not as useful as an eyewitness report.

"I'm going to chase some leads, but this scene is clear. Make sure CSI looks around for the missing heart, but don't hold out hope for it showing up."

He nodded and I pulled out a card for him, "I'll talk to your superiors about getting our witness some protection. In the meantime, If you hear anything, I'd appreciate a call."

The officer nodded as he took my card. "Of course."

I smiled, encouragingly I hoped, and set off into the early morning. The only person I knew with a larger thumb on the crazy and oddities of the world than the US Marshals worked for the local FBI office.

So, I pulled out my phone and called my contact in the Chicago FBI.

Chapter 3: Old Friends

Miles, being a busy man, didn't answer his phone. So, I loaded up, and started heading towards the FBI building on the Near West Side[11] calling Miles' office en route. Instead of Miles picking up the phone, however, I was greeted by an angry and dismissive prick who wanted to know how I got this number. Apparently, Miles had stopped working for the FBI three months ago and the new guy was sick of people calling his new office. By the time I had convinced him I wasn't some kind of crank caller and had gotten information where Miles was, I was sitting in line to be checked into the secure FBI parking lot.

Frustratedly, I pulled out of the line, earning me several odd looks, before rerouting to the nearby University of Illinois. I punched in the number the prick had grudgingly given me, and got directed to a slightly bored sounding woman, his new secretary at the University. Instead of trying to set up the usual lunch date, with a trip to Serendipity for burgers and drinks that was half business half catching up, I pumped the woman for information.

The secretary jumped on the chance to gossip and filled me in. I tuned out the inane chatter and focused on the details. Apparently, he had been on a raid with a tac-team, ran into a couple of young vampires, and it had ended poorly.

"How poorly?" I asked, worry uncomfortably slinking into my voice.

The secretary's voice turned conspiratory "When he interviewed for the position," she confided, "He was on

---

[11] Or, more specifically, in the Medical District. But no one really pays attention to that.

crutches and missing a chunk of his left leg. Now, he's moving so well, you wouldn't believe that he had ever been crippled." There was a pause before she corrected herself, "Handicapped, I mean. Still, he doesn't let it phase him. When he walks, you can't even tell that he was ever hurt and it's clearly not affecting his research. He's working on it at all hours."

Hearing that, I immediately became suspicious. Encounters with vampires of any age usually ended in fatalities for normies like Miles.[12] Hearing he was already up and moving made me wonder if he had become some kind of metahuman now. Coupled with the fact that I wasn't told about it until now, and it made all the paranoia come out. I mean, a few months without talking wasn't unusual for Miles and me. We were good enough friends that we didn't sweat downtime, and both had busy enough schedules that regularly meeting up was a hassle. However, we weren't so distant that I expected his hospital stay to completely miss me.

I asked the nice lady where I could find Miles, and she helpfully gave me the building and room number of Miles' first class of the day along with the warning that campus might be a bit busy, with today being only the second day of classes.

Seven short minutes later, I parked, used one of the local maps to make my way across campus, and into an average sized lecture hall. I surveyed the room and picked a seat in

---

[12] A newly made vampire was generally three times as strong as your average man and twice as fast, at least. Couple that with the ability to shrug off bullets like they were spit wads and the fact that they hunger for blood but don't know how to get it without killing people, you could see how it was a bad day for anyone unprepared. Or, even the prepared.

the middle of the row, but towards the back of the hall. I wasn't the first to arrive, but I guarantee I was the only one there who wasn't there for class. The detective dress of slacks and a button down stood out amongst the swaths of shorts, polos, and occasional sweats. Even fifteen minutes early, the pile of knots that passed for my back, and still not having slept, I resisted the urge to catnap. Miles was my friend and I needed all the information I could get my hands on about this sudden change.[13] There enough crazy and spooky things out there that could've commandeered his body or compromised his mind that I didn't want to risk missing anything for a for a few z's.

Which meant that despite it being 1045 on a Tuesday morning, scanning every student who filled in the hall and mentally running through explanations for his spontaneous recovery. Vampires were mostly out, especially as young as Miles would be. They normally didn't get the sunlight resistance until they broke 150. Likewise, Alips, Ghouls, and the other things that go bump in the night. The lunar calendar said that most of the new moon creatures were out, they'd be too tuckered from the nights past to be teaching classes. Though, with the full moon so far off most of the furry options were still on the table. Werewolves healed fast regardless of how furry they were at the moment. Not a realistic option, mind you. Even this away from the full moon, most freshly turned were-creatures had poor impulse control

---

[13] Miles and I went way back. Our fathers had served on numerous army bases together, each looking to transfer with the other as a way of keeping their friendship alive, the new locations tolerable, and providing some sort of stability for their respective families. Our mothers were good friends, Miles and I were good friends and our sisters were good friends. The only odd ball was Miles' brother, who didn't have a corresponding pair in my family, but he had dated my sister at one point. It was one of those odd moments you wanted to cheer for and but also hated. Thankfully, it hadn't lasted long.

and I hadn't heard anything about mood swings from the gossipy secretary.

I carefully fingered the rings on my right hand, making sure they were in place while considering other options.[14] It was a bit late for a Mayan gift occurrence in Miles. Post Mayan empowering events were possible, but unlikely. And given the Keane Act's position on any event resulting in powers, Miles wouldn't be sitting pretty in a Bureau feeder classroom teaching classes. He would've been Section 13'd so hard and fast it would've made his head spin so the Feds could figure out if the process was replicable. I paused going through my mental list when I noticed a low murmur raising through the classroom and checked the clock. Miles was running about 12 minutes late at this point and the lecture room was full. Annoyed at myself for losing track of time, I pulled myself from my thoughts and started listening to the student's whispers. It involved a bit of leaning, some cursing, and a lot of curiosity about why they were whispering at all in a teacherless lecture hall.

Apparently, University policy was that if a teacher was 15 late, the students could leave, and the teacher would personally pay them back for their lost time. A few were hopeful for the refund, but most were frustrated at being stood up on the first day of this class.

---

[14] The only reason I wore rings back then was because they could be used as an early detection system for some supernaturals. Shake hands with a werewolf regardless of form while wearing a silver ring and they'll be marked with rashes. Cold Iron would do similar things for some faetouched. I tried to avoid relying on them since: One, you had to touch skin, putting you in arms reach of something that might be angry at being outed. Two, people with metal allergies would present a false positive. And three, more powerful supernaturals could either hide or suppress the responses. But sometimes that extra half second they provided was all the time you needed to keep you on this side of the grave.

I was mildly concerned, as Miles was generally a punctual person. Then again, Miles had never been exactly excited for "research projects." Given, or in spite of, the secretary's warning, I figured he'd be here any minute.

Sure enough, right around the time the impatient students were getting ready to leave the room, in sprinted Miles carrying a stack of papers almost as large as he was, his short black hair barely visible over the haphazard pile. He was dressed in denim jeans, a wrinkled polo shirt, and sports shoes, all several sizes too big which just made him look unhealthily thin. Not exactly what you'd expect a Doctorate to wear, let alone a teacher. He stumbled over the door frame, spilled the papers all over the floor and planted on his face.

Despite the slapstick of the moment and the barely restrained laughter of the students around me, all I could think was, "Huh, no crutches."

Quickly, he kneeled up and started gathering his papers into a haphazard stack while he began talking. About halfway through the sentence, he seemed to realize that his microphone wasn't on and paused his shuffling, dropping the papers once again, to turn it on. Immediately, feedback cut through the hall, and his voice uncertain and slightly shaky, "Ah… sorry about that. As I was saying, my name is Mr… sorry …. Dr. Cross and welcome to… uh…. Behavioral Analysis two-seven-five." He paused to stand up with the disorganized pile, talking as he went. "I apologize for my tardiness," he continued, "but the copy machine was slightly occupied when I went in there." He moved to the table at the front of the room and dropped the papers on it. Straightening his shirt unsubtly as he continued, "I don't have your syllabus on hand as I was already running late. Our topic for today is...." He stuttered, shuffled through his notes, and paused hand on a frayed yellow legal pad, he flipped through the pages, seemingly at random. "Where was it? I know I put it here somewhere?"

While he looked, I hazarded a glance around the room. The students were somewhere between disgust and shock at the state of someone who had literally written two of the textbooks the course had required them to purchase. A few had taken out notes and one was on his phone taking a video. Miles showed up clearly, his round face clearly flustered, which I both noticed and filed away for later,[15] before turning my attention back to Dr. Cross as he spoke again. "Ah!" he exclaimed, "Cognitive biases. Please take out a piece of paper that you won't mind turning in and something to write with."

He glanced over the room as students slowly started responding to his requests. If he noticed or cared about me, he certainly didn't show it. Following the classroom trend, I pulled out a notepad and pen, prepared to take notes.

The projector, seemingly unlike everything else in Miles' day, worked like a charm. A small bit of text showed up on screen.

"A man is under investigation for potential political candidacy. File states that he's a decorated war hero, vegetarian, doesn't smoke, infrequently is a social drinker, and has no extramarital affairs.

---

[15] The number of things that screw with cameras made them a wonderful spot check against some groups of metahumans. It wouldn't catch anything serious like a doppelganger, but it would totally identify a young vampire or someone using fae illusions.

1. Based on that description, would you vote for him?"

I smirked slightly, and put "No." After a few moments, 75 pairs of eyes looked up at Miles.

"Question 2," he said, face placid. "How about now?"

The slide wiped into an image of Adolf Hitler with the caption, "Political Candidate". A small swell of discomfort crept into the room as the students sheepishly changed their responses to no., I could even see two students trying to discreetly change their first answers.

"Question 3," Miles continued, this time showing the image of an attractive young blonde woman in a small-town cheerleader outfit, clearly posed on the bleachers for what was probably yearbook photos, "Would you want to be friends with this girl?" Immediately, a flurry of pencils wrote.

"Question 4," asked Miles showing the next slide, with cheerleader image adjacent with the wanted poster of the most wanted Necro-Terrorist in the world, Mary Morbid.[16] Frantically, students looked from image to image, trying to reconcile the innocence with mug shot next to it. You could

---

[16] Any person who used what were traditionally called Necromantic powers in a manner similar to a terrorist. Mary Morbid had raised the entirety of Kentucky Veterans Central Cemetery and marched them into Fort Knox where she killed and then raised a good chunk of the soldiers there, broke into the vault, stole two tonnes of gold, and then disappeared while her now unled zombies ravaged the Louisville suburbs for days. Four years later and she's still at the top of at least seven U.S. most wanted lists, 3 international lists, and others of lesser import as the second most deadly terrorist attack in world history, with a death toll of 1,252 people. Every agency in the US had shoot on sight orders. Officially for her and unofficially for anyone else who could raise the dead.

feel the tension as the discomfort turned from a creeping sensation to a cloying flood.

He waited for the disgust and resignation to take hold, before asking again, "How about now?" Once again, sheepish pens and pencils marked the page.

"Question 5," Miles offered, trying to hold back a smile, "Write down your first impressions of me. Don't hold back anything. It's part of the exercise."

I smirk slightly and start writing on the page, starting with the disclaimer, "NOTING THAT I KNOW THE SUBJECT AND THUS AM BOTH ADVANTAGED AND CLEARLY BIASED." The hall rapidly wrote, trying to redeem their seemingly poor judging of character with observational skills.

After about three minutes, he interrupted our silent scribing, "When you've finished translating your impressions to the sheet, go through and star any of them that are lacking evidence."

When the last pencil clicked down, he let the hidden smile shine through, and he began the lecture. "They often say that first impressions matter. And that's true. Research shows that even after interacting with people personally, your first impressions color how you interact with them, regardless of whether or not those impressions hold up. As potential Psychological profilers, it's your job to be able to recognize cognitive biases and check them against reality." I smirked, sat back, and learned.

****

1215 came, and Miles was just wrapping up the lecture, "Up here there are three areas for piles. The warmup activity goes in the first, then grab a syllabus from the second, and your homework from the third. Have a good day, I'll see you Thursday." I sat back as the mad dash for the exit began and looked around the room. The tension had faded away and notably, none of the students were laughing or disgusted now.

They all seemed rather happy, or at the very least content with the lesson. As the last person made dropped their paper off, I stood up and approached the desk, handing my scrap paper to Miles personally. He smirked slightly as he took it, "Tennant," he said as a way of greeting.

"Cross," I offered along with my right hand. His head cocked in curiosity as he carefully assessed the rings on my hand before firmly grasping it and giving me a prolonged shake. There was no screaming or tell-tale sizzling sound, so most of the cursed types were out. Still, something was off. I'd have to get him to bleed for me later to verify my suspicions[17], but for now, I was just happy I wouldn't have to worry about putting a bullet in his brainpan. Whatever his "research" was, it certainly was paying off. I immediately pulled him into a tight hug, "What the fuck happened man?"

He hugged me back before responding, voice muffled by my shoulder, "Life. We'll talk about it over a few beers."

I wasn't entirely happy with the response, but I knew that's as good as I was going to get right now. Plus, that response was so perfectly in character for Miles that I was willing to kick my paranoia to the curb. I gave a satisfied nod and he asked the obvious question.

---

[17] Bleeding eliminated about two-thirds of the abnormal types. Faeborn, for instance, tended to have translucent streaks in their blood while werewolves healed faster than they bled. All sorts of information could come out of a simple finger prick test.

"What are you so stuck on you came to me for advice?"

"Well, that was originally the plan. But I'd imagine being a teacher has granted you some more free time."

He scoffed, "Spoken like someone whose classroom experience ended with college."

I shrugged, conceding the point, "If you say so. Still, since you're officially badgeless it wouldn't be that hard to have you brought in on as a consultant. You could actually tag along this time instead of being remanded to desk duty and research."

He laughed, "Do private citizens get a check? Teacher salary is much thinner than what I was getting from the bureau."

"Do you take IOUs?"

"Only from you."

"Well, then yes. You get paid in IOUs"

He nodded, turning from joking to business as he neatened the stack of warm-up questions, "Right, so what's the case?"

I rolled my shoulders slightly, trying hard to keep details of the morning from resurfacing and knotting my stomach, "I've got something eating just the hearts of people and has super strength to boot. Any ideas before I dive ass first into the fire?"

He pursed his lips and nodded, "A few. We worried about running into this monster?"

27

"I don't know," I honestly responded, "But best to be prepared."

His voice turned skeptical "And what's in this for me again?"

"My continued well-being and a chance to catch up. Plus, a chance to pay back for abandoning me in basic AND not letting me know you were in the hospital." I adopted a mock pleading tone, "I spent five years arguing with Afghani Tribals about where it was appropriate to carry rifles and you don't even call me when you're knocked down?"

He looked genuinely hurt, before conceding, "That might almost be worth it," He turned away from me to stack his piles into a single larger pile, the ruffling disconcertingly loud in the empty lecture hall. That more than anything verified it was my Miles still rattling around in there. Man had one hell of a guilt complex. When he spoke again, his voice had turned formal, "Take it there are no Metas in the area that fit the bill."

I took his lead and moved past the tension that had filled the air. "None registered at least," I stated with a shake of my head.[18]

---

[18] This wasn't necessary entirely conclusive. While there was no mandatory requirement for registration. Rather than trying to force a registration requiring people to register and living through Marvel's Civil War, someone had a bright idea. Any metahuman, supernatural, or otherwise abnormal person could receive assistance from the government for dealing with their powers, provided they reached out and registered themselves for said assistance. People signed up hand over fist to join this system if it meant that they didn't accidentally blow holes in walls or crush door knobs. Or to get those repaired with government money when they inevitably happened. These programs often served as doorways to becoming an EEP for the government for people with

He pursed his lips in thought, "Not a ghoul I take it?"

I shook my head, "Nope. Operates during the day, or at least close enough to sunrise that most ghouls wouldn't risk it. Also ruled out most types of zombies and skinwalkers too. No one's going crazy and the drizzle would've stopped the animating effect."

Miles just nodded knowingly, "I figured as much based on you coming to me, but still good to ask. You got a lead you want me to take a look at?" I pulled my phone, loaded the recent pictures, and handed it to him.

His face turned sharp as he considered the images, but I could see the steel enter his spine and the wheels start spinning in thought.

"Fun times," he said handing back the phone, "Let me grab my fun bag and some spare ammo and let's go."

the right gifts, killing many birds with one stone.

Chapter 4: Information Gathering

Miles' "fun bag" was a large duffel bag with his ballistic vest, tactical harness, and a slew of customized firearms. When the second shotgun was pulled out of the bag, I raised my eyebrow as I looked at him in the rearview mirror.

"What?" he asked defensively cradling a shotgun that was almost as large as he was.

It wasn't the number of guns. I counted two shotguns, three handguns, and what looked like a subgun. I had grown up on military bases and around gun nuts. Number of guns owned hadn't surprised me in years. Granted, Miles had certainly upped his gun count since he got jumped, but I didn't blame him. Having a tool to fight off the bumps in the night probably was comforting.[19]

No, what was bothering me was the piece of artillery he had in his lap. I tilted my head slightly trying to get a better look in the back seat, not quite believing my eyes. "Is that a drum fed shotgun?"

"Well, yeah," he said confusedly as he started checking the weapon in question, "Not sure what the Marshals do, but FBI metahuman containment and engagement procedures dictate an automatic shotgun with a 20-round drum minimum for dealing with unknown threats. Figured I'd at least adhere

---

[19] Plus, a number of people had taken to faking abilities to get them out of dangerous situations. 'Playing wolf' had become so prevalent that the standard response to claims of abilities was to shoot first lest they come true.
Plus, the local gangbangers often respected force they could see, such as a gun, instead of the threat that may or may not come true.

to that if I'm watching your back." He hefted a drum covered in green tape," Do you think I should bring the silver slugs?"

I blinked rapidly and then sputtered, "What? How did you…" I took a breath to center myself, "No, in fact I don't think you should bring the shotgun at all."

He didn't even look up from his inspections, "Why not? It's legal, I have permits for it, and an open carry license."

It said something about me that not only was I not surprised but I had no problem with any of that. Still, I kept my eyes on the road as I responded, "And while as an officer of the law, I appreciate that. But as I can't, justify you being that heavily armed to morgue security you'll need to leave it in the car."

Officially, no one outside of local security forces were supposed to be armed in any government building. Anyone with the Marshals tended to get a pass at the morgue given the new and disturbing tendency for the dead to get themselves off the table. Only needed a single zombie scare to convince all but the most stringent of sticklers that some exceptions needed to be made.

No one wanted to deal with a vampire or zombie barehanded.

He glared at me through the rearview mirror. My hairs started to stand on end, and I shrugged sheepishly. "Look, I don't make the rules here. If it all goes sideways at the morgue, you can totally say 'I told you so'. For now, keep it low profile."

He seemed mollified at that, putting the shotgun back in the bag and pulling out a Beretta.

"This okay?" he asked me in the mirror.

I took a quick look and nodded, "All I'm bringing."

He nodded back at me and then went to work stripping out of his professor clothes and putting on his ballistic vest, changing topics as he suited up. As the shirt came up, I winced at the flash of ribs. He had always been skinny, but he looked particularly emaciated today. He had a tendency to forget to eat, which is why when we met up, I always made sure it was at a restaurant with a lot of food. Miles would stuff his bird stomach and then have leftovers for another meal.

Part of me wondered if his lack of height was due to his constant malnutrition. It had already sunken his eyes, paled his skin, and made his hair far stringier than it had any right to me. Keeping him at 5'6" when his father was nearly 6'6" would just one more blow from a lifetime of long hours and forgetting to eat. We had been using alarms to remind him for a while, but that hadn't exactly panned out. Still, it was relieving in the oddest of ways. This was the same man I had spent most of my life around, the emaciated body serving as a darkly humorous proof of identity. I shook my head as he started talking and focused on the situation at hand.

"So, you've already ruled out the werewolves and the standard fare," he said conversationally, "Let's talk abnormals. Merfolk?"

I glanced at the traffic around me and shrugged, "A bit far from the lake, but close enough to the river I could see it."

"Ghost?" he said, tightening the straps on his vest.

I shook my head, "Too many physical effects and again, too close to sunrise. Unless we've got a Revenant. But that seems unlikely. No goo at the scene indicating ectoplasmic residue."

Miles shook his head as he pulled his shirt back on over the body armor. If I didn't know better, I would've sworn he was just wearing a thick shirt. I'd need to get one of those I thought, as he continued the logic, "Could've dissipated. We'll file that away as an unlikely option for now though. Vampire? Either trying to frame another metahuman or a new breed."

I paused and considered that. Vampires, with all the myths about them, were just as diverse as humans when it came to weaknesses, requirements, and gifts. I wouldn't put it past the group that one of the bloodsuckers to have started eating flesh instead. "No idea. We could go up to Serendipity and ask around?"

He nodded, pulling his jacket and holster on. "Later," he offered. "The O'Dell's won't be up yet. The day staff will just refer us to them."

I shook my head, "You're out of the loop. Apparently, O'Dell, Cris that is, has started keeping daytime hours. Don't know if she's finally that old, or she's just been faking for a while."

I pulled my arm to the side as Miles crawled into the front seat, dressed and armed. "Faking," he said, "She's got an oddity in her speech pattern that puts her closer to the 1700's than she's ever admitted. Pops up when she's angry."

"Isn't she always angry?" I asked, carefully making a right turn.

"Facade. She's playing the bad cop to Jim's good." He said by way of explanation.

I turned and stared at him for a second. Miles was always really good at getting reads on people. Part of the reason why the FBI had poached him out of basic for their profiling division.[20] Still, the ability to get a read on vampires was a rare fucking gift. The entire group prided themselves on excellent poker faces and duplicity.

"Eyes front. Red light." Miles interrupted my thoughts. I slammed on the brakes just in time to avoid rear ending a flashy sports car. I shook my head and once the light changed, we moved on to the morgue.

****

The Cook County Morgue is possibly the simplest building on the planet. Seriously, the thing looked like someone took a solid square, sunk it half in the earth, chiseled out two floors of square row windows, and called it done. I thought it

---

[20] Since Miles and I had been friends before going into the military, we decided to go into the military together, looking to use the buddy system. It had failed spectacularly, with him getting poached by the FBI really early and me getting picked up for linguistics work. Neither of our fathers were happy with where we ended up. Dad wanted me to be an engineer, not a linguist and complained, mostly jokingly, that I never actually ended up in the military. Just spent five years in the sand on government dime. My retort generally involved disparaging remarks comparing him to a hammer that hit things until they worked. At which point mom would quip about how they should've spanked me more as a kid, and we'd all laugh. Miles's father Donovan, on the other hand, refused to talk about the service with Miles at all. Apparently, the idea of a son who worked with the spooks was too much of an insult to bear.

was a wonderful statement of how pragmatism still had a place in the world. Building was functional and plain, which warmed my heart. Miles shuddered nervously next to me in the August heat.

"Really? All the blood and gore in those photos, and a plain government building is what gives you the heebie jeebies?"

Miles glanced sideways at me, "Too much death stored in one place. Leaves a stink."

I cocked an eyebrow at him. Talking about mystical auras and feelings, and that Feng Shui stuff never would've come out of his mouth back in basic. I chalked it up to a near death experience and went to comment, but he had already started moving into the building. Things for later.

Three security checks and a gun argument later, we were armed and in the Vault. The Vault was a retrofit to the Cook County morgue to contain any bodies that were involved in supernatural or metahuman events on the odd chance they stood back up and started causing issues.[21] Officially, all

---

[21] After the Detroit Zombie outbreak in 2014, this was a standard practice. Thick doors, air-tight seals in the vents to allow complete suction of all gases and prevents anything that goes misty from escaping that way. State of the art fire extinguishing systems to help deal with the odd infernal ticker. And state of the art incinerators that would pump the entire floor full of purified oxygen and incinerate everything for four minutes straight to help deal with any regenerator or undead issues that couldn't be contained under conventional means. Great for dealing with problematic issues, but often at the cost of the lives of whoever was working there, which was why they had loosened up regulations on who could bring guns in.

It was argued that the death of one person in the vault was worth preventing another Detroit. Which is why being assigned to Vault duty was often considered an execution warrant. Still, anyone who

coroners were expected to work the Vault on a rotational basis. Practically, or at least in Chicago, there were two people who worked regular shifts down here. One day, one night, with people picking up the gaps. Not a lot of vacation time was signed off on for Vault workers. The day shift worker was Dr. Lindsey Niccols.

Lindsey is of average height for a woman, somewhere around 5'8". Her natural dirty blonde hair was generally up in a bun to keep it out of whatever corpse she was dissecting at the time, but when she let it down it framed her face beautifully and really drew attention to her sharp and discerning hazel eyes. You could tell her body was well toned and in shape even through the scrubs, as there wasn't any bulging and the scrubs looked particularly baggy. This was coupled and confirmed with my knowledge of her outside of work. We often attended the same conferences on supernaturals, the best way to stay up to date in a rapidly evolving world. And since she treated the conferences mostly as weekends off, she'd often go to the bars with us after the lectures were done.

She didn't drink much, but she certainly loved dancing and often pushed the tamer and more reserved[22] out onto the dance floor. She had a love for life that was often disturbingly contrasted with her understanding of how the human body would break under strain. It was a great deterrent to people who wouldn't take no for an answer, as she had once demonstrated in excruciating detail to a creepy drunk frat boy when we attended a conference at Arizona State.

---

worked in a vault had a sizable life insurance policy provided by the government as part of their hazard pay. Proof that not all politicians are completely horrid bottom feeders.
[22] Read: the unable to dance and nervous about that. Deeper read: McCoy, myself, and Danvers.

In case it wasn't obvious, I had a bit of a crush.

As Miles and I walked in, Lindsey was elbow deep in what looked like the splattered remains of a werewolf mid transformation. The wide-tread truck marks could see over the crushed remains of the legs. Lindsey acknowledged us as we walked in and pointed with her head towards the corner before continuing her autopsy.

I turned to Miles, politely tuning out what was going on over on the table. He turned from the spectacle to face me. "Alright, Lindsey said she had something important for us, so play nice."

Miles regarded me with a polite scorn and amusement, "Just because you want to hook up with her doesn't mean that I have to accommodate."

I shot him my best puppy dog eyes, but all he just shrugged noncommittally as Lindsey walked over. I turned and smiled wide, "Dr. Niccols, you said you had something interesting for me."

She smiled her plastic professional smile, raised an eyebrow, and cocked her head at Miles. I picked up the message, "Do I have to act for him?"[23] I simply shook my head.

---

[23] Some background there. From what I could tell, Lindsey's boss hated her for the simple reason that she was a woman and thus was unqualified for the workplace. Thus, he had stuck her in the Vault hoping that either she'd quit out of fear for her life or get roasted one day. Lindsey, who had delayed her graduation to get a metaphysical anatomy minor added to her degree, took this in stride. She wanted to be in the Vault anyways, so it was really a win for her. Less time with her boss, access to what she wanted to

Immediately, the smile dropped, and I could see the stress in her eyes. Apparently, it had been a busy week, and her eyes were dulled with tiredness and frustration. "Thank fucking God," was all she said as she walked back over to the freezers. I heard Miles chuckle under his breath as I followed her over.

"I finished with your body about an hour ago. Name is Craig Masters, 37. Dentist from North Lawndale." She began as she slid out the former Doe's tray and started pointing with a scalpel.

"Very few things that I'd imagine will surprise you Silas. Damage was done by something with beyond mortal strength. But that thing was largely human. Or at least humanoid. Indents and tearing suggest human like hand structure. Male, if I had to guess, given the width of the knuckle gouges." She moved her scalpel up to the shoulder, "Shoulder wound increases the probability of male, as the hand size that goes with these wounds place the perp's height somewhere around 6'2". Crushing motion indicates someone using a vise grip. Which given the amount of force it would take to not only break, but crush the humeral head like it has been, was suggests someone at minimum 30 times stronger than an average human. Given the ease this

---

do, and to top it off she filed a complaint with HR. The boss had wormed out of it and now spent every chance he had trying to catch her on regulations to get fired. Part of the reason why she didn't party outside of conferences. Ultimately, this meant there were two Lindsey's. The work-slash-professional-flawless-and-polite Lindsey who was boring but unfireable and the actual I-know-how-to-cut-all-your-vital-parts-and-hurt-you conference goer who I had a major crush on. The fact that she was able to keep the facade up so well only increased my respect for her. And the crush. But mostly the respect thing.

was done with, I'd guess that our perp is possibly stronger."

I let out a low whistle at that. On a good day, my full telekinetic kick was somewhere around 7500 newtons[24]. This man apparently could do at least double that. With crushing motion. Which meant if he got his hands on me there was about fuckall I could do. Note to self, don't get crushed to death. "That's a lot of info. Thanks Lindsey."

She audibly snorted, "Silas, please, I didn't call you down for that. I called you down for this," she said, pointing at the half-wolf corpse. "This is the worrying part." I cocked my head and followed her over to the corpse, sparing a glance over my shoulder at Miles who was curiously, but cautious not to disturb any work Lindsey had done, poking Master's body. I went to call out, but heard Lindsey snap some gloves on and decided I could ask him later. I turned just as she opened the half-wolf's cavity with a sickening squelching noise. Undeterred, she talked as she propped the cavity open.

"This thing came in a few nights back. I had already cut it up as best as I could and written my report, but policy says to hold them for a few days in case we need to use his saliva.[25] I wrote it off as an oddity at the time when I saw it, but seeing Mr. Masters got me thinking." She pried the chest

---

[24] Official government record had me at around 4000. So I held back. Sue me.

[25] Recent scientific breakthroughs had given us the Heisenholtz remedy to werewolf infections. Frederick Heisenholtz had figured out that if you could get the DNA from a werecreature that bit you 72 hours before the next full moon, it is possible to brew up a sort of antitoxin to counteract the lycanthropy "infection" and stop someone from turning. The things had something like a 42% success rate, which was astounding, but still a way to go to fully perfect. Federal government mandated that any werecreature's corpse had to be kept for one full lunar cycle in case it might save anyone.

39

flaps open revealing a cavity in the creature's chest. Where a heart should've been was a series of broken blood vessels. "I figured at the time it was part of an Alpha challenge and wrote as much in my report." I nodded along. Such things weren't unheard of, especially since some werewolf packs, mainly first-generation, believed that eating the heart of another gave you the consumed's strength.

I'd imagine with that report, the investigation hadn't gone much farther. Even though the official marshal policy was to investigate any homicide that might involve an EEP, werewolf pack disputes often mysteriously found their way to the bottoms of paperwork stacks. No one wanted to deal with a group 300 pounds of fangs, claws, and fury that regenerated and responded to police investigations with violence. "But after poking around a bit more, I found similar scooping indents in this one's chest. And, the knuckle width matches."

"Fuck me sideways," is what I thought. But, not wanting to look like an idiot in front of the pretty woman, I instead said, "So, whatever did this is also tough enough to slug it out with a werewolf." I paused and looked at the tire marks, "Or at least smart enough to play dirty."

Lindsey shook her head, "Those are post-mortem. Near as I can tell, the werewolf survived getting its heart ripped out, but without the blood flowing started to revert. They managed to make it out to the overpass where they finally lost consciousness, passed out fell over the edge and into traffic. One eighteen-wheeler later, it ends up here.

"Are you fucking shitting me," I said aloud this time, decorum be damned. "Since when can a werewolf survive being literally heartless?"

If Lindsey was offended by my outburst, it didn't show. With a shrug and a wave of her hand in the direction of the corpse, she said, "Near as I can tell, they can't. At least not for long."

Razor wit to boot. Be still my beating heart.

"Which means that someone killed an Alpha," Miles said, suddenly behind me. "They're known to be stronger, tougher, and extra powered[26] compared to the average run of the mill werewolf." Lindsey just nodded looking slightly concerned herself. "I've written a report for you and sent a copy to Slate. Whatever this is, it's dangerous, scary, and resilient."

I bit my lip in thought, while Miles continued the train of thought. "And I guarantee the local werewolf packs are ready to tear someone up over this. Losing an Alpha always sets them on edge."[27]

---

[26] I.e. They had more odd gifts. Like surviving the plot to <u>Temple of Doom</u> apparently.

[27] That might just be the understatement of the year. San Antonio SWAT had kicked in the door on a believed gangbanger. When he resisted arrest, they shot him, which only pissed him off enough to go full on werewolf. Seven dead officers and 300 normal rounds later, the werewolf was down. Unfortunately for the San Antonio PD, the man they killed was the local Alpha. Seeking vengeance, his pack strolled into the San Antonio police station, went furry, and assaulted the station, killing nineteen other officers and maiming four before they were pushed back. The US MCD Marshals organized a massive manhunt for the members of the pack and to date have killed, since capture is damn near impossible, nine of the twelve perpetrators while suffering only four more casualties. I had been part of two of those raids and had been very grateful that I didn't need to test if advanced healing meant healing from werewolf infections yet. Officially, the werewolf community condemns the actions of the San Antonio pack, but wouldn't you just know that those last three have proven damn impossible to find. The werewolves may be carnivorous monstrous

"Fuck!" I cursed again. This is not how I wanted to spend my day off. Goddamn emergency protocols. Fucking Slate. Fucking werewolves and most importantly and relevantly, fucking werewolf killers.

I took a deep breath and centered myself. Lindsey looked concerned. Miles just looked bored, but I could tell that was a facade. He was not happy either but didn't want to show it, I could almost feel his unease in the air. "Okay, well then let's go find the local pack representatives and see what information we can get from them. At the very least telling them where their Alpha went might keep them off the streets and away from the innocent."

"And where is that?" asked Lindsey.

"I don't know," I responded, "But I know people that do."

___

bastards, but they're a tight knit family and gun to any of their heads, I guarantee every last one of them would've done the same if their Alpha was killed.

Chapter 5: Tension

I then proceeded to make two phone calls.

The first was to Jacob Danvers, our local IT guy and research specialist[28]. He answered the phone professionally and businesslike, "US Marshal's, Chicago's MCD Office, Tech Division. This is Jacob Danvers, how may I help you?"

"Jakey boy!" I said as unprofessionally as I could.[29] I could imagine Jake smiling on the other end. I even thought I heard a laugh. "I need some info if you can spare some time."

"Sure thing Silas," He spoke in clearly a lighter mood, "Hit me."

---

[28] Jacob was an EEP actually. Low grade technopath, which made his Google searches twice as efficient and his ability to troubleshoot tech difficulties almost legendary. This had made him the go-to guy for finding things out, which is why we kept him in the office as support staff instead of a proper deputy. Well that and the fact that he couldn't shoot straight.

[29] Jacob was also a horrific nerd in the worst way. The first conference we went to, instead of coming out to the bars with Lindsey, McCoy, and myself; he tried to stay in and Skype into a DnD session. I say try because once McCoy found out about those plans she made it her personal mission to teach the boy how to have a "proper good time." Which, in McCoy speak meant getting horrifically drunk and letting your inhibitions out into the wind. I didn't find out about how she had wrangled him until Jacob was at the bar and four shots in. Apparently McCoy had literally kicked in his hotel room door, stole his laptop, and stuffed it in her room, refusing to give it back until Jacob came out drinking with us. She then plied him with as much alcohol as she could handle, which was enough to reduce the poor kid to vomiting and left me to clean up the mess. He was extremely grateful for both the care and the fact that I didn't let any pictures be taken, and we've been friends ever since.

"Three things, in order of importance. Firstly, I need to know if either of the local pack's Alpha's are currently missing. We've got a body down at the morgue we're pretty sure is one of them and we need to let the wolves know asap before they think that we're trying to obfuscate the information, and thus in on it."

I could practically hear the color drain from Jacob's face as he fought every urge to wet his pants right there. Personally, the only reason I hadn't is because I was too sleep deprived and worried about Lindsey judging me. I wanted to say it was because I was made of tougher stuff, but I don't feel the need to lie. I gave him a second to process before I continued.

"Secondly, see who's in the area and free. I need back up at the morgue for when the pack comes in to ID the body. Some tempers might flare. Slate hasn't approved it yet, but I want to get that ball rolling before he does cause we'll need people ASAP. And thirdly, we're looking for something not yet documented that has enough strength and toughness to go toe to toe with werewolf and handily win. Key phrases: 'Eating hearts' and 'humanoid'. Current perp is probably male."

Miles tapped me on the shoulder and added, "Another key phrase: 'Ravenous hunger'."

I gave him my best bug-eye look and mouthed, "How?"

He pointed at the phone and then when I didn't relent, mouthed "Later."

"Also, Ravenous Hunger," I added after what must've seemed like a horridly bloated pause to Jake.

"Right. One list of horrific hungers of days gone by, fairy tales, and myths that now are reality coming right up," He said before pausing and adding, "The fact researching that list is the least scary of the three jobs is worrisome on its own."

"Oh, you're telling me Jakey boy," I said with a sad chuckle, "You're telling me."

My second phone call was to Slate. Jeremiah Slate was a man who sounded as rigid and unflappable as his name suggested. He was perpetually dressed in an ill-fitting suit that hung poorly on his athletic body. The man was a lead on the DEA's door kickers back in the 80's and 90's and still had the physique to match it despite the salt and pepper hair. He perpetually scowled and saw no reason that the fact half of the deputies he supervised could kill him with but a thought stop him from being the most terrifying person to work for ever. He had this uncanny knack for knowing your weak points, vices, and attempts to hide things from him. Which made him the perfect person to lead the local division. Specifically, it meant he could keep everyone in line, even Carlson who had authority issues. Couple that with his ability to pull blood from stone for our budget, making Chicago one of the most capable and best funded MCD's in the nation.[30]

---

[30] Officially, we were supposed to be very well funded. When the MCD was founded, the U.S. Marshals were supposed to double their budget to accommodate the new division and responsibilities. Unfortunately, how to pay for that increase had resulted in several government shutdowns and was always pushed off to future budgets. As such, we generally lived off the meager increase to funding the Marshals had received at creation and the scraps other Marshal offices could supply. The argument in Washington was the same one that had been raging on every budget complaint for years. The Dems wanted more taxes. The GOP wanted to cut money from anywhere that wasn't the military.

"What do you have for me Tennant?" he asked by way of introduction.

"A lot and nothing at the same time Sir," I said as I filled him in on my day. When I was done, I stayed on the line waiting patiently for him to consider the information.[31]

I didn't have to wait too long. Slate started rattling off our marching orders at a pace that wouldn't be out of place at boot camp, "I am dispatching four deputies to the morgue to back you up on the off chance the werewolves get violent.

Additionally, once I am done with this phone call, I will fill out the paperwork and have Marshal Wilcott sign off on deputizing Cross so that he can officially help you out.

Further, I'm officially waiving the State's right to hold the body. If the pack wants their dead Alpha, let them have it. Not worth a burn protocol over.

Regarding research, I'll see if we can't pull in Jennings to help Danver's do the archive trawl and contact my people

---

All the arguing meant that the MCD ran more like a task force than an actual section within the US Marshals, pulling resources and people in from where we could to supplement our meager supplies. Despite those struggles, Slate was able to not only extract our operating funds out of the Marshal's budget, but was also able to secure the regular donations from some wealthy business owners to help us out. I wasn't exactly sure if it was legal for Beretta to donate 75 handguns and 50,000 rounds of ammunition, but I wasn't complaining. Especially to Slate.

I mentioned he was scary, right?

[31] I was humming the "Bumblebee song" on loop. It was my personal hold music. Got stuck in my head 12 years ago and never got out. By this point, I had grown attached to it in the weirdest form of Stockholm syndrome ever.

abroad. When you're done at the Morgue, go over to Serendipity and see if the O'Dell's know anything. You're authorized to give out information that will end up in the papers within the week, but nothing case sensitive.

When you're done, report both what information you traded and received to me as soon as possible."

About what I expected. One of the nice things, possibly the only nice thing, about working for Slate is that he likes brevity, procedures, and protocols. Generally, that meant that I could guess his action plan before he put it in place. It was comforting in an odd way, but it made the deviations all the more shocking. I smiled and nodded, "Of course, Sir."

"Department briefing tomorrow at 9 am. See you there." And then he hung up on me.

****

Jake texted me the contact information we had on file for the two Chicagoland packs.[32] The city-based pack was a bunch of second-gen werewolves under Katelyn Walker. Thankfully, or frustratingly, they responded to our call immediately and offered to schedule a meeting with Katelyn for tomorrow. Good news, it wasn't her. Bad news, it wasn't her.[33]

---

[32] Werewolves are so territorial that most metropolitan areas don't have more than two packs. One pack for first-gen werewolves and one pack for second-gen. Smaller packs are either absorbed into a larger pack, run out of town, or killed off. There are a couple areas, Portland in particular, where there was only one werewolf pack. Those tend to be bloody affairs where one generation kills off the other. Werewolf generations do not know how to play nice with each other.

[33] Katelyn Walker was the heir to John Walker's Walker Incorporated, a series of investments and ties to the local unions, community groups, and associations that put them somewhere just

47

So, then I called our point of contact for the country-based pack.

Sydney "Syd" Larsson was an oddity for a Werewolf, let alone a first-gen one. First of all, she was the curator for the Burpee Museum of Natural History out in Rockford. First-gen werewolves were generally too feral for jobs. Sure, they were faster and stronger than a second-gener, but impulse control and moving past basic needs was not their forte.[34]

Secondly, while she was affiliated with the pack, I had never seen her with a pack member nearby. Most werewolves tended to move in, at the very least, pairs. Every time I met her, she was alone. Moving around alone occasionally

---

south of full on organized crime. If it wasn't for the fact that the Mayan Event made them turn furry once a month, the Walkers were well in line to become the next Daley's or Kennedy's. After the Event they started going the way of the Gambino's or the Bonanno. As a cynic, my response was largely, "What's the difference?" If someone had clipped Katelyn Walker it would take a lot of stress off the Chicago PD's Org Crime and VC units, provided the power vacuum could be handled graciously.

[34]Some terminology for a second. First generation Supernaturals, including werewolves, are things you see in movies and myths that were part of the long existing supernatural community prior to the Mayan Event. That community kept to the shadows and was largely kept out of the public's eye due to secrecy, our tendency to censor anything subtly weird, and our tendency to make conspiracy theorists into outcasts. Second generation supernaturals were those made by the Mayan Event. In many cases, second generation supernaturals were still faster and stronger than humans, but less so than first-gens.

However, almost to compensate, they picked up weird abilities not commonly associated with their mythos. Second-gen werewolves, for example, were able to use whatever mental state was appropriate for the situation, could fade out of existence, and were more likely to manage a job, which kept them off the radar.

happened with the second-gens, especially those who never found a pack to begin with.

But, first-gener's were all about the pack and that bond. For her to be out on her own was akin to blasphemy, which just convinced me that she was the exception that proves the rule. But probably most damning was the fact that she not only willingly gave her phone numbers to the police but answered when we called. First-geners had almost a pathological hatred for any outsider that attempted to impose order upon them, which included cops, priests, the government, all the way down to queueing lines. This issue was exacerbated by the fact that many first-gen supernaturals were forcibly dragged into the light by the fact that once the second-gen popped into existence we started paying attention to the conspiracy theorists and the weirdness censor went right out the window. This had caused a large amount of animosity particularly in the werewolf community. All that combined with the fact that Larsson was a point of contact for the police, gave me the impression she pissed someone off years ago and being a go between was her prolonged punishment.

"This is Syd Larsson, how may I help you?" she answered in a brusk yet clear voice.

I paused, considering my options one last time. Ultimately, I decided on honesty. "Hello Ms. Larsson, this Deputy Marshal Silas Tennant with the US Marshal's Metahuman Control Division. I have the body of a deceased werewolf who I have reason to believe was someone affiliated with your pack. Could you contact someone to come down to the Cook County Morgue to identify the body?"

I heard the faint clatter and crinkle as something was dropped and broken. When Larsson returned to the phone, her voice had dropped several octaves to something just short of a guttural howl. "I see. When did this body come in?" I bit my lip in concern.

Most first-gens tended to turn when they got scared or angry or really anything that got the adrenaline pumping. I didn't know where exactly Larsson was, but images of a suddenly furred monster tearing through the museum made me pause before answering.

I considered dancing around the question, but it'd probably only piss her off, which would definitely lead to a werewolf rampaging through a museum. I settled on a compromised truth. "Two nights back. We just finished doing DNA analysis which confirmed it wasn't a lone wolf." Technically speaking, I wasn't lying. Lindsey did just finish the DNA analysis, which told us that the werewolf wasn't in the ARCHIVIST system.[35] It's just that there was no way a lone wolf would show up in Chicago.[36] Larsson knew that. I knew that. Larsson probably

---

[35] Lone wolves had a slightly higher than average chance of registering for government aid in managing their powers since they couldn't rely on their pack to help them.

[36] Werewolves rarely, if ever, left their packs and became Lone Wolves, as the act somehow marked them as outsiders which caused a very large aggression response in pack wolves. This meant that any werewolf that either chose or was forced to become a Lone Wolf tried to stick to the unclaimed territories, cut off from anyone who might understand what they were going through, which lead to staggeringly high depression and suicide rate. Those who didn't off themselves, almost inevitably went to find a pack that was accepting of Lone Wolves. One was in Colorado, and the other was in the Northwest Territories Province, and both were founded by Lone Wolves who felt they were kicked out falsely. Apparently, the call of kinship and understanding won out in the long run. Interestingly, Werewolves who had never been part of a pack didn't provoke the same aggression response and had far better mental health. Jennings and Danvers had theorized about that for hours on end, but I'd be lying if I said I paid attention the entire time.

even knew I knew that. However, it was an excuse that allowed us to cover for not calling them sooner and gave the werewolves a reasonable explanation to not go all San Antonio on us.

Her voice, while still low, started to climb back up to human registers. "I see. Someone will be there in 40 minutes."

"Of course Ms. Larsson. Please remind your pack that we don't want any trouble and are fully willing to cooperate."

A sound that was somewhere between a bark and a laugh festered through the phone. "I think that will depend entirely on you, Deputy Tennant."

Before I could answer, there was a click as she hung up on me.[37] I settled down to prepare for the werewolves.

****

Thirty-eight very tense minutes later the werewolves arrived. The Marshal at the door radioed their arrival about two seconds after Miles started getting jumpy. I had tried to talk to him about all of his lifestyle changes and how he knew about the ravenous hunger during the wait, but he refused to talk around the cameras. It was mildly annoying, but understandable. Plus, I was too nervous about the thought of being up close with pissed off werewolves to really push.

A minute after the radio warning, a man and a woman swept into the room. Dressed and built like rural bar bouncers, tight jeans and leather vests. After a quick assessment of the room, the man went back out while the woman stared

---

[37] I was starting to get annoyed by everyone hanging up on me at this point, but couldn't think of a way to exact my vengeance upon those who had wronged me. Yet.

daggers at the four other Deputies in the room with me. Unfortunately for me, these were non-MCD Deputies, which meant push came to shove, it was ultimately our job to hold the vault long enough for the doors to lock and the burn protocols to go into effect. I wanted to blame Slate, but I really couldn't. If shit hit the fan, it was the right call and the seven of us in the room were worth keeping three First-gen werewolves from going on a killing spree in the middle of downtown Chicago.

However, it was my job to make sure things didn't go that bad. Tact was the order of the day.

That was immediately complicated by the sudden urge to run from the man the bouncer escorted back in. He was shorter than Miles, around 5'4" if I guessed correctly. Dressed in an unassuming pair of jeans and a tight white t-shirt that would've looked average at a distance, I would've dismissed him as just another dude. But up close, he had this haughty animalistic aura that screamed to the primal and prey part of my brain, "RUN YOU DUMB ASS! RUN!". I looked around the room and saw the rest of the Deputies looking similarly panicked. Lindsey and Miles were doing a better job of concealing their panic, but it was still there. The longer he stayed, the more amplified the effect got. I swallowed hard, fighting the panic down as the shot man caught my eye.

Smiling wolfishly, he walked right up to me and looked me straight in the eye. "Deputy Marshal Tennant, I presume. Thank you for placing the call. I'm Ipsen."

His voice was so rough and gravely that the hairs on my neck instantly stood up in fear. Some, foolish, part of my brain thought "This man could make a killing as a voice actor for villains." And my consciousness, looking for any excuse not to be afraid clutched onto the thought. It helped, but not nearly enough.

Still, it gave me enough clarity to realize that he had extended his hand to shake. His arms were oddly long but muscled to the point it could've easily been a Bowflex commercial. I finally found my wits and grabbed his hand, "Pleasure to meet you," I said before stopping myself from adding "Sir." My brain screamed that I was a horrific idiot for not taking my chance to run. I pointed over to the autopsy table. "This is the corpse we wanted to show you.

At that cue, Lindsey stepped forward and pulled the sheet off the half-wolf. The bouncer twins audibly gasped, but Ipsen just squeezed my hand a little harder and nodded before releasing to walk over. The moment he let go, I could feel my blood rush forward to return normal circulation accompanied by the annoying tingling sensation you get when your foot falls asleep. I shook my hand a few times as I walked over by him, careful not to distract his silent contemplation of the scene before him. Curiosity finally over road my panic and I took a careful look at him

He looked melancholic. I expected rage and frustration, at the very least a little anger. Distraught would've made sense. Instead, Ipsen looked like he was trying to comprehend this new emotion that he had never encountered before. And all that did was drive my run responses higher. Something was off with this guy. Well, more off than normal for a werewolf and it was seriously bugging me out.

Still, I couldn't bring myself to interrupt his contemplation. The silence was so intense, you could hear the clock tick. The fear and unease I felt only ratcheted up as time went on. I busied myself by counting the ticks.

After a few minutes that felt like an eternity, he turned to me. "I will confirm that this man was the former Alpha of our pack, Steven Hotchkiss. He went missing three nights back and we felt him slip from us two nights ago. It is my understanding that you need to hold him to the next new moon?" he said in an almost mechanically even tone that somehow still made my neck hairs do their freaked-out dance even harder.

I nodded numbly. Felt him slip? Did they already know he was dead? What the fuck was going on here?

"At the next new moon, Sibor," he said motioning at the male bouncer type, "Will come collect him for a funeral. Thank you for the phone call and your time."

And with that, he turned and walked out followed swiftly by his two flunkies. I just stared.

About a minute later, Lindsey finally broke the silence with a cough. I turned and finally noticed the rest of the deputies also looking at the door in nervous shock. That went well. Almost too well. I shook my head to recollect my thoughts and began to the deputies in the room, "Thank you for your time gentlemen, you are dismissed. Sorry to disrupt your day." They snapped out of their own shocked states and filtered out of the room.

After they had all left, I turned to Miles and Lindsey. "I don't know about you all, but I could use a drink."

Chapter 6: Serendipity

Serendipity was one of the best bars in town. I say this because not only was the food amazing, but also because it was relatively unknown to the people not in contact with Vampires in some shape, way, or form. Couple all that with the owners, and it was solidly at the top of most lists.

James "Jim" and Cristina "Cris" O'Dell were vampires, sure. But not only were they affable, they were also legal bloodsucking citizens. When the truth came out during the Mayan incident that vampires and other types of supernaturals existed, but had just been hiding, public consensus was torn. The O'Dells, and other enterprising vampires, very quickly went into business securing their place in society.

For the O'Dells that meant paying all their back taxes and spending more money than I could fathom on lobbying.[38] It helped that Jim had an American birth certificate (from 1893) and Cris had immigration papers (from 1872). Which meant that they came here legally and had never actually been legally declared dead, and that went a long way into

---

[38] As a Deputy Marshal, I wasn't exactly privy to tax records. What I was privy to was the Risk Assessment documents provided on every legal vampire and registered metahuman in the United States. The O'Dell's had paid 1.2 billion dollars in back taxes, through 1913 when the Income Tax was legally introduced, including their incomes from investment and return and interest on amounts unpaid and inflation adjustments effectively in cash as one lump sum. Apparently, they had set money aside for this very day. Even when the government waived those amounts after heavy legislation in hopes of encouraging other vampires to become legal citizens and get access to their income taxes going forward, the O'Dells didn't want it back. And that isn't including the amounts they spent on lobbying to be citizens. Conservative estimates of their net wealth put it around 20.2 billion dollars.

navigating the legal nightmare that was becoming citizens in the post-Mayan United States. Furthermore, they made a point that Serendipity was neutral ground and those who caused trouble here had to deal with Cris directly. She might look like an Italian supermodel, but I've seen her throw a 300-pound man literally out the door and across the street one handed. Pretty looks be damned, woman was strong and more dangerously, unlike your average supernatural heavy hitter, actually knew how to use that strength.

Couple that with their bar being pretty much exclusively the place where metahumans, humans, and supernaturals[39] could meet up and discuss things in a non-formal manner under the guise of getting dinner, which meant that many people liked both the bar and the O'Dells. So, ending up on the O'Dells shit list meant you probably ended up on the majority of the city's movers and shakers shit list. I personally loved it because it meant I could go be a person outside of being a Deputy Marshal. Miles liked it because he got to people watch people who were normally unwatchable.

We walked down the unobtrusive alley and into an unremarkable door, which lead us to the front room. Cynric Adel, the mountain of vampiric muscle who served as the bouncer, checked us over before letting us into the bar proper. A few people smiled and waved at me when I walked in while others paused their conversation while I walked by. I smiled and moved through the busy front room into the back. No need to hold people from doing business.

---

[39] Supernatural is a descriptor that vampires use to describe creatures and people that were around from before the event and is slowly being adopted. To date, this includes vampires and werewolves among other things. Unfortunately, that list is far from complete. It turns out even vampires and werewolves have their myths and legends.

The back was covered wall to wall in enough memorabilia and signatures from blues and rock legends that you could take all the decorations down and stock three different Hard Rock Cafe's with it. Jim had made friends all over the music world and signs of that could be seen on the wall. From a signed Chuck Berry guitar to one of Louis Armstrong's trumpets. It was a rather standard showing for a Tuesday night as Miles and I grabbed a seat at the bar and watched the man on the stage play.

Jim O'Dell was a slightly tall man, just short of six feet tall, but you couldn't really tell that as he stooped over his guitar tapping out a soulful and complex beat. The guitar was probably a century old but sounded perfectly in tune, and it had a twang that went well with Jim's subdued Irish brogue to make a wonderful harmony. Jim would tell anyone that asked, he was alive back when the Blues had come to Chicago and had met numerous big names, such as Alberta Adams, Lester Davenport, Bo Diddley, Otis Rush, and more.

If you listened to him play and sing, you wouldn't doubt it for a moment. Some people claimed that undeath killed your soul and creativity, but Jim O'Dell just laughed that idea off. He had put out an album the year prior that had revolutionized the Blues Industry and occasionally did shows down at the House of Blues. Since he didn't travel outside the city due to his "condition", those shows always drew in people from all over the world and sold out faster than you could blink. Those of us who knew where Serendipity was generally got free shows and appreciated every damn minute of it.[40]

---

[40] Near as I could tell, not a single cent from those shows ended up in either Cris or Jim's pockets. Jim donated the money to various charitable organizations. This past year alone he had raised 1.4 million dollars for Breast Cancer research. In an interview, he was asked why. He simply responded, "I love playing.

I unfortunately couldn't sit and enjoy his craftsmanship while I was on the clock. I passed a note to the bartender and a few minutes later, when Jim ended his set and left the stage, Miles and I were ushered into a small office. Jim was sitting behind a desk with Cris standing in the corner leaning on a filing cabinet.[41] Her face was blank, but she always radiated a slight aura of, 'I'm really unhappy to be here dealing with you, so don't waste my time.' Considering what Miles had said earlier about good and bad cops, I could see how that would work. Now all I wondered is how much of it was an act and how much of a misanthrope she actually was.

I took a breath to prepare for the verbal fencing match that was about to occur. Every vampire I have ever met acts as if every conversation is a way to both establish dominance and as if the meeting is being bugged, which meant there was far more implied than ever said.[42] Normally I'd have McCoy do this for me while I chased down other leads, since she had a

The simple joy of it. The fact that other people want to hear me do it is enough. But, they insist on giving me money for doing what I love. Money that, I quite honestly just don't need. So, I give it to someone who does and go on doing what makes me happy." I nearly vomited when I read it, given how saccharine it was. In my professional opinion, he was playing the nation for good PR and they were buying it. Disgusting how gullible some people can be sometimes. Doesn't stop me from enjoying the shows however. He really is a damn good musician.

[41] The O'Dells are frustrating to me on a personal, and very petty level. There are two of them, with the same last name and I need to distinguish between them which means I need to use their first names. It was a mental struggle with my military training and it made talking to vampires just that more stressful.

[42] Apparently, centuries of living in the shadows, playing a long game of politics, and the ability of some vampires to turn invisible had made paranoia, innuendo, and doublespeak a way of life. The fact that most sane people couldn't keep up was seen as a failing on their part by the larger vampiric society. Welcoming bunch, aren't they?

knack for this vampiric politics thing that I just couldn't fathom, but she was probably at the bottom of a bottle right now after the long weekend of sobriety. Jim smiled warmly and motioned to the seats, "Greetings, how might I help two fine gentlemen tonight?" he inquired in a voice that was smooth and gentle like the night tides on Lake Michigan. Translation: *I'm the person you will be talking to this evening until otherwise indicated. Am I talking to the US Marshals or private citizens?*[43]

"Good evening Mr. and Mrs. O'Dell. I am Deputy Marshal Silas Tennant and this is Deputy Marshal Dr. Miles Cross. We're here looking for some information about a case and were wondering if you would be willing to help us." Translation: *I recognize you as separate and equal powers. We're here on official business and people will notice if we go missing. I am the superior in this situation and you will address all questions and discussion to me. We need information and while we know that no formal payments will be exchanged, we are both ready and willing to exchange information for information.*

"Ah, of course Deputy Marshal. I am always ready to aid the US government. Tell me what are you looking into?" Translation: *I have acknowledged that you represent an authority greater than yourself and I am amenable to providing that information to that greater authority. Provided*

---

[43] Vampires made a huge thing about whether you were speaking for yourself or for a higher power. Jim could've hated my guts, but if I was here as an envoy of someone he respected or representing an office he held respect for, he wouldn't touch me. Vampires respected the office of a person even if they didn't respect the person, and it had started to rub off on those who worked with them, myself included. Personally, I thought it made a lot of sense. Had Donald Trump actually been elected president, I would've probably done the same thing.

you can demonstrate an ability to pay information that would be valuable to me.[44]

"Of course, Mr. O'Dell. We're investigating a local homicide that occurred last night in the local area. For mere formality sake, could you please tell me where you and your wife were all night?" *Something supernatural is killing people in the area. It's at least strong enough to rival you or Cris. I don't actually think it was you, so I'm asking for an alibi I'm sure you have.*

"I spent most of the night inside on stage. My bartender's would verify that, though if you'd prefer there are numerous guests who would place me here the entire night," he said before nodding at Cris. *I am intrigued. I, of course, have an alibi. I even have one that has sources you can trust. Cris is not under my thumb. I am not her superior, and thus she can speak for herself.*

Cris snorted before offering, "I spent most of the night bouncing the front door since Cynric had the night off. I can tell you everyone who came through that door if you really want to make something of this." Her voice tight and restrained, with a hint of an Italian accent from her decades long past. She was harder to read than Jim, but that might just be because I had trouble cutting through the menace surrounding her. Best Translation: *"I too have an alibi from relatively unbiased sources. Stop yanking our chain and get to business. I can crush you both physically and socially if you dance around too much."*

---

[44] Information and favors were the commodities of the vampiric world. I knew the O'Dells weren't at the top, but given the popularity of Serendipity and the amount of gossip here, I had to imagine they were somewhere close.

I smiled politely and continued, "Wonderful. I'll make sure to talk to some people before I leave, but I'm sure it will all work out. A humanoid creature has fought and killed at least two individuals in the city. He has done so by crushing their body parts to restrain them as he ripped through their chest until he was able to reach in and rip out their heart. The Marshal's office would be very grateful if you could help with any knowledge gained in your long existence about such a creature." *I don't doubt you, but for appearance sake I must verify your alibis. Here is the information I'm offering. There is a male supernatural serial killer with superhuman strength. He has enough strength to crush human bones and gains power from eating hearts. Have you ever had to deal with something like this or is it a new supernatural thing?"*

Jim pursed his lips, in a way that was just this side of theatrical. "I might have some information, but I'd hate to lead you astray. What else can you tell me so I can direct you in the right direction?" *I have information that could be useful, but you haven't paid me enough information. Give me more."*

Smile still affixed to my face I continued, "Of course. The creature is, at minimum, thirty times stronger than the average human. We also have the indication that this creature is supernaturally tough. He was able to duel and kill the former Alpha of the First-Gen werewolves in the area, Steven Hotchkiss. The corpse was confirmed by the new Alpha." *He's stronger and faster than a werewolf and probably you. Head on combat is not advised. More importantly and interestingly to you, one of the local power groups in the area are undergoing a leadership transition which you might be able to take advantage of.*

Jim's face went from expressive to blank. There was a full three seconds, an eternity in vampire politics, passed before he continued. "I see. I can think of a few possible options, but most have either gone extinct or are rare enough I find them unlikely. However, if my reading is right, this killer has only been working here a few days, I can point you in the direction of a group that this killer probably came from." The silence spoke volumes, so I chose to translate this as: *Are you kidding me? What the fuck? This is the kind of stuff that tends to make up myths and legends to myths and legends. However, I am not going to screw you. You paid me and thus I am obligated to pay you. However, I need some assurances this won't come back to me directly.*

I let my smile fade and nodded, "That would be greatly appreciated." *Of course, I can be discrete. Now pay up.*

Jim nodded, "Look into the Racine County Fairgrounds where the Moloch Menagerie Circus is performing. They've got a bit of a reputation for adding some realism to their exhibits. I'd suggest going tomorrow during the day. They're the only new group in town I know of." *There's a circus in town that has actual supernatural and metahumans in their show. There are vampires or other creatures of the night amongst their numbers, so it would be intelligent to wait until the morning. I stake my reputation as a knowledge broker that they brought your killer into town."*

I nodded, "Thank you Mr. O'Dell for your information. Thank you, Mrs. and Mr. O'Dell, for your time." *I consider this transaction complete and satisfactory. I acknowledge your excellence as being a knowledge broker and do not question your abilities. I am now requesting permission to leave.*

Jim smiled civilly, "Have a good evening Deputy Marshal and good luck in your investigation. We look forward to your next visit. "*I am also satisfied with this transaction. We will gladly do business with you and your superiors in the future. Permission to leave granted.”*

I stood and left, letting Miles get out the door first. Right before the door closed behind me, I heard Cris call out, “Good luck.”

I wasn't sure how to translate that.

Chapter 7: Traveling

The O'Dells' alibis, unsurprisingly, held up. No less than fifteen regulars confirmed they had spent last night at the bar. Cynric even confirmed he had the night off and provided us information so we could check his alibi too if necessary. I dutifully wrote it down and then left, filing it away for the unlikely event of needing to look into him. But that was a task for tomorrow. It was getting close to 2200 and Miles had to teach the next day. I pulled onto 90 heading towards Miles' condo in the Near West Side. Miles stared out the window as we drove, clearly exhausted. I bit my lip in thought, considering the day. Later had officially come, but I wasn't sure if I wanted to open that can of worms right now. Still, I needed to know. Softly, I asked.

"Miles, you've been awfully quiet about your new life choices. What's going on man?"

I saw him reluctantly pull away from the window and frown in thought. I gave him time to think as I maneuvered through the late-night drivers. We were exiting 90 before he finally spoke up.

"Shortly after the Mayan event I started getting hunches. Really good ones. At the time I thought it was simply being in the field long enough. Wasn't until my clear rate nearly tripled the department had me looked at. Turns out I had got low enough grade psychic abilities that they were missed in the chaos that winter was. Initial results suggested it was an unconscious form of precognition."

I couldn't help it, I winced. Precogs had an alarmingly high tendency towards depression, psychotic episodes, and strokes.[45] He nodded knowingly but moved past the twitch.

"Turned out to be a low-grade unconscious form of psychometry.[46] My hunches were reactions to my unconscious ability to pick up on the anger or fear someone was putting out. The FBI immediately shuffled me into their EEP division, which was not fun. Close quarters, lots of supervision, and treated like second rate citizens for a few years there. I didn't figure out why until about nine months ago. Psychics in close proximity to another create a resonating effect between the two psychics. A prevailing theory was that this resonance could either amplify psychic abilities. So, they took a group of us, manufactured a reason for us to be in close proximity by making us live in a barracks and watched."

---

[45] Precognitives were a major boon to the Physicists of the world as they pretty much verified that the many-worlds interpretation of quantum mechanics was actually correct. Your average precog saw snippets of the future. However, the farther in the future they attempted to see, the more possibilities they saw and the less likely the mind could handle it, leading to the aforementioned issues. The most successful precog in existence was the now deceased Warren Caravaugh. Warren was caught in a hostage situation and managed to take out all twenty-three hostage takers in a non-lethal manner while unarmed just by being able to find the perfect spot to be at any second to avoid any setbacks, from gunfire to broken glass. He then died from a massive brain hemorrhaging due to the amount of strain that put on his brain. The U.N. has officially banned any research into precognition with promise of heavy sanctions to any nation that defied the order. Smart money still said that any nation with a pocket book was doing that research on the lowdown. Precogs, if ever mastered in a meaningful way, would render nuclear weapons and most forms of conventional warfare obsolete. They would be, in theory, unstoppable. As if I didn't have enough to worry about.
[46] The formal definition of psychic abilities was long and mired in painful legal speak. Depending on who read it, my telekinesis was either absolutely psychic or not at all. My rule of thumb was: If you can feel something you couldn't before with your brain, it was psychic. Thus given my t.k.-fingers, I tended to say I was psychic.

I slammed on the brakes and ignored the frenzied honking of the people behind me. "You mean to tell me they figured out how to make powers stronger?"

Miles shook his head slightly, "Not really. The growth is small. Over the two years I was in the program, we saw a two-percent increase over the expected growth amounts from using the powers. The ultimately couldn't determine if that was from increased use or the collaboration." He shuddered despite the August heat, "Could you drive please? The anger of the people behind us is starting to get to me."

I shook my head to clear my thoughts and pulled back into traffic. Almost immediately, Miles calmed down. After a few moments and deep breaths, he continued. "Needless to say, people weren't exactly happy. The research was shut down and I was released back into a task force, which was right about the time you joined up with the Marshals." I paused, searching my memories for a few seconds. Miles did mention that he just moved into his office when I joined up with the local Marshal's two years back. I interrupted his story for a second, "That doesn't add up with what you've been like since the vampire attack. What happened there?"

Miles shook his head, "Fast forward a year and a half. One of the people I was in the program with, Carla Rose, was abducted and held ransom by a group out of rural Indiana. FBI got the call and was asked to come into help with the situation that the locals weren't equipped to deal with. I volunteered to be the profiler helping track the sons of bitches down"

He paused, and I watched his lip tremble as he was clearly struggling with the trauma of the events. The entire car felt tinted, as if I was viewing everything through the blue cellophane of his memories. "We knew they were bad folks, but we thought it was a human trafficking ring, not vampires. And they were bastard vampires at that, force feeding people their blood out of what we later found was the hope of amassing a force large enough to take over the Vampire hierarchy of Indianapolis."[47] This time we both shuddered, but he kept going, "When we kicked in the door, she was one of three chained down. The vampires started swinging hard. I personally got knocked through a wall and both my legs were broken. I passed out. When I came to a few days later, I found out that the raid had been successful with a very low mortality rate. It was a bit disconcerting given that my legs were in casts after being plowed through a wall."

He sniffled twice before continuing on. I parked the car next to his condo and sat in the AC while gathered the energy to go on. "Apparently, Carla had used her abilities to fix mortal wounds and stitch people back up. She didn't have that ability before she got kidnapped. She could do cuts and scrapes on other people, but not broken bones and mortal wounds. The working theory was that the vampiric blood caused her abilities to kick *way* into overdrive. The evidence was in aftereffects of the raid. The two officers who were letting her out of the chains were fully healed from just

---

[47] Vampire blood has a number of properties that make it very dangerous for the average person, especially since it is powerfully addictive. The exact effect depends on both the person imbibing the blood and the specific vampire donating the blood. Possible effects included: Hallucinations, temporary vampiric powers, sun sensitivity, increased healing, decreased aging, heightened senses, increased strength, increased speed, increased stamina, increased libido, and often death. More sadistic vampires used it to leash humans to them much like sex traffickers did with heroin, either through controlling the source of the human's addiction or through the fear of introducing the addiction. Doing so was a capital offense which meant any vampire that wanted to be a citizen, such as the O'Dells, didn't do it. At least openly.

touching her. And not just the stuff they had gotten in the raid. Old surgical scars, that kink in their back, old football injuries. All just gone. A miracle."

Normally, when you hear that line, it's said in a sense of wonder. His was full of anguish, foreshadowing the tragedy to come. He sniffled again, "However, the atrophy and vampiric blood withdrawal knocked her into a coma almost immediately after healing the two officers. She collapsed, giving her more damage on the way down. She hadn't healed herself. She never could. There had been a push for that in the program, a possible place of growth, but she had never gotten there."

He paused again, brushing aside the tears that were welling up in his eyes and loss filling the car. From the outside, I could piece together why he volunteered for the mission and why the blow out had hurt him so. He was in love with Carla. I gently laid my hand on his shoulder, offering some silent support. He patted it appreciatively and after a few moments, continued on.

"When I was cleared to use crutches and move around, the first thing I did was head over to her room. She was still in coma. Doctors couldn't do anything for her. Prolonged exposure to the vampire blood had burned out large chunks of her nervous system and made her unresponsive to most treatments."

He stuttered for a second, now full on crying. I opened my mouth to tell him that it was alright to stop, but he just barreled on, wanting to get the story out. "There was a theory, a hope, that I could use my psychometric powers to interface with her unconscious mind and provoke an emotional response that would induce her into healing herself so she could wake up. Unfortunately, it wouldn't work at my current power level. But now that we had evidence that vampiric blood could give me a power boost. And wouldn't you know it, they had some spare blood on hand.

I could have the vampire blood, but it would require me signing numerous waivers and a whole bunch of other risks that I just kind of ignored. It was a chance to save Carla. I took it. I signed the papers. They gave me the blood, right there and I drank it down just as fast. It felt so good, so phenomenal. I felt like I could take on the world. I wanted more, but first I had a job to do. I could feel the hurt in her soul, the concern of the nurses, and the satisfaction of the governments that they had got me to do what they wanted. I didn't care. I reached out and tried to contact Carla." He stopped, his heaving sobs making it impossible to get the words out.

I moved my hand on his shoulder, in small comforting circles, and whispered, "You don't have to tell me now. We can wait, Miles."

Stubbornly, Miles shook his head, and wiped his nose, tears fading away. When he spoke again, his voice was detached just like mine was when I was dealing with a corpse. He took his memory and reduced it to facts and objects so the suffering would stop. The cellophane filtering effect started to fade as his voice grew more distanced.

"It worked, but not as intended. Well, not exactly as I intended. Maybe it was the hallucinogens in the blood or maybe it was because I didn't have enough control over my power level. Whatever it was, the reaction was painful and radiating. Almost like the feedback you get from a microphone when it gets too close to the speaker. There was a moment where it all looked good. I remember looking at Carla face to face, her eyes open and her smiling. And then I remember waking up to the fire alarm going off and fully healed. We were pulled out of the hospital and the doctors had looked us over."

He sniffled again, voice ragged. "With the vampiric blood, we were able to achieve the positive feedback loop the suits had been trying to manufacture. The issue is that it worked too well. Once I had healed, she started trying to heal other things touching her body. The linen sheets started to grow roots as it turned back into flax. The rubber wristband on her arm started to grow leaves like it was a tree again. Annoying, but not dangerous. The issue was things that weren't exactly organic to begin with. In particular, the metal of the bed responded negatively to the healing effect. The energy poured in just started pumping higher and higher until the metal exploded and the bed caught fire. She lived but is now in an arguably worse condition than she was previously. EEG's show less going on than there was previously."

Cleared of snot and tears, his face had turned into a robotic and immobile facsimile of humanity. This wasn't Miles, at least the Miles I knew. He was expressive even in his silences. Now the silence hung like a technical drawing, illustrative but emotionally blank. His voice had an alien tone; crisp, methodical, and completely divorced from anything human. How bad was his guilt complex that this was the only way he could talk about the situation?

"I failed her. I failed to help her and now she's worse off. So, I left the profiling department and started teaching so I had more free time to figure out how to fix what they did to her. And how to fix what I did to make it worse."

Chapter 8: Briefings

Needless to say, I spent the night at Miles' so I could keep an eye on him. I helped him up his condo where he almost immediately went into his bedroom and closed the door. I wasn't too worried, so I set about tidying the couch and getting ready for bed. When I checked in on Miles twenty minutes later, he was still half dressed and curled up in bed asleep. I quietly turned off the light and made myself comfortable on the couch. It wasn't the best couch, but it was a far cry better than the cots I had spent the weekend on, and my head barely hit the pillow before I was out cold.

I woke too many hours later to the sun streaming through his living room windows feeling rested and relaxed. It was saying something that I slept better on Miles' bachelor couch than the military cots. It had been so effective, that I only had tiny knots and issues instead of the single giant one. Apparently, karma worked mighty quick in these parts.

Gingerly, I let myself into the kitchen and started to make breakfast for Miles and myself. I'm not much of a chef, but I can do cheesy scrambled eggs and coffee well enough.[48] Within the next ten minutes, Miles made himself present in the dining room and I served him the eggs and coffee. He silently took both and we sat down and ate together, maintaining the comfortable silence. Nothing really needed to be said, the fact that I had stayed and was helping take care of him spoke louder than any words and we both knew

---

[48] I can do plenty of things over a campfire fire and with MRE's. You had to get creative in the military to stop yourself from going insane. However, even the best MRE salvage operation was far worse than anything people could do at home. My skills at home largely involved frying pans and attempting to apply my military cooking on the stove. The results were mixed at best.

it. We finished breakfast, I grabbed a spare change of clothes from the car, we got dressed, and then hit the road.

The silence persisted through the crowded streets of rush hour as I took him from his apartment to the University of Chicago on my way to the Marshal's office. We didn't even listen to the radio, instead enjoying the relative silence between the occasional muted car engine. When parked, I reached out and put a hand on his shoulder. He looked up at me, face creasing slightly in a very human concern. My lips quirked in relief before I spoke, "You gonna be alright man?"

He paused, honestly considering the question before nodding, "Yeah. Thanks for listening. And crashing." There was another pause as he looked for more words, but they wouldn't come. Eventually, he shook his head, "I'm done with classes at 1530. If you need backup, come grab me then."

I bit back the urge to wince at the idea I might need his help so soon, so I nodded instead. "I'll let you know man. Have a good day."

He leaned in for that awkward car hug, gave me two sharp pats on the back and headed in. Once I saw him safely inside the building, I pulled back into traffic and towards the Chicago Regional Marshal's office.

****

The US Marshals, and thus the MCD, follow the District Court's divisions. Chicago and the surrounding areas fell into the Northern Illinois District, which actually had two Marshal's Offices.
The main office was in Chicago, but there was a sub-office out in Rockford due to the population densities. We largely split along Illinois 47, which was largely considered to be the

boundary of the Chicago sprawl. Inside 47, the Chicago were the first responders, outside Rockford was expected to respond first. What this meant is that any impromptu, and most planned, all-office meetings were at least in part conference calls. Danvers had offered to set up video conferencing, but Slate hadn't approved it yet.[49]

By the time I arrived in the conference room, most of the staff was already there. I grabbed some coffee from the corner and set aside a donut for McCoy. As I did so, I nodded hellos at the assembled, each in turn. Slate was sitting, of course, at the head of the table. On his left were Jodi Chalmers and Malcolm Brooks, our other two non-EEP members of the MCD. Chalmers was somewhere north of 45 and starting to show the grey in her hair. She used to be part of the Witness Security Division, but got tired of all the traveling, so she volunteered to be transferred to MCD so she would be more localized. Brooks was a local police officer who had decided that volunteering for the MCD Task force was the best way to get promoted. The times I had interacted with him, he was quiet and kinda bland but had gained a bit of a reputation as a bit of kiss ass. Most days I just ignored him.

Next to them sat Jacob Danvers and an open seat. Officially, Jacob was support staff on loan from the NSA and thus not

---

[49] Kyle Jennings, our local research contractor, had several fascinating theories about that. He theorized that there was some kind of supernatural or Mayan dark secret that Slate had that a video call would expose. He was always going on about things like that, even with the far more reasonable explanation of Slate being old and not wanting to adapt to new technology and methods. Before the Mayan event we would've called him a quack or suffering from paranoid fantasies. Now, we hired people like Jennings to give us access to their encyclopedic knowledge of myths, legends, and other such things come to life. Funny how fast some things change.

mandated to be here, but he always showed up since he inevitably got looped in on any situation we encountered.

On the final side of the table sat Trevor Carlson, with his legs thrown over the other unoccupied seat. Carlson had a face that only a mother could love, which came from it having been through the grinder a few too many times. If you asked, he could tell you where each crack, scar, and break had occurred during his fifteen years of being a bail bondsman. He wasn't exactly trusted in the office especially since he had been more or less blackmailed into being a deputy.[50] His gift was being strong enough to wrestle a vampire. I wasn't sure what his MARA recorded strength was or if he could match our perp, but I didn't think too much about it. He had been in Keane county with me. No way he had been able to rip both Master's and Hotchkiss' hearts out from across the country. I looked between the two seats for half a second before I took the seat next to Jacob. Carlson could deal with sitting next to McCoy, who inevitably would be late.

If Carlson was the one that no one trusted, Angela McCoy was the one we all actively despised. For starters, she had been forced upon us by the FBI in what clearly became an effort to offload her. Add in the fact that she was a telepath with a bad case of power incontinence, one of the most horrific combinations in existence, and you could see where the hatred came from.

---

[50] From what I can tell, Carlson had been working out West when he got arrested for illegally bounty hunting. Either the person he was picking up wasn't who the papers said they were or something, but regardless, he got pinched. His choice was either going to Citadel Prison for metahumans or working as a Deputy for the US Marshal's. Some days, I think he wishes he would've gone to Citadel.

74

She could hear every dirty thought people had about her and every errant rage filled impulse loud, clear, and without stop and often responded to them as if they had been spoken aloud. For those not in the know, it made her seem crazy. For those in the know, you had to police your thoughts lest she go off on you. Horrifically irritating and frustrating, which is why no one wanted to work with her if they could avoid it. The feeling seemed mutual, given her preference of working alone.

The final problem was that the only solution she had found to her power incontinence was alcohol. The fog reduced the number of errant thoughts she received, or at least muted them to the point where she could feel silent. That wasn't too bad on its own. I knew several infantry men who needed to numb themselves to sleep and knew how to work with the type. The real issue was that she had been self-medicating for the better part of 5 years at this point, which meant that her tolerance was astoundingly high. Only place she never drank or was drunk was on the job,[51] which was the only reason Slate hadn't fired her yet.

Given the impending sense of departure and general irritability, you could see why she wasn't anybody's favorite person. Personally, the only time I could tolerate being around her is during conferences and office parties when it was socially acceptable for her to be drunk. When she

---

[51] According to McCoy, during work she didn't really need to drink much. Most EEP's had a low grade interference with her powers. She didn't get their thoughts without trying. The non-EEP's in the office were either relatively harmless or not offensive enough, so she didn't feel the need to drink. I was willing to believe her given how hard Slate cracked down on the department, but I didn't trust it would last. Deeds, one of the aforementioned infantrymen, always had said that he was one bad day away from sticking a flask in his bag and I couldn't imagine McCoy was any better.

drank, McCoy loosened up, wasn't glaring at you for thoughts you never said, and actually became a fun and nice person to be around. Sadly, those events only happened once every few months.[52]

When I had settled in, Slate started the conference call. I idly wondered if McCoy had told him that she was going to be late, before deciding that Slate wouldn't have let it slide if she hadn't. The phone rang twice before Gale Delanch picked up the phone.

Delanch was one of the few existing Deputies to be empowered by the Mayan event, which meant he was a shoe in for MCB leadership. While he officially reported to Slate, he was largely given free reign over the Rockford office, which made him the highest placed EEP in the Federal Government. He was always ridiculously energetic, possibly a side effect of being a living tesla coil. "Good morning Chicago!" He crooned in a passable imitation of Robin Williams, "How are we coming through?"

"Good," Slate responded firmly, "How about us?"

"Fantastic!" Delanch said, "Let's get this show on the road. I'll go first."

Delanch then proceeded to fill us in on his stretch of

---

[52] Quinn Eckles, for all I talk about her, doesn't actually work in Illinois. She's off in Vegas, but we get along well enough that we try to stay in contact and schedule trainings together. It generally makes them more bearable to have someone you know suffering through them. We joked about one of us moving, generally her to Chicago given the density of people she liked out here, but the idea of having to deal with snow was too much of a no go for her. Jennings guessed that it interfered with her pyrokinetic abilities, but I think she was on the level about not wanting to live where the wind hurt her face.

Northern Illinois. He mentioned the reported shake up in the first gen werewolf hierarchy, I told him that we could corroborate, but left the story until later. There was something going on with the vampires of the quad cities they were keeping an eye on. Lots of 'wait and see' which meant busy but easy work. Right around the end of their presentation, McCoy snuck in, sporting a pair of sunglasses that obscured her probably bloodshot eyes and looking very haggard. Carlson reluctantly took his feet off the seat and she flopped into the chair, her dark chestnut ponytail bouncing once before falling over in a deflated lump. The rest of her body shortly followed suit. I slid over her donut and went back to listening. I might not like her, but there was no reason to be petty enough to steal her favorite donut. Besides, she'd remember this niceness the next time we went drinking and might take pity on my liver.

Chalmers went next. Apparently, while the EEP deputies were down in Alabama, there had been a series of disappearances in South Shore, especially near the lake. They were working with the Coast Guard to talk to the Aquatics[53] in the lake to see if someone was to blame. Smart money was on the merfolk, but we couldn't act without a warrant. Slate assigned Carlson to help out, which largely meant he was on arm wrestling duty if the merfolk wanted to try to establish dominance.[54] I went next.

---

[53] Anything that lived primarily in the water. Merfolk, amphibious people, and the odd sentient animal.

[54] Displays of strength were the traditional merfolk way of settling disputes. Anything from who got the last portion of dinner to the authority to arrest one of their people for a crime. The average merfolk was stronger than your average human, but Carlson was stronger than both put together. Man seriously went out and won money arm wrestling vampires when he was bored.

I filled them in over the last day of activity. Much like Jacob and I, they were all in a large state of shock over how much shit had actually hit the fan. Well, except Slate who never seemed surprised and was at least partially in the loop.

Brooks spoke up first, to the point and surprisingly talkative today, "How many other victims do we suspect are out there?"

Jacob jumped in, "Dr. Niccols has gone through her archives for the past three months and found only one other possible event besides the two I just reported, but that was inconclusive. Based on what we've seen, the killer is new to town, which matches the information from the O'Dells."

Brooks seemed slightly disturbed but took the information in stride. Chalmers, however, was not letting it go from there, "So, when do we get warrants for the Circus?"

Slate interjected, "We can't go off the rumors of two vampires. While they have established themselves as a good source of information, by Tennant's report they are working on supposition as much as we are. Still, it does merit an investigation. Tennant?"[55]

-----

[55] I had to bite back a scoff at not being able to go to the judge with the O'Dell's information. What Slate was actually saying was that he didn't want to spend that particular political capital quite yet.

Getting warrants based on supernatural, particularly vampire, information was always a dicey thing. First, most of them weren't exactly in good standing. While the O'Dells certainly were, most of the vampires were seen as little better than a gang member who'd sell out their mother to keep the cops off their back. Or worse, point us at one of their enemies because they could. Think SWAT-ing, but with the SWAT team being just as likely to die as the person being SWAT-ed.

"Already on the docket for today," I sharply responded. Slate nodded in approval and I let myself relax. Man gets scary when he thinks you're slacking off.

"So, what exactly are we dealing with?" McCoy chimed in, speaking for the first time all morning. Practical woman McCoy. Made me almost like her if she wasn't so insufferable to work with.

Jacob responded, leaning forward and reading from a yellow legal pad as he went, "Well, there are numerous mythologies that we could be drawing from. Kyle Jennings and I ran through as much of the internet, archives, and library as we could, and we've got a few strong contenders. Immediately discounting non-humanoids, such as the Wakwak and Ammit, and the narrow profiles, such as the eating of Albinos in sub-Saharan Africa, we're left with a few options.

First option is some kind of werewolf or vampire. Both are humanoids and are strong enough to do the damage described. However, both the vampires and the werewolves in Chicago have not done this in our recorded history. Additionally, Walker reports that there are no new Werewolves in the city and Vincent Madoc's Magistrate reports similarly for the vampires, which reduces the likelihood of either severely.[56]

---

[56] An insight into Vampire politics for a second. Previously, there was a head Vampire who ruled over the shadowy part of the city who was often referred to by an official title such as Governor, Prince, or Master. They ruled through a combination of information, bribes, connections, age, personal power, and favors. The person with the largest combination of those was generally on top. These days, that power was also supplemented by the endorsement of the US Government who tended to support vampires who played along with the policy of "I don't care about your internal power structure, you ultimately report to us," rhetoric. Madoc, with the support of the O'Dell's, had overthrown the previous structure to

"Next, we have the Manananggal, which is a female creature from the Philippines which is said to seduce men and eat their hearts. They can shape shift, which would explain the indentations in the two victim's chests and why only males have been targeted thus far."

He paused as he traced his finger down the legal pad, "The American Indians have a tradition of doing this. In particular, the Quechua of modern-day Bolivia and the Iroquois of modern-day Great Lakes did such things as part of a victory ritual. It supposedly gave them strength in the face of their ancestors.

If we discount the hearts, and limit it to conventional human eating, we're left with," Jacob paused, as he flipped through his notes "the Rakshasas of Indian, the Wendigo's of Algonquian myth, the Muma Padurii from Romanian, Baba Yaga from Slavic folklore, Whaitri from Maori mythology, the Khakhua-Kumu from Papua new Guinea, and the Brahmarkashasa one again from India. If we only allow for male supernaturals, that discounts the Manananggal, Whaitri, Baba Yaga, Muma Padurii. I've got a limited file on each of them here. Jennings is off doing more research right now, but it's kinda hard since we don't know what exactly we're dealing with. We'll need more details to start narrowing the search"

---

put one in place that would be amenable to that logic. In exchange for being an early adopter, he was allowed certain flexibility in internal policing. His magistrate, a man by the name of Dominic Torres, was that local law. While the O'Dells were our official contact with the vampiric world, anything coming directly from Torres meant that it was also coming with the full support of a man who was able to keep the vampires of Chicago under his thumb.

Slate pensively waited to give orders as Jacob handed out folders to each person in the room. A quick thumb through revealed that inside was most of the information he had just provided. Just twice as long and in blocks of printed text. I closed it, resolving to read through it in detail later and focused on Slate, who was nodding slowly and giving us marching orders.

"Right. Delanch, report in if you can spare any people, because it sounds like we need back up. Chalmers, Brooks, and Carlson go get back to work on the missing people. See if you can't wrap it up quickly so you can be back up on the man-eater case. Danvers, you and Jennings get back at those books. If I need to start pushing for silver bullets or some other weapon to make sure this thing can be dealt with, I want to start on that sooner rather than later."

I looked up from my folder and inwardly cursed. We didn't normally do partners around here, too much ground to cover and not enough people to do it. But if he was assigning everyone else a partner that meant….

"Tennant, take McCoy and go check out that circus. If we can get a lead on our killer from there, let's do it. Get to it people." Fuck me, I had been hoping to avoid this by having Miles deputized. Stupid classes. I sighed and breathed out. No reason to be angry at a man for having a steady job.

As I calmed myself, there was a rush for the door which left McCoy and I sitting alone in the conference room. She pulled her glasses down, revealing that her eyes were surprisingly not bloodshot, but tired and a muddy brown. Her face was flat as she looked me dead in the eye. "Joy," she deadpanned.

Glad to know I wasn't the only one who was unhappy with this assignment.

Chapter 9: Moloch Menagerie Circus

It took McCoy and I the better part of an hour and a half to make it out to the Racine County Fairgrounds traveling along I-94. McCoy[57] had spent the trip alternating between catnapping and skimming the files and reading the important identifying bits to me while I drove. By the time we reached the Wisconsin border, Slate had texted us on route to tell us that we had been cleared by the Eastern District of Wisconsin to conduct an investigation on their territory, which was good. Last thing I wanted to deal with was jurisdiction friction.[58] I said as much to McCoy.

"I don't know. Spending the day at a circus just seems like some kind of personal hell to me. Hard to see any silver linings."

----

[57] McCoy is tall for a woman, somewhere around 5'10". Makes her about three inches shorter than me and far too tall for your average man. She was also several pounds overweight, but it didn't seem to ever phase or slow her down at all, which suggested there were some muscles hiding under there. Still, the entire appearance was slightly off putting.

[58] I suspected that part of that was due to the fact that Milwaukee's MCD was two guys who had barely made it through the training and didn't do it full time. If Chicago was one of the best funded MCDs, Milwaukee was one of the worst. Part of that was because Wisconsin's Governor, Bart Lancer, had run on the promise of not spending a single penny of state money to support the MCD, arguing that the existing Marshals and police departments could handle any issues. Which largely meant that metahumans in Wisconsin were not well regulated and we in Chicago had to pick up the slack. It also earned the universal ire of the MCD, but Governor Lancer didn't seem to care. His unwillingness to give money to what should be a federal expenditure got him lots of votes, which is all that really mattered to him.

See what I meant about hard to work with? Still, the monotony of the car ride was starting to wear on my nerves, and I prided myself on at least attempting to be civil. "I'm not sure about hell, but I could see where you're coming from. I don't know what it was, but it always seemed like it was raining when the carnival came within fifty miles of whatever base we were at. Which was a shame, because military bases and projects aren't exactly kid friendly."

McCoy snorted a small laugh, "I suppose my childhood didn't suck that much." I paused, waiting for her to continue, but she didn't. Annoyed, but too bored to be quiet, I tried another approach. "I take it the hatred of circuses is a more recent thing then?"

She just shook her head wistfully and turned to stare out the window, "Yeah, it kinda is." And left it at that. So much for civility. I took the hint and we spent the rest of the drive in a pained silence.

****

The sign at the edge of the fairgrounds proudly welcomed us to "The World Famous Moloch Menagerie Circus, home of the Real World Wonders!" It was adorned with images of people doing things once seen as impossible, such as contorting into knots while flying, and previously impossible people, such as bearded ladies and strong men. The grounds were surprisingly packed with people, mostly attendees from the look of it. I thought it was a bit cold for August, let alone a carnival, but apparently that didn't stop the cheeseheads from showing up in force.

From my right McCoy snarked, "I wonder where they're hiding the Colossus of Rhodes."

I blinked for a second in shock, staring at her incredulously. "What?" She replied defensively, "It's one of the Seven Wonders of the Ancient World."

I shook my head, "I got the reference, I'm just surprised you made a joke and willingly talked to me."

She shrugged and put her sunglasses back on, "You got me a donut this morning. Don't get used to it." And with that, we walked into the park.

The circus was your standard fare. Cotton candy, popcorn, clowns, and animals. McCoy and I made plans to search the grounds and meet up at the big top tent. She went towards the animals, I went towards the funhouse. It might've been wiser to stick together, but after the awkward car ride, I was grateful for the break.

About halfway there, I spotted a crowd moving towards a tent, proudly proclaiming "Freaks and Mutations! Shock your senses and expand your horizons." I grimaced and went that way.[59] If our killer had come from this Circus, this might be the best place to start.

---

[59] Many metahumans had notable physical mutations that made holding down a legal job effectively impossible. While Muldoon v. the State of Texas had ruled that the Civil Rights Act protected metahumans and as such discrimination against them was illegal, it didn't stop people from discriminating against them the same way women, african americans, and other minorities had suffered for years. As a result, a number of metahumans with physical mutations had to find other alternatives for employment. An alarming number of them had found their way to the circus, carnivals, and other freakshows of the world. I tended to avoid them for the simple fact that no one likes being confronted with their privilege.

The tent was dark and cramped as people walked pushed through the hall, going from one exhibit to the next. The first two displays, more like cages really, featured your standard Circus fare. A bearded lady sat across from a two headed snake. Once sights of wonder, most people moved past them quickly to see the new and exotic mutations the world had made. I smiled politely at the bearded lady and she smiled back, nonplussed by the people passing her by. It made me consider stopping to talk, but realized I was just stalling. I didn't want to see what my life might have been like had I not been so fortunate with my gifts. With a nod to no one in particular and against my better judgement, I followed the crowd deeper in.

The third exhibit was much more tightly packed and attended. I poked my head around and saw a man slithering along the walls and fake trees of the cage, much like a snake. Apparently, his Mayan "gift" was to turn him into half an anaconda. HIs arms and legs had shrunk to the point of being laughable, but his torso and newfound tail belied a sinuous strength. He smiled and coiled around a log two feet thick. A ripple of muscle ran down his twelve-foot frame as he started constricting. The first contraction didn't seem to have a notable effect, but the second was followed by the distinct sound of wood breaking and the top of the log being split into a web of cracks.

There was a dramatic pause before the third pulse. When he sent the cascading pulse down his frame this time, the entire log exploded into a shower of splinters. Most of them flew upward, sailed over the wall of the cage, and rained down upon us. After a second of stunned silence the crowd turned to furious applause. I joined while idly wondering how many practice logs, they had gone through to get the cascade just right.

The snake man propped himself up on his tail and took a bow, serpentine tongue slipping between his lips as he soaked in the applause. As the applause died down, he began to move again. This time moving to coil himself around a metal barrel that had been discreetly placed into the cage while we were all distracted.

As impressive as the man's strength was, he couldn't possibly be our killer. No way those shriveled hands could punch through a rib cage and scoop out a heart. Quietly, I pushed past the gawkers to find the next exhibit.

The next room was poorly lit and empty. Framed against a painted backdrop of withered trees there was a woman who looked like something out of a horror movie. Bleached white skin, long stringy black hair, sitting easily upon a simple swing, her eyes scanning the room. Watching, assessing. Measuring. Almost immediately, I could tell why her room wasn't crowded. The room oozed a sense of discomfort that only grew more intense the closer you got to her and her mannerisms were clearly designed to make that feeling more pronounced.

I became acutely aware that my tongue didn't sit right in my mouth, the sensation of my heart beating, the fact that my toes were slightly too tight in my shoes and countless other minor disturbances that ultimately added up to an unending sense of unease. I watched a young couple rush past me, fighting the urge to run myself, and walked up to the display. This was the first, and probably only, carnival worker I had found alone and the way her eyes moved made me think that she was in the habit of watching for details.

The woman seemed surprised that I hadn't run on to the next room, which quickly shifted to cautious. I smiled as warmly as I could with my jaw not being able to line up properly, "Good afternoon."

She smiled warily, "I suppose it is. What do you want?"

I suppose a few years of making people uncomfortable would make anyone skeptical about willingly talking to you. I got it. Even though my gifts hadn't exactly had the same overt effect hers did, I knew what it was like to find trouble for them.[60] Given the skepticism she was already showing, I could tell any attempt to pull the wool over eyes would go poorly. With that in mind, I decided to go with the truth.

"My name is Silas Tennant. I work for the US Marshals and I'm investigating a crime. A lot of fingers are pointing at this circus and I'd hate to see you all get in trouble for it."

She sneered at me for a second, "What do you care? All you cops want to do is lock us all up at the Citadel."

The sudden shift from panic to creeping menace in the room caused me to sputter, "Well," I started before having to breathe and get my train of thought under control, "I care

----

[60] There was a period of time where I was pretty much mandated by the government to donate blood and my cells to science to see if my healing factor could translate to other people, via things such as blood transfusion. It doesn't. Apparently, with my super healing comes with a super aggressive immune system. If they transferred my blood wholesale, the white blood cells went into overdrive killing everything "foreign" in the new body. Man they tried it on doesn't have functionality in his right arm at all any more. If they filter out the white cells, whatever makes the healing go doesn't work anymore, so that's useless. They tried cutting hair and taking skin samples, but those didn't grow back or heal. Thankfully, the government mandate stopped short of cutting off body parts. I'm still not exactly sure if those will grow back. Nor am I in a hurry to find out.

because I'd hate for fingers to get pointed in the wrong direction just because you're different."

There was a scoff and a glare as she looked away from me dismissively. "Like I've never heard that one before," she said, biting off her words with contempt that could only come from experience. My hair started to stand on end as I became convinced that someone was watching me. "You're just trying to pretend you care long enough to get what you want."

I winced at the scorn and sad acknowledgement that her assessment was probably true for most people in law enforcement. Badges weren't trusted here, which meant my honesty had been a mistake. I took a breath and fought the urge to look for the person behind me, forcing myself to stop and think of a rebuttal. She didn't think I could possibly understand her pain. The suffering she had experienced and isolation she had felt because of it. That I didn't know what it was like to be different.

But, I did get it. Honesty had been the right play; I had just chosen a bad topic to be honest about. Closing my eyes, I dug into my telekinesis, directing my invisible hands to push down evenly on the ground. There was a wobble as my left foot came off the ground, followed by my right. Her aura made it, so I felt the discomfort of weightlessness more keenly than I ever had before and distracting me. A well of panic bubbled within, nearly causing me to drop.

I clenched my teeth, refusing to be bested by some nerves, and felt the copper taste of blood in my mouth from exertion. I swallowed hard and held out for a few more seconds, lifting myself even higher. It felt like I was a mile high, but I knew it couldn't be more than six inches. Didn't have the mental muscles for much more. When I felt stable enough, I opened

89

my eyes to see her face somewhere between wonder and fear. Careful not to let my teeth show, I stated, "I care because I get it."

The impressive display was immediately undercut by someone saying, "Wowwwww," behind me.

I promptly lost control of my telekinesis and fell flat on my ass. Coming from the snake room, there was a small kid and his parents looking at me. Sprawled on the ground, I smiled sheepishly, trying not to die of embarrassment. They smiled back and waved before moving on.

 turned to the woman, who was politely covering a laugh that ruined the entire horror movie aesthetic. I chuckled a bit, and that just set her off. Soon, we were both on the floor laughing our asses off. It felt good. And what made it better is that I felt all the little aches and nuisances fade away as she laughed. We stayed like that for a good minute before we were able to compose ourselves.

Still smiling she offered, "Fair enough there Deputy. Don't know about crimes, but a few days ago, our strongman, Curtis Voigt got into a fight with the ringmaster about something and stormed off into the night. Right after that the animals all calmed down, even around me. I don't know if that's exactly helpful, but it's the only odd thing I've seen recently."

I picked myself up off the ground, starting to dust myself off, "Know how I'd get into contact with Mr. Voigt?"

She shook her head, "No. And I wouldn't ask the show runners either if I were you. They're bloodsuckers in more ways than one and never learned how to play nice with outsiders." She tilted her head in though, "Although, Charlie

Keitner, our giant, was fairly close with Curtis and might know where he ran off to."

I stood up, trying to figure out why a circus had both a strongman and a giant, and handed her a card, "Many thanks ma'am. Call me if you think of or notice anything else."

She took the card, shaking her head and chuckling all the while, "You're welcome. And the name is Emily."

****

I found McCoy looking at a pair of guinea pigs. One of them was dressed in a taco outfit and seemed relatively normal. The other was dressed up to look like he had a cyborg eye and a mechanical arm as he stood on his hind two legs. From a distance it almost looked like the standing guinea pig and McCoy were talking. I walked up eyeing the guinea pigs contemplatively and considered the two animals. Clearly, they were some kind of props, puppets, or maybe good animatronics. The mechanical eye swung to consider me, and I swear the guinea pig smiled. Really good animatronics then.

"Disney, eat your heart out," I said.

Which was a mistake. McCoy apparently didn't hear me come up and responded to the sudden presence with a blur of motion. The world spun and before I realized it, I was flat on my back with a gun pressed discretely against my chest and a knee on my diaphragm, "Fre…. oh, shit. Sorry, Tennant." She apologized, looking appropriately embarrassed. I just sat there shocked and to be completely honest a little winded. Eventually, I found my voice, "I'll make a note not to sneak up on you ever again and forgive you provided you do one thing."

She cocked her eyebrow,

"You get off my chest and stop pointing a gun at me."

"Right," she said sheepishly. She stood up, the gun went back into its holster and the ability to breathe returned in a merciful rush. I coughed a little and then took the hand she offered me up. "Didn't know you were so jumpy." I said, dusting myself off.

She shrugged, clearly wanting to move past the entire situation, "I guess old habits that die hard."

I contemplated that and decided I didn't want to probe any further. "Well, whatever those habits were, it certainly gave you some solid practice. I don't think I've seen anyone not enhanced in some way move that fast."

She smiled slightly at the compliment, looking around a little as she filled me in. "I didn't find much. The carnival seems to be run by a few vampires who are societal rejects. Explains why the O'Dell's recommended coming during the day. Near as I can tell, they aren't forcing any feeding, but I'd like to get a warrant just to be sure."

I nodded in agreement and considered it before responding. Not strictly protocol and certainly more than we had time for right now, but definitely the right thing to do. "We'll pass it along to Milwaukee's division and offer to be back up if need be. We're in the middle of a case right now and can't spare the time," I suggested with a tilt of my head.

McCoy nodded in a satisfied manner before moving on. "Fair enough. What else did you find out besides how good my quick draw is?"

I filled what I had seen, leaving out the embarrassing bit of falling on my ass. She listened and nodded, "Well, certainly more than I found and this strongman certainly matches the information we have." There was a pause where she rolled her shoulders, "But so does half the state. Where do we find this giant?"

I wanted to point out that we had a bit more than 'male', but decided it wasn't worth the argument and instead pointed towards the trailers behind the big top, "Emily said the giant camped out over there during the day, normally working on repairs. Just follow the clanging."

McCoy cocked an eyebrow, "Emily? First name basis already?"

"It's the only name she gave me," I flustered at her before turning to walk towards the trailers.

McCoy laughed, "Did she give you a phone number too?"

I felt myself blushing, "No, I gave her mine." McCoy doubled over laughing at me. I could feel the blush traveling down my neck as I valiantly tried to defend myself, "In case she remembered anything else or saw something weird!"

"Sure, that's the only reason why," McCoy managed to get out between fits of giggles.

"Shut up," I muttered sullenly.[61]

---

[61] I had considered lying, but while I know she normally couldn't read my surface thoughts, I didn't put it past her to be actively reading my mind after that little throwdown. Plus, we needed some levity after a near shooting.

Chapter 10: Keitner

By the time I had circumnavigated the circus enough to be by the supply trailers, I was slightly sweaty and very annoyed. Apparently, being flipped onto your back aggravated knots. Who knew? McCoy seemed to be in a better mood, but whether that was because we were moving away from people or because she flipped me, I didn't know. Regardless, I was just happy to finally hear the clanging sounds Emily had pointed me towards.

Still, McCoy and I had to pick our way through the maze of trailers and RV's before we finally found Keitner. Keitner, in addition to being the giant, apparently also did part time work as a blacksmith. As we walked up, he was hammering away at something working at an open-air forge. Even hunched over the anvil, you could tell he was large the slope of his back raised well above my head.

I stepped forward, "Mr. Keitner!" I yelled to be heard over the din of work. He put up a single finger indicating we should wait and went back to hammering. A few minutes later, he picked up the red-hot item with tongs and burrowed it in a bucket of water. A rush of steam later, he pulled out a very recognizable horseshoe. He appraised his work for a second before nodding satisfiedly to himself, setting it down and walking over to us.

Okay, large was an understatement. Man was easily seven and a half feet tall and had wide stocky shoulders. His right arm was notably bigger than his left, probably from a life working at the forge, but both were bigger around than my head. His arms swung casually as he walked, almost creating a hum from the sheer amount of air they displaced. I sized the muscles carefully, idly wondering if he might be our killer. He looked like he might be able to give Carlson a run for his money, but his hands were too big for the chest wounds. When we were a few steps away, I looked away from the arms, craning my neck to look him in the eye. He met my eyes and smiled warmly. His voice fit his frame; loud, boisterous, and affable. "Good afternoon folks! What can I do for ya?"

I stepped forward to introduce us, "Deputies McCoy and Tennant. We're looking into a series of crimes and we're hoping you could help us out."

His face and shoulders visibly fell before I had even finished talking. "Oh," he stated quietly, "I figured this was coming." There was a moment where I was wondering if he was going to try and run before he shook his shoulders out, "We should sit down for this. Beer anyone?"

I shook my head in a polite refusal. McCoy visibly hesitated and then followed my lead. "Suit yourself," Keitner said before making his way over to a collection of chairs at the edge of the clearing his forge sat in. He dropped himself into a large and sturdily built wood chair and immediately set about fishing through the cooler next to it. After a moment, he pulled out a Miller, opened it with his forearm, and threw it back in one go. There was a pause followed by a burp before he turned to us. "You're here about Curt, right?" he asked cautiously, fishing out another beer.

"That is my understanding of the situation, Mr. Keitner," I responded in my best professional tone as I stepped forward and took a seat.

Keitner smiled, "You can call me Charlie, most everyone does."

McCoy stepped in, "Okay Charlie, what can you tell us about Curtis Voigt?"

Keitner nodded solemnly, "A few years back Curt was in the hospital for cancer. It was everywhere. Pancreas, liver, lungs, and a few places I don't recall. Anyways, a man came to Curt and offered him a way to cheat death. Fight off the cancer and live again."

I raised my eyebrows. This screamed dangerous magical pact thing but the idea of being able to cure cancer would be truly phenomenal. There were half a dozen labs throughout the nation who were looking into magical remedies and methods to see if they could be applied to the average person, hoping to push the boundaries of modern science and redefine the cutting edge.[62] Keitner saw my surprise and shook his head solemnly with the despair of a man who's had to tell this story before. Hope cut out, I could feel a knot forming in my stomach as I started putting the pieces together.

"Curt, not wanting to die overly much, readily agreed. Man then gave Curt what Curt describes as the single tastiest steak ever, whole pound of it. Thing was barely cooked, but Curt ate the entire pound in one sitting and promptly fell asleep. When Curt woke up, he was cured. Cancer was gone, he was fit and happier than he had ever been. He got a clean bill of health and was sent home with no issues." He let that sentence hang ominously, the unspoken truth ringing out.

---

[62]Well, maybe not redefine. Metahumans and the such had cast the definition of cutting edge into question and there were so many new ideas and research that it was hard to keep up with. All I was hoping for was that people would stop trying to requisition my blood.

Nothing in life worth having comes easy.

Keitner sat back and sipped the beer contemplatively, "Apparently, the fix was temporary. About a month later, the cancer came back. Curt went out to track down the man who fed him the steak about why it wasn't working. The man told him if Curt didn't keep eating the meat, he'd start relapsing. Curt asked where he could get more. The man just smiled and told him where to get it." The knot was fully formed and sinking fast in my gut. "He just had to find someone to eat."

McCoy let out a low whistle and I fought the urge to gag. Apparently, the green reached my face and Keitner, nodded sympathetically, stated, "Bout what I did when I found out. Anyways, Curt didn't want to die, but he didn't want to eat people. So, he started doing what he could to survive. Turns out that if someone died in an accident, as long as he started eating them before they rotted, he was good. So, he started listening to APBs and bribing folks to donate bodies to him for science."

McCoy cut in, 'You're aware that's like seven different crimes right there? If you knew about them, we have to charge you for aiding and abetting." Her tone was probably meant to be informative but came across accusatory.

Keitner shrugged resignedly, clearly not concerned with the implications. "Ma'am, you do what you feel you need to. I'm more worried about what's going on with Curt."

That's an odd response. Probably a man dealing with some guilt. I put my hand up at McCoy, "Let's hear this out before we do anything. I don't think Mr. Keitner's done with his story yet."

I paused before thinking in her direction, "Besides, I think he knew that going in. Looks like he wants to atone." I hoped that actively directed though would help her pick up something despite the troubles me being an EEP normally gave her. McCoy caught my eye and nodded and Keitner took that as a sign to continue.

"Curt went on like that for a few years, but I'd imagine about six months ago he figured out something else. He started coming in, stronger and bulkier. Thought maybe he had started doing extra workouts or doing some steroids or something for the act, but the strength came in too quick and didn't have nearly enough muscle to back it up. He started getting distant and reclusive. Turns out that he was eating more. The more he ate, the stronger he got. But also, the more the hunger built."

He paused, staring off into the flames. After another sip or two he forced himself forward, "Turns out he was getting more distant because he was looking at us like food instead of people. I'd like to think that he was disturbed by that and trying to get away from us and those thoughts. Or maybe it was a predator recognizing you couldn't be friends with your prey." He sighed, and leaned back waving a hand airily, "Didn't matter. The ringmaster and show runners found him with fresh bodies in his freezer about a week ago and kicked him out. Never bothered them before, but it had never been more than one before now. Apparently, that's their line in the sand." There was an undertone of disgust when he said that that was full of raw emotion. Uncertainty and confusion undercut with betrayal.

I felt McCoy simmering at my side and quickly interjected myself before she started doing something horribly stupid, but probably morally right.[63]

"Would you be willing to go on record stating that the showrunners knew and covered up Voigt's predilections so that we could officially charge the show runners with a crime. Perhaps for a plea deal."

Keitner looked solemn, "Hell, I'll do it for two concessions. Small ones."

Anger started radiating off McCoy. I could hear it in my brain. Seething, festering, and threatening to overcome my thoughts and infect my mind. 'Fuck him,' it hissed, 'He deserves no quarter!'

I took a breath and sectioned her out. "What condition would that be Mr. Keitner?"

"Two things. One, you leave the rest of the carnies alone. Near as I can tell, it was only me and the show runners in the know. Two, I don't get a plea deal."

McCoy's anger abruptly cut off and my thoughts were clear once again. Her shock was clear. Apparently, the idea of someone wanting to atone for their sins was horridly alien to her. I personally got it.[64]

---

[63] I was all for morally right. Just not stupid. I wanted back up.

[64] I spent some time down at the VA working with people suffering from PTSD and survivor's guilt, while working through a few issues of my own, so I was used to seeing it. Carlisle, a Vietnam vet, sprung to mind. Sweetest guy I knew, came down every morning with donuts to help out and volunteer to get the new people talking about their troubles. I also know that he spends months working for habitat for humanity and building houses. Back in 'Nam he was a bomber pilot and when he had finally seen the photos of how much damage he did, it nearly broke him. Get him drunk enough, and he'll loudly proclaim to anyone that he deserves to be put on trial and put down for his sins. He largely channels it into doing good

"We can manage that. We just need to know where Voigt is now so we can stop him from hurting more people."

Charlie nodded, tears welling in his massive eyes. "Of course. He's..."

A crunching sound broke us all out of our reverie. Walking into the clearing was a man and a woman dressed in leathers and with their muscles clearly showing. My thoughts jumped around for a moment before connecting them to where I had seen them before. Ipsen's bodyguards.

"Fuck," I mentally cursed.

The woman smiled toothily, seemingly in response to what I had thought. Or more likely, what was on my face. "Oh, don't stop," she said mockingly, "We want to know where he is too."

Quietly, I started reaching for my gun, chewing myself out as I went. Of course, the meeting with Ipsen had been too easy. He was planning on playing us for the location of the killer so he could get vengeance himself.

McCoy's gun was already in her hand, as if by magic. "I'm sorry, I'm going to have to ask you to leave. This is a Federal Investigation."

The man smirked, showing his elongating teeth, "Like we care."

---

community service to atone, but I know that he thinks there's no hope for him. And he's not the only one with that much accumulated guilt. Breaks your heart.

Chapter 11: Werewolves

Tactically speaking, we were fucked. Even outside of the full moon, werewolves were faster, stronger, and meaner than humans. The fact these werewolves were shifting right now, in the middle of the day so close to the new moon, meant that the bouncer twins were either particularly powerful werewolves too.[65] Presented with a bad situation, McCoy did the right, proper, and sane thing.

She shot them.

Two bullets, center of mass, for each werewolf. Say what you will about McCoy, you can't deny she's wonderfully pragmatic.

It wouldn't stop them, in any shape way or form[66], but it would slow them down while they regenerated, draw

---

[65] Werewolves, regardless of generation, are tougher and stronger in their base human form. When they shifted into their wolfman form, their strength and toughness increased again and they grew claws that could shred metal. Now, during the full moon all werewolves shift, but young werewolves **only** changed during the full moon. As werewolves got older or if they were particularly powerful they could push those initial conditions and start doing things like shifting outside of the full moon or controlling when they shift. I had never seen a werewolf keep their pronounced canines outside of a morph, but ARCHIVIST records indicated that partial transformations like that suggested a high degree of control and thus a high degree of danger.

[66] If we had silver rounds on us, maybe. But carrying silver generally required special requisition orders and time. I had the standard shotgun in the trunk of the car loaded with silver slugs for situations like this, standard operating procedure since San Antonio. No matter how tight budgets were, no one skimped on silver ammunition anymore. But the car might as well have been on the moon given that the werewolves were ten feet away from us.

attention to the situation which would mean possible help, and buy us time to run. The man folded over from the double tap in the stomach, but the woman started moving towards us undaunted.

Extra fucked then.

McCoy continued to fire into the woman, but I lowered my peashooter. Bullets clearly weren't doing us much good, so it was time to cheat.

My parents insisted that my sister and I take martial arts from a young age. I had replaced most of that knowledge with US Army Combatives, but one of the things I had retained was that the ankle is not particularly sturdy. From soccer players to figure skaters to horses, the ankle was disturbingly easy to dislocate. And hurting your ankle? It was often as simple as your foot being slightly out of alignment with the rest of your body as you stepped. Such a vital joint, undone by nothing more than your full body weight. Twisting your ankle like that could knock someone out for days.
I could apply a force roughly 10 times greater than a human falling. With my brain.

It took me a moment to focus my full strength into a tight fist, wait for an opportune moment, and then drive into the female bouncer's ankle. My focus and patience was rewarded with the distinct cracking sound of bone snapping and the werewolf shifting from confident to surprised as my telekinetic ball peen hammer hit her right ankle just as she lifted her left foot to step. Her howl of pain covered the thud as she hit the ground hard.

That would buy us some time.

But every second mattered when dealing with werewolves, so we needed to stretch the advantage. With fear of the werewolf closing on us, McCoy and I raised our guns and emptied our magazines into the crippled werewolves. By the time I clicked dry, McCoy had already started running and I wasn't far behind her.

Keitner, showing remarkable self-preservation instincts, had already taken off. Even more impressively, he was moving away from the mass of civilians and through the twisting confines of the tents, heading away from the park. All the twists and turns would mean that the werewolves speed advantage would be minimized due to the inability to accelerate or keep a speed. Also, we wouldn't have to worry about errant claws finding small children.

"We need to get to the parking lot!" I yelled at him. He nodded, and started changing directions, easily bounding over the tent ropes and poles with his long strides. McCoy and I struggled a bit more due to not being giants, but started following along, struggling through the tent corridors. McCoy was only three inches shorter than me, but she was far more nimble meaning that she could duck under most of the supporting wires without bending over much. I, on the other hand, had to either fully stoop and duck under most of the wires or weave around to where the ropes were mounted in order to maintain pace, letting her pull ahead.

I was cursing my height when I heard it. A piercing noise that caused me to stutter in involuntary panic and made the hairs on my neck stand up. A hunting howl. Louder than the wolves, and with a menace that wormed right into my brain. My stutter turned into a stop as a shudder rippled through my body. The Neanderthal part of my brain knew that howl was for me and was panicking.

But panic would only get me killed.

Cursing, I kicked myself back into motion, noticing that McCoy and Keitner had also stopped. I moved my tactical assessment from 'extra fucked' to whatever was on the spectrum below that. That howl meant the bouncers were both fully regenerated and shifted. Bouncing back from fifteen rounds, even lead ones, in that time frame was beyond anything I had ever seen before or even read about before. I caught McCoy looking over her shoulder, her grimace revealing she had made the same conclusions as I had. The contained terror on her face nearly made me freeze again, but I pushed that aside and started thinking action plans. McCoy reached into her belt and pulled out a spare magazine to reload. I pulled out my phone.[67]

The phone rang once before it connected. "This is Slate."

I took a deep breath as my very little combat training took over. McCoy and I were probably dead, but at the very least we could pass our information on to someone who could use it to get the job done and avenge us if this indeed went sideways.

"Deputies in danger at the Racine County Fairgrounds. Have custody of an informant who can point us towards our man-eater. Informant name is Charles Keitner, suspect name is Curtis Voigt. Keitner has implied that circus owners complicit

---

[67] Classic difference between people who were in the military and weren't. There were days where it was joked that taking a break to piss required calling it in for approval. I think that has something to do with the reality that any most military units rarely acted without support somewhere nearby. A phone call was vital for making sure that support knew when to roll in and that it was a position to do so. Even though I wasn't in active combat, calling for support early was ground into us in basic.

in the murders. Currently pursued by two werewolves attached to the Rockford pack who want to find Voigt themselves. They are transformed and have demonstrated rapid regeneration, shrugging off fifteen bullets in under one minute. You are first contact. Please advise."

I ducked another low hanging wire, short hopped a stake, and used my telekinesis to lash the phone to my ear while I exchanged my spent magazine for a fresh one while Slate took the eternity of two seconds to respond.

"Weapons and powers free," he eventually commanded, "I'll get support there as quickly as possible. Do what it takes to survive until then."

"Affirmative."

There was a click as Slate hung up the line, looking to get that support rolling as fast as possible. As much as the man terrified me, I was always appreciative of how he handled a crisis. No superfluous orders to be wary of collateral damage or discussions of the impracticality of response times. The sharp efficiency warmed my probably doomed heart. Procedure followed, I stuffed my phone back into my pocket and barreled around a corner leading into a clearing. Keitner was already there, making a break for the wire fence that separated the tent city from the parking lot, with McCoy not far behind. Thankfully, this meant I was able to see the werewolf bounding up on her and yelled out before she was blindsided, "Behind!"

McCoy turned, assumed a firing stance, and started putting bullets into its head. Lead found purchase, opening a few cuts and bleeding the wolf, but not slowing it down in the least. That wasn't to say they were useless. Blood in the eyes would quickly inhibit the werewolf's vision. Grasping her intent, I skidded to a stop and pulled my telekinesis to the ready.

True to intent, the werewolf's leap was wild and likely blind, aiming for where it thought McCoy was. McCoy rolled the moment the leap began, down and towards the fence, as far away from those extended claws as she could manage. My telekinetic limbs reached out and gave the airborne werewolf a hard push up and over, increasing the claws clearance from McCoy.[68] As an extra benefit, the push caused the werewolf to tumble as if McCoy had done a sacrifice throw.

The guttural growls turned into an almost comical yip of confusion as the werewolf spun into the wire fence face first. Once again, seconds mattered. I took a deep breath and the extra second to crumple the fence into a makeshift net around the werewolf while conveniently tearing a hole for McCoy and Keitner to get through, hopefully gaining us more than I spent.[69] I wheezed like I had just run a 100 yard sprint, heaving for air. Telekinesis was a muscle I just didn't exercise that much.

"MOVE IT TENNANT!" McCoy yelled at me from the fence before turning and running. Ungrateful much? Wheezing, I pushed myself forward into a jog looking to catch up. Thankfully, the parking lot had long corridors that I could

----

[68] How becoming a werewolf isn't exactly well known, and it seems to vary from case to case. Common consensus at the moment was that it had something to do with the saliva and an infection of some kind. Unfortunately, that didn't account for all the transmission cases. Jennings posited it had something to do with mystical energies and belief structures and something. I had kinda tuned out at the technical details, but got the major takeaway of: "Treat every contact with a werewolf as if it might turn you into a werewolf."
[69] I was rather impressed with the double utility there, but I'd be lying if I said I had thought that out in advance.

open my stride in, letting the longer pace compensate for my windedness.

A few moments later, just as I was catching up to a tired looking McCoy, the werewolves howled again. I didn't stop this time, but I did take a moment to focus on them and consider where the howls were coming from. One was from behind us, probably the one I wrapped in the fence. Howl like that meant it was probably free. The other sounded like it was somewhere to our right. "They're trying to flank us," I yelled to McCoy, unable to do anything else.

"No shit!" she turned to yell at me, jumping slightly when she noticed me right behind her. I didn't comment and just handed McCoy the keys, "Shotgun on the far right is the wolf gun. Take it, you're the better shot." She didn't even argue, lengthening her stride to take the lead in front of me and Keitner, leading the way. Keitner, looking slightly nervous but determined, let her pass and started following her to the SUV. I took the rear, looking around as I ran out of habit and mild paranoia.

There were civilians in the parking lot, but most of them had cowered in their cars. The people in the park apparently had seen the furry monstrosities making their way out here and stayed far away until the werewolves were gone. Little miracles. Downside was there was shit for visibility and maneuverability was very limited outside of the defined corridors. Getting caught in here would be less than ideal. I was trying to figure out what to do about that when I felt a mountain hit me on my left side.

I went flying and bounced off the edge of a particularly sturdy feeling car, pain cascading through my still knotted and tender back. I cursed myself for letting adrenaline tunnel vision me enough that I could be blindsided.

That turned out to be a poor use of my time as the werewolf
buried its claws into my gut and gave me all sorts of new
things to complain about. I fumbled for the gun and managed
to get a shot off before it sliced my arm and my fingers
stopped responding. The gun hit the ground next to me,
within easy grabbing distance.

So close, but so useless.

While I could feel my tendons starting to regrow, there was
no way I would be able to grip that gun before I was dead. I
didn't heal that fast.

Desperately, I gritted my teeth and tried my damnedest to
focus through the pain, looking for any little bit of fight I could
muster. I kicked with my feet but found nothing meaningful,
so the werewolf ignored it. Pain made bringing my
telekinesis to bear nearly impossible, but I tried anyway. It
would be weak but would be something. I envisioned a
telekinetic fist balling beside the werewolf's head, solidifying
enough to strike.

Unfortunately, the werewolf claws breached my abdominal
wall, causing my innards to start oozing towards my outards,
shattering what little concentration I had and shattering my
telekinetic limbs. Refusing to give up and just die, I started
again.

I didn't get far when there was a sudden thunk and the
werewolf went flying off me before cratering into a nearby
car. Vision blurring, I cast a glance around.

Keitner stood next to me, 4x4 post gripped like a baseball
bat. Taking my breather, I finished my desperate struggle
and formed two telekinetic arms. They were wobbly and

wouldn't last long, but they were stable enough for now. The two of them slapped onto a nearby SUV. With a lurch, it slid forward and slammed into the werewolf, pinning it between the cars.

I snorted in satisfaction as the telekinetic limbs faded away. Job done, I could feel the shock setting in as I tried, and failed, to stand up. Keitner grabbed my arm with one of his enormous hands and hoisted me to my feet. Then, with surprising grace, he then tucked his arm under mine and started staggering us towards our car. We were moving way too slow and I nearly fell over the struggle between gravity and my natural regeneration caused as my intestines to bounce like a yo-yo. I groaned and put hands to my stomach, looking to hold them in place long enough for the regeneration to do its job. It hurt and caused my knees to buckle, but Keitner held me up.[70]

Fortunately, in all the worst ways, that pause gave me enough time to hear the other werewolf coming. Cursing my bad luck, and using the fading clarity of adrenaline, I fell to a knee and turned. Keitner, not in the know, went to pick me up, but I waved him off. "Get out of here, I'll hold them off." He hesitated, confused and palmed his fence post.

"Go!" I screamed pointing at the approaching werewolf. They were leaping across cars to faster, "Get out of here! We need you to find Voigt!"

He hesitated for another second before nodding solemnly and started lopping off towards the SUV. The werewolf

------

[70] I think I heard Keitner gag, but to his credit he didn't comment or vomit. Better than most people do. Pretty sure the only reason I didn't vomit is because the muscles required for that weren't attached.

altered course to chase after him, and I cursed again. Fucking intelligent werewolves screwing up your distraction ploys. Quickly, I calculated and realized there was no way Keitner was going to make it to safety before the werewolf got to him. Worse, McCoy was nowhere to be seen.

Grimacing, I took my hands off my reforming intestinal wall. I immediately regretted the decision, but I was committed. Using my hands to direct my waning focus, I imagined a wall between the werewolf and Keitner. I focused in and slowly my imagination became reality in the form of an invisible barrier of solid will sectioning the werewolf away from Keitner. As the werewolf approached the empty air, I braced and watched the werewolf slam into my manifestation at full speed. The wall, and I as a result, shuddered but held strong.

The werewolf then staggered to its feet and pawed at the void for a few seconds. I felt the pressure as the claws dug into my external will and nearly collapsed from the effort of holding the wall in place. Blood flowed from my mouth, but I managed to keep my focus. I would've whooped but was too busy trying to keep the barrier up.

Besides, that would've just ended with me coughing blood.

The werewolf started looking around for the source, and eventually, spotted me. Recognition crossed its lupine features and it started stalking towards me. It seemed slow, but with that much adrenaline in your system, time gets all kinds of wonky.

I let the wall drop and loaded my brain one for final swing before the werewolf dismembered me. I'd go for the toss again, best chance I had to stagger away and most likely method to incapacitate it, all I had to do was wait for the right....

BANG!

Fighting the impulse to turn, my vision blurred but I could make out the werewolf staggering sideways. Another shot rang out and the werewolf staggered again. The immediate threat handled, I let myself look around and found McCoy, shotgun shouldered and working the pump action in slow motion like a B action movie protagonist. Two more shots rang out, and I saw the werewolf start to go blurry at the edges. Fucker was trying to fade out and run.[71]

McCoy, however, was having none of that, and put the next shot in its head, which snapped it back to this world. I wanted to cheer, but I had just started floating off the ground. I turned to see Keitner picking me up.

"I thought I told you to run." I said. His face crossed into confusion. I apparently was slurring my words. I tried again, but my jaw wouldn't work right. Instead my tongue just lolled to the side. I resigned myself to being a rag doll. After a few

---

[71] One of the rarer powers second gen werewolves displayed was the ability to "fade out". Where they went, no one's really sure, but we knew it wasn't invisibility or anything. I had once gotten caught listening to Danvers and Jennings argue about what they thought happened when something faded out. Danvers posited that our world was a lot like a Dungeons and Dragons world where there were many different planes and forms of existence stacked on top of each other and werewolves went there. On the other hand, Jennings guessed that since had effectively there were infinite worlds by the Many Worlds Theory, werewolves ducked into one of the other planes of existence when they faded out. I liked Jacob's better, but only because it came with the supposition that these alternate planes weren't exactly easy to navigate, which is why we didn't have random werewolf attacks. That, and I feel that shifting between realities would make physics cry too hard.

seconds, he placed me as delicately as he could in the back seat and folded himself into the passenger seat. I blinked, and then McCoy was in the driver's seat looking back at me. She looked nearly angelic with sunlight behind her, but her face was too worry stricken for that. She spoke in a genuinely concerned tone, and I nearly passed out in surprise there. "Christ, Tennant," she murmured, "you look like ground beef."

I smiled weakly and tried for a quip but failed.

She shook her head, "Don't worry about it Tennant. Just *sleep*." I felt the press of her mental command upon me and since that was kind of my plan already, saw no reason to argue.

I was out cold before she even turned the engine over.

Chapter 12: Hospitals

I came back to consciousness in a hospital bed with the dull glow of fluorescent lights pounding into my brain.[72]

"Fuck," I said in a voice far hoarser than I expected.

"You're telling me," said a voice in the corner.

I turned as best as I could but got snapped back by something holding my wrist in place. I fell back onto my back and the faint metal clink told me what was going on. I was handcuffed to the bed.

Miles appeared in my vision, armed and looking vaguely dangerous. "You were clawed," he said by way of explanation. I nodded solemnly in understanding. Didn't need another Providence[73] on our hands. I'd be held here until I was cleared of werewolfism.

"How long have I been out for?" I asked, stifling a cough.

---

[72] Not the first time this had happened. Between a nasty bicycle accident when I was 9, a car accident when I was 17, and a few other incidents, I had spent my fair amount of time in hospital beds. Granted, that amount of time had pretty much flatlined since the Event.

[73] Providence's Miriam Hospital received a young man come in, severely mauled during a full moon. Doctors tried their best to save him, but eventually his heart started fibrillating, which meant they had to shock him. That shock caused him to transform into a werewolf immediately instead of waiting for the next full moon. By the time the MCD had arrived on the scene, there were 4 dead and 19 maimed. Of those 19, 15 were infected. Unfortunately, Heizenholtz wasn't a thing yet, so come the next full moon, we had 15 new werewolves. It was a minor crisis to say the least.

He checked his watch before answering. "Around nine hours," he stated with a shrug, "I came in at 1700 and relieved Danvers. Danvers had been here since you got in around 1300."

I sank back into the bed, anxiously waiting. Nine hours meant that the test results were going to come in any minute, unless they were horribly backed up. My throat scratched again, and I coughed. "Any chance of water?" I asked finally piecing together why I was so sore and hoarse.

He nodded and grabbed a glass and straw that had been set by the bed, probably for this very instance. "They tried to get you on a saline nutrient drip when they found out you were a regenerator.[74] Didn't stick in your body long enough to really give you anything. After the second stick didn't hold, they just gave up."

I drank deeply, while I started doing an internal assessment. My stomach, unsurprisingly, felt sore. Still, I didn't feel any gaping wounds or bandages, which meant that I had probably entirely healed and was just dealing with the new and unstretched skin. My arms felt solid enough and it didn't hurt to move my arms, which spoke well for the new tissue that had grown in after Alabama. Also, my back was hurting less. All in all, I was probably in better shape than I had been when I arrived at the Circus, minus the lack of food.

I looked up at Miles who was watching me carefully from his bedside position. His face was riddled with concern that was pouring through an unconvincing mask of bravery. Poor guy, he was probably blaming himself for this. Something along the lines of, "If he had been there, he could've stopped this"

---

[74] Regeneration is well known to burn a lot of calories. It's theorized that's why werewolves eat so much meat.

or something. Guilt complexes, I decided, were absolutely awful.

"How you holding up?" I asked as gently as I could.

He rolled his shoulders, trying to figure out an appropriate way to state his concern without casting stones. I waited patiently and tried not to show any judgement in my face. Finally, he responded, "I got really used to the idea of you being functionally immortal and not having to worry about you. Today scared me and reminded me that you aren't nearly as immortal as you or your regeneration makes you out to be." He shuddered, stifling a sob, and I felt his worry start filling the room, "You're not allowed to die."

I received images of him at my funeral, brought on by the blanket of sorrow. It wasn't hard to understand where he was coming from and to be dragged down into the despair he was clearly feeling. I almost started crying in sympathy, which set him off. We bawled for a few minutes before my rational mind finally caught up. I don't cry, or at least rarely do in front of people. It makes me all sorts of uncomfortable. Something was going on here.

With that in mind, I focused on the sorrow I was feeling and found it almost synthetic in taste. Stale, like old bread and distinct from my own emotions of concern and anxiety. I breathed and shook myself from the intrusion, tendrils of melancholy falling away like spider webs. Almost immediately, the tears dried themselves. And looked at Miles, putting two and two together. It hadn't been that sad until he started expressing it. Probably a secondary effect of his psychometry then. Right, time to pull out of this sorrow hole. Tears were okay, but they could be shed later.

I forced a cough, and he looked up with a tear laden face. I
smiled slightly, "It'll be okay man. I'm still alive and I have
every intention of outliving every last one of you pricks."

He chuckled, and the sadness got a little less cloying.
Looked like I was right. "Besides," I quipped hoping to lighten
the mood further, "Slate wouldn't let me die. He'd tell me that
I hadn't filled the proper paperwork."

The chuckles became full blown laughter and the blanket of
sorrow was gone and was slowly being replaced by a warm
feeling of happiness. That in turn fed our laughter, which
amped up the happiness.

By the time the nurse came in a few minutes later, you could
practically see sunshine and rainbows filling the room. He
proclaimed me clear of the werewolf infection, and all was
well in the world.

****

Turns out that the world being well doesn't last long. The
initial test seemed to indicate that I was clear, but apparently
my super immune system had done something with the
werewolf infection that was curious, and they wanted me to
stay overnight to run more tests. Miles had taken the bet that
it was just them being safe and wanting to make sure. I,
being the cynic, raised it from a friendly bet to a trip to Uno's
that it actually was because they wanted to see if they could
replicate it to make Heizenholtz more effective. We shook,
and then my stomach growled. I was stuck here, which
meant hospital food. Thankfully, I was ambulatory and able
to put on actual clothes, a change Miles had raided from my
apartment, so I could go down to the cafeteria myself.

I was halfway into my third tray of food when McCoy arrived,
looking weary. I noted that she had put on a bulletproof vest

117

under her shirt and was carrying both the shotgun from the SUV and extra magazines for her pistol. She caught me eyeing the weaponry and raised a single eyebrow in challenge. I, intelligently if I do say so myself, didn't comment and she rewarded my restraint with a bag she pulled from behind her back. She, by the grace of god, had brought me actual food in the form of Portillo's, immediately raising her twenty points of status. Without a second thought, I shoved the cafeteria slop away and began digging in.[75] While I ate, she started to fill Miles and me in.

"So, Keitner has spilled all the beans he has. Brooks is officially looking into what to charge him with, but that's not going to last. I already heard Slate talking about handing the case off to the local PD's and getting him off the hook, despite his wishes." I cocked my eyebrow as I worked to devour a Chicago dog. McCoy noticed and added, "Yeah, surprised me too, Slate being generous. But, I'm thinking it's a bit more about Slate wanting the vampires running the Carnival and not having enough to prosecute on. I bet he thinks Keitner is holding out and thus needs to be guilted into telling us the whole truth."

I chewed in contemplation. It didn't seem entirely in line with the book Slate, but then again, given the fact I wasn't exactly

---

[75] McCoy wasn't a slouch when it came to putting calories away herself and had probably put away a comparable meal herself. One night of drinking she confessed that she used to be a health nut and very active in high school sports. By all appearances, that muscle was still there, just hidden behind the weight that had crept in when the sports had stopped and the metabolism slowed down. I was personally convinced that if she stopped eating donuts and drinking, she'd start turning heads. Which is why I also thought she kept eating donuts and drinking. Still, it didn't get at all in the way of her job, which proved that the BMI was just utter bullshit. In fact, it probably helped her since by acting as a natural deterrent from the creeps and their disturbing thoughts.

118

sure how legal our donations from Beretta were, I could see it. I didn't have the energy to really dig into that exchange, so I shrugged and started on my shake while McCoy continued.

"Regardless, with the information we've got from Keitner, it seems like Jennings and Danvers have narrowed it down to a Wendigo. Which is good and bad for us." She paused to steal some fries, which Miles took as a need to drive the conversation forward, "So, the good news is that we know what it is. Let me guess. The bad news is we don't know how to hurt it?"

McCoy shook her head before carefully talking around the mouthful of french fries, "Nope, we know that. Apparently, Wendigo are just people. Granted, they're people who eat other people. Which makes them stronger, sturdier, regenerating, and faster than your average man. The trick is hurting them enough."

I cursed. Or more accurately, I tried to curse, which caused me to choke on my shake. After a coughing fit, I looked up at a concerned Miles and a bemused McCoy. With as much grace as I could manage after nearly choking to death, I asked McCoy, "How much damage are we talking here?"

She shook her head, "No clue. Jennings' sanest sounding theory states that we'll have to kill him once for each person he's eaten. According to Keitner, if we're being cautious, at least 70 times."

I, having learned from my mistakes, didn't choke on my food this time. Miles, however, nearly fell out of his seat. I let him flail while I considered the implications and methods to handle this.

Drowning, explosions, or going all Terminator 2 molten steel works on him might just do it. Still, something was bothering me, "What about the hearts?" I asked.

McCoy shook her head, "I've got no idea. Jennings and Danvers are still looking into it, but nothing like that has shown up in their research thus far."

I pursed my lips in consideration, trying to piece it together. Miles, next to me, was doing much the same. McCoy just ate french fries and let us think. After a few moments, she interjected, "There are two silver linings to all this. Thin ones, but still there."

Miles and I looked up almost in unison, curious.

"One, we're too busy for me to be put on desk duty after discharging my weapon, so you're stuck with me[76]," she said with a smug smile, "And two, we're weapons free. Based on Keitner's testimony and Niccols' report, Slate has deemed Keitner too dangerous to take alive and it's been signed off on by Porter.[77] Shoot to kill is authorized."

---

[76] Standard operating procedure for most law enforcement agents who have discharged their weapon is to have them put on desk duty until the matter can be investigated. The MCD, while accepting of this idea, tended to be a bit more pragmatic about it's implementation. Ever since the Mayan event, the amount of things where lethal force was the appropriate response had shot through the roof and as such the investigation was either postponed to slower times or was waived altogether in the cases of things such as werewolves and ghouls.

[77] Porter is the Director of the US Marshals and the only person allowed to authorize kill orders. He only did so only when the threat to the public was severe enough to merit lethal force. The legal methods for such things were so convoluted and widely debated that it didn't happen often.

Often Associate Director Meyers, who was officially in charge of

I let out a low whistle. Shoot to kill was generally only authorized for werewolf packs, Mary Morbid, or other such threats. McCoy's smirk reappeared, "Like I said, thinnest silver linings ever."

I chuckled and shook my head, "I don't know, getting stuck with you instead of Carlson is a solid competitor."

She put her hand to her chest in mock shock and gasped. We held our serious faces for all of five seconds before laughter filled the cafeteria. There were a few stern glances, but we didn't care, we needed the laugh. McCoy looked around and her smile turned sly.

---

the MCD, would pass along directly to division heads a directive that "Officers who feel threatened for their life need not bring the perpetrator in alive," or "The deputies need not worry about the perpetrator's wellbeing." Such unofficial orders weren't 'allowed' but didn't need such clearance and were a lot easier to manage. Especially framed as an extension of a police officer's right to defend themselves in the light of a 'reasonable belief of a threat.' No one was going to argue that a mass of muscle with six inch razor blades for hands wasn't a threat. There was no cry of 'Metahuman Lives Matter' or some such equivalent.

Still, I didn't find much solace in the statement, since one day it might apply to me. What was worse, is that I actively benefited from the legal gray area. As a former military man, the criteria for self-defense were a lot stricter than they were for most police agencies, which meant my hesitation to shoot was a lot higher than most officers. And sure, I would probably heal from the damage, but that extra second of hesitation could mean the difference between an injury I could heal from and one I couldn't. Especially when dealing with something much faster than the average human.

To call the entire situation uncomfortable was a massive understatement. Even back then, I had already lost count of the nights of sleep I had lost trying to figure out how I was okay living under rules that could justify my death.

"Say," she asked, "have you heard the joke about the orphan and the priest?"

Chapter 13: After Dinner Activities

The cafeteria was nearly empty when they finally came to kick us out almost two hours later. I hadn't noticed that people had been leaving without more people coming in, having both watched and participated in Miles' and McCoy's contest to out joke each other.[78] There had been a couple good laughs, but the one that warmed my heart the most was when McCoy and Miles offered, almost in unison, to walk me back up to my room. I was too amused by their embarrassed flushes and concern to make snarky comments and tilted my head towards the stairwell in a silent admission that they could both walk me up.

And so, we moseyed over to the stairwell, having no desire to be trapped in a small space after the werewolves earlier. Plus, I needed to stretch my legs after the two-hour gorging. Eager to move past their brief stumble, Miles and McCoy moved to continue their joke fest.

"And, then I turned to the lady, and said," Miles recalled through some stifled laughter, finishing a particularly off-color story, "If you want her to stop, you can tell her yourself."

I chuckled carefully, having both heard the story before and having a very sore and freshly healed abdomen. McCoy, however, nearly hit the floor laughing, stumbling on the stairs. "Oh my god! And how red did she turn?"

---

[78] I knew it was coming. I was banned from two different Chinese buffets and a Golden Corral due to my impressive caloric intake after regenerations. Still, Eckles generally out ate me. If regenerating was a high calorie activity, I'd hate to think about how many calories setting things aflame was.

Miles shook his head, "I don't know, I was too busy hightailing it out of there before she decided to take my advice."

I paused to let McCoy find her legs again and found myself smiling wider despite myself. The past two hours had shown me that McCoy wasn't all that bad, even without the alcohol. Apparently, some honest laughter and being away from large numbers of assholes did wonders for her demeanor. I made a note to hang out with her again outside of work and away from people. She caught me smiling at her and looked at me curiously, "How are you not laughing Tennant?"

I shrugged, "I've heard it before. Also, I had to pick him up from the apartment since he didn't have a car. Had to stop so I didn't get us into a car wreck on the way home."

There was a pause and then she looked as if she was about to double over again, "Oh my god, that's right you were stranded Miles." She shook her head chuckling, "I honestly think I could hear that story a thousand times and laugh every time I heard it. Thanks Miles, I'll make sure to spread that story around."

"Oh, please don't," he said with a slight grimace, "I think the poor woman has suffered enough."

"Oh, stop. She deserves it. She totally...." McCoy trailed off, stopping in the stairwell, a shadow of confusion crossing her face.

Miles, who had noticed it first, asked, "What's wrong?" a second or two before I could

"Shhhh," she cautioned, with one finger up, cocking her head as if she was listening, eyes closing in a focused trance.

Reflexively, I started digging for my telekinesis. Not activating it yet, but certainly having it nearby. Miles produced a pistol from somewhere and handed it to me. I took it, checked to make sure it was loaded and removed the safety, while he unslung his shotgun and switched the safety off.

McCoy snapped out of her trance and her hands were already pulling her shotgun to bear, and with a voice so hoarse, it might've been a whisper, "The entire floor is quiet. There's no one alive up there that I can detect."

I felt my eyes go wide. There had to have been dozens of people on that floor. Nurses, other patients, night doctors. Where did they all go? I felt Miles quiver besides me as the follow up thought hit us both, "So, did they go somewhere, or did someone kill them?"

We all looked at each other in contemplation, each knowing what we needed to do but not wanting to do it. I decided to offer them an out.

"Technically, we're all off the clock," I said, testing the waters.

McCoy looked at me in disgust for even suggesting such a thing while Miles had a solemn look of determination on his face.

"Figured as much," I said, "Onward and upward. McCoy, take point while I call it in. Miles, you're on rearguard. Take it nice and safe people."

McCoy handed me her phone and we started creeping up the stairs. From memory, I dialed a number. It was late, and

125

most sane people would be asleep, but the phone only rang
twice before it was picked up.

"This is Slate."[79]

"Deputy Tennant reporting in sir. Cross, McCoy, and myself
are at the Lovell Health Center, West Campus. As of 2323,
Deputy McCoy is reporting no signs of mental activity on the
4th floor where my room is. We are currently in the North
West stairwell and ascending to investigate."

I could practically hear Slate processing through the phone
as he started typing on a computer. Maybe he didn't sleep
either. "Understood. Welcome back Tennant. There have
been no triggered alarms in the past 5 hours and their
servers are unresponsive to my pings, which suggests some
form of sabotage." He paused. Based on protocol, he would
tell us to stand down, which I don't think any of us were okay
with. I decided to interject before he could.

"Sir, the rest of the building seems unaffected, which
indicates a high degree of sophistication. Regardless, the
longer we wait the more likely this can cascade into a
disaster. We'll focus on scouting out the situation and
disengage if faced with a threat."

That was a lie and one that Slate knew was a lie. However, it
was a lie that Slate knew he could do nothing about, which

---

[79] The concept of waking Slate up or disturbing his personal life
didn't even cross my mind. Slate lived for the job and was always
on the clock, and I've never seen him enter or leave the office. I
always imagined these late night conversations as Slate moving
from his unending reverie at his desk, disturbing the spider webs
that had started to form on his statuesque body, to deal with the
intrusion to his quiet staring contest with the wall.

meant I might pay hell for it later, but right now all he could do was support us.

"Scouting only. I'm contacting Great Lakes Naval to see if we can get you some actual back up. If you can, evacuate the building to ensure safety."

Wow, he wasn't messing around. Normally, I'd expect him to call in the local police. But then again, given that we had a shoot to kill order and had already had a run in with the local werewolves, it was probably the right call.

"Acknowledged," I said, pushing those thoughts aside. Responses would take time, and we had a job to do between now and then.

He hung up and handed the phone back to McCoy, filling them in as I slipped into the point position.[80] Gun at low ready, I climbed the stairs, pulling the first fire alarm I saw, and continuing upward as the sirens began to wail. I could hear the bustle and grind as people started pouring into the stairwell, but I didn't pay that much attention. I was too busy being worried that no one was coming through the fourth-floor door.

As I reached the top of the stairs, I pushed the sounds of evacuation out of my mind, and paid attention to the thin door window to the floor. It was dim, which told me that the main lights were out, but the emergency lights had taken

------

[80] Three reasons I took point here. 1. McCoy was the better shot, which meant I wanted her easily able to pivot between watching our back and our fronts. 2. A pistol is more maneuverable than a full barrel shotgun, which made me better at going around corners. 3. The point person is generally the one something awful happens to. I was the person most likely to survive that encounter without being permanently crippled.

over. Worryingly, there were no flashing lights or sirens typically associated with fire alarms. I peered through the window but couldn't see anyone or anything through the small gap in the pale light. I fell back and made some hand signals to the group, both of them nodding in understanding.[81]

On the count of three, Miles opened the door, I slid right, and McCoy left. My side was clear, but I heard McCoy gag. Before I looked, I checked my corners and then turned to find a bloodbath.

Two nurses were leaned backwards over the central station, arms twisted at awkward angles and their chests splattered in blood. From our spot, 15 meters away, I could see the grizzled off white of human bone protruding from the bloody chests. I couldn't tell from here, but there was probably an empty cavity and there was only one thing I knew about was running around ripping out hearts.

"Voigt," I cursed.

In response, there was a crackle of static as the PA system turned on, "Oh, hello Deputy. I've been expecting you." The voice was honeyed and strident as it poured over the intercom.

Well that wasn't good. Such a prompt response meant he was likely close enough to hear me. McCoy and I exchanged glances before turning to check the nearby rooms. Miles was

---

[81] There are some differences between Military and Police hand signals, but since they come from the same tactical roots and considerations, learning one allowed you to generally communicate with someone who learned the other. Personally, I was grateful we had reviewed them in Keane County since my time in the military had been less tactical and more about translating the nuances of idioms.

still in the doorway, making sure we could escape. My room was a similar bloodbath to the hallway, but no sign of Voigt. McCoy's shake of her head indicated her room was identical. Meanwhile, Voigt continued on the PA.

"When I heard that you had stopped by the Carnival looking for me, I was a little concerned and was considering leaving town. But then I heard that you could regenerate, and I had a thought." I paused, considering our options. There was no way we could fight Voigt, but he was talking, which meant he was both giving us information and unlikely to be moving. I had seen Alien enough times to know that going looking was an awful idea, so I spun my pointer finger in a circle above my hand and we grouped back up by the door, ready to leave as soon as shit inevitably hit the fan.

"You see," he continued, "I realized that you were the solution to all my problems. This hunger I feel just will not go away, but I don't want to kill people. But you? I could just keep eating you forever and then I wouldn't have to die."

I felt bile rising in my throat and swallowed hard to keep it down. That sounded even less fun than being a science project for the government. Still, if he was focused on me maybe we could get out of here and keep him from killing anyone else. I held up a fist for us to stop, circled around the stairwell scanning for threats. McCoy tapped my shoulder and looked around. Not a standard sign, but I got her point. I nodded, and she let her gun go down and closed her eyes once again. I could see her eyes rapidly twitching under her eyelids, so I turned and focused on the hallway to see if he was approaching us.

"But when I got here, you were already gone. I decided to wait, but then the hunger set in. And once the first bone snapped and someone screamed. After that, well, they really all had to go."

I felt my hand twitch as the adrenaline started pumping. This man had killed people just because they had the misfortune of being on the same floor as where I was supposed to be. Shooting him would be wonderfully cathartic but not the only thing my brain wanted to do. I wanted vengeance for his victims.

I shook my head and reasserted logic and training. Voigt was stronger and tougher than the three of us put together and we didn't have nearly enough ammunition to make a dent in him. I bit my lip, using the pain to bring my attention back to the present and refocused on the hallway.

"Thankfully," he said, then the air filled with a pregnant pause. It took me a moment to realize what was going on, but with my refocusing I could hear him chewing in the background. He was still eating people and talking to us between the bites. I took half a step forward before I realized what I was doing and stepped back into formation. I hazarded a glance over my shoulder, McCoy was still in her trance and Miles was still watching the doorway but had turned a few shades paler. The chewing stopped, and he finished the sentence, "you're here now, and we can play!"

The PA clicked off. Fuck this, we were out of here. I moved backwards, grabbing the concentrating McCoy and tugging her towards the stairwell. That apparently, broke her out of her fugue and she immediately started moving forward. "No, not that way," she cautioned.

"We've got to move before he comes down that hallway," I argued in confusion.

She just shook her head, standing firm. "He's not on the floor. I was trying to find him."

I blinked in confusion, letting go of my grip on her arm, "Well then, where is he?"

Miles answered for her, "Contact in the stairwell."

"Oh, fuck me," was all I could say.

Voigt's honeyed voice carried calmly from the cracked doorway, "If you insist, but normally I have dinner before sex."

Chapter 14: Voigt

Miles apparently did not approve of Voigt's wit and opened fire into the stairwell. He seemed determined to burn through his full drum of ammo and I wasn't about to stop him. I turned from the hail of fire to McCoy, signaling her to scout for an exit ahead, not daring to hope the barrage of gunfire would kill Voigt. We'd need to beat a hasty retreat at some point in the near soon. She nodded and I moved towards Miles, waiting for him to run dry.

After several seconds, Miles ducked behind cover having spent his thirty-round drum. My hearing reasserted itself as I hazarded a glance into the stairwell. Amidst the smell of cordite and splatters of blood, Voigt stood there on a bent metal step in his shredded clothes and mountain man beard, looking vaguely disappointed. He caught my eyes and flashed his teeth at me in a slasher smile, muscled chest unflinching, breathing calmly and completely unmarred by the sustained fire. "No foreplay then?" he inquired. I slammed the door shut and telekinetically twisted the door frame in on the door to lock it in place. Holding my telekinesis close, I pulled Miles up from his reload and started to run down the hallway, looking for McCoy.

After a dozen steps, I heard a whump and slam. I couldn't help myself and looked over my shoulder. The metal door and frame were across the hallway embedded in the wall and Voigt was casually strolling onto the floor. He saw us, waggled his fingers hello, and started walking towards us in a methodical and predatory manner. I turned back and moved from a run to a sprint.

I tried to stop in the hallway just past the nurses' station to figure out which way McCoy had gone. I say try because with the blood on the floor, I slid past the hallway. Still, McCoy was down that way slamming her shoulder into a door. I gave Miles and myself a telekinetic push to get us moving in the right direction and opened up my stride to get to her asap.[82]

McCoy saw me coming and cried out, "It's jammed. He must've done something to the doors to pin us in here."

Keeping my telekinesis active was tiring at best, but spared me the seconds it took form the arms. Pulling the telekinetic around me, I formed a battering wedge and worked into a sprint towards the door. "Move!" I cried as an afterthought.

She hurried to the side and I started to push the telekinetic barrier forward. At the moment of 'impact', I shoved the barrier into the door and blew it out of the frame. Not quite as impressive as Voigt, but just as effective. I heard the door clatter over the railing and started running down the spiraling stairs with Miles and McCoy right behind me.

When we hit the second-floor landing, I saw a blur whiz past us followed shortly by the slam of something hitting the ground hard enough to make the stairway shudder. From behind me I heard McCoy yell, "It's Voigt. He jumped down!"

"Are you fucking shitting me?" I yelled in frustration. Seriously, what the fuck were we supposed to here?

"If she is, it's an awful joke," Miles deadpanned before opening the door onto the second floor. I wanted to chastise him as I back peddled from the stairs down, but realized his snarky commentary was probably one of the only things

---

[82] I was also suddenly glad for over-eating like a pig. I had calories to spare, at least for now.

keeping him from pumping out panic. Once McCoy dashed through the door, I followed, slamming the door shut behind me, and bent the frame in place around it.[83]

As we ran through the blindingly bright hallway[84] I started thinking long term. We couldn't run forever. Eventually we'd run out of ammo or places to run and then Voigt would catch us. Unfortunately, all that was running through my brain was Terminator 2 reruns. The scene in Sarah Connor's mental hospital in particular. It was less than helpful. "What I wouldn't give for a vat of molten steel," I lamented.

"The fuck are you smoking?" McCoy growled at me, her voice dampened by the ongoing fire alarm.

Miles, god bless his soul, caught my reference, "Seems unlikely," he said with a single shake of his head. There was a pause and his face brightened, "How about a pressurized boiler?"

Cogs turned in my mind, running through my mental archives. Desperate and stupid, but it might work. Well, at the very least, it could buy us time. "Basement," I stated to Miles.

"The fuck?" exclaimed McCoy.

"Basement," he agreed with a nod.

McCoy looked like she was about to blow a gasket, "Would someone fucking explain what's going on to me?"

---

[83] In hindsight, I should've just run. Blocking the first door was totally ineffective, but in a panic situation you think about what would stop normal people, not monstrosities.
[84] Actually normally lit, but my eyes had adjusted to the emergency lighting on the 4th floor.

I was about to explain the elegance of James Cameron to the unenlightened, but the door behind us went clattering off its hinges, and I decided running would be a better use of my breath. I could enlighten her later.

****

Five minutes later, we were in the basement of Lovell Health Center and were looking at the hospital's industrial grade water boiler. You see, my father was an E.O.D.[85] for the US army and a career military man, which meant a variety of things.[86] Most relevantly, it meant that both Miles and I had been treated to numerous stories about how situations had gone sideways and my dad had to improvise a solution. The one Miles had been referring to was the story about how my dad earned his Purple Heart for putting shrapnel in his own leg.

The details change every time, but the general gist is thus. When pinned down at one point in his military career, he decided the best option was to remove all the safeties from a water heater, over pressurize it, and use it to blow through the wall and the enemy forces. Unfortunately, dad caught some shrapnel in the leg. Which had gone through the solid concrete wall to get to him. The idea here was to replicate that with a hospital sized water boiler in the hopes of stopping Voigt.

---

[85] Explosive Ordnance Disposal Specialist. As he said, he was in charge of making the enemies explode and stopping the enemy from exploding them.
[86] Including, but not limited to, my desire to go into the service myself (continuing the legacy), my lack of consistent education (we moved between the bases frequently), and my general introversion (hard to make friends when you move every eight months).

McCoy had taken to our plan the same way I had the first time dad had told this story, "Are you fucking nuts?"[87]

"Well, clearly," Miles quipped. The false positivity, while necessary, was really starting to grate.

"Oh, shut up," I rebutted, "I just don't like the idea of being a chew toy for the rest of my life."

Miles looked at the boiler contemplatively, "I don't think we have enough time to rip all the safeties out. Hell, I don't even know where to begin."

I pursed my lips in consideration, "I'll just clamp the output valves and hope for the best. Not like I have the training to do the full on job dad did," I started locating pipes while asking McCoy, "Where's Voigt?"

She paused and tilted her head in a gesture I now associated with her accessing her telepathy. "About 500 meters away, still walking towards us. We've got maybe thirty-five seconds," she bit her lip in concentration before adding, "Building seems to be otherwise clear though."

I nodded towards the door, "You all get going. I'm going to stay behind and make sure this goes off."

Miles went to argue, but McCoy just grabbed his arm and pulled him towards the maintenance stairwell out.[88] I dug down and started doing some of the most prolonged telekinetic work I had ever done. First thing I did was crimp

---

[87] Causing my father to swear in shock had earned me: a laugh, a scolding, and a pat on the back. In that order.
[88] Thank god for practicality. I was worried that I'd have to convince them to run. Make a big heroic speech like they do in the movies or something.

all the outtake pipes, which would cause the internal pressure to skyrocket. I could almost see the strain as the pressure gage started creeping towards the red. Looking to control the blast, I wrapped the full strength of my telekinesis around the boiler, looking to reinforce the walls, funnel the inevitable blast, and stop the trap from springing too soon. It took so much of my mental energy, I almost didn't hear Voigt enter the room over the klaxon of the fire alarm. I strained my teeth and waited for him to get further into the room.

"Tired of running?" he called out.

I could feel the boiler bulging against my telekinetic fist. I couldn't hold it much longer. I hazarded a glance at Voigt, who was slowly making his way down the catwalk. Just a few more seconds.

If he found my lack of talking weird, he didn't comment, but just kept going. "Ah, I see. Torn up by the fact your friends abandoned you. I get it, these things can be disheartening. It's okay, I have a perfect place for you."

I twitched at the thought of where that 'place' might be and nearly lost my hold on the boiler. I mentally scrambled and pushed back on the boiler hard. If it started bulging it might give away my plan. He was only five steps away, I didn't need to hold it for long. "I told them to run," I managed, hoping to keep him focused on me instead of the odd quietness.

Four steps, "Oh. a sacrifice," he nodded, with a tone of understanding. Three steps. "How noble."

Two steps, "Not getting them away from you."

One step, "Oh? Then from what?"

He paused, and where we stood buckled underneath his weight. I let the telekinetic hand go, collapsing it into a shield on my body. I was too focused to throw down the appropriate one-liner, but the boiler answered for me, hissing and starting to erupt the moment I let go.

Voigt's eyes went wide for half a second before one of the pipes I had missed ruptured and blasted steam into the air, venting pressure, and stopping the explosion I was hoping for. He both stared dumbfounded at the steam that was billowing into the ceiling for a second, before turning to look at one another.

Voigt spoke first, "I take it that wasn't your desired result."

I shrugged sheepishly.

Before Voigt could start moving again, I snapped out with my telekinesis, grabbed the pipe, and bent it towards Voigt. His smug grin was rapidly scalded away by the torrent of pressurized steam, showing for the briefest moments muscle and bone. Then, his Wendigo nature asserted itself, presenting a fully healed face only for it to be peeled away again, flesh and muscle flayed away. I'd have time to be horrified and contemplate the information later. For now, I turned and ran.

The doors at the top of the stairs were open, which meant that I could hear the sirens from Slate's backup finally arriving. The joy was cut short by Voigt's screams echoing behind me, filled with rage instead of honeyed words. "I'M GOING TO MAKE THIS HURT, TENNANT!" I double timed it up the stairs as Voigt started stomping up the stairs and actually moving at an increased pace, as opposed to the confident prowl he had the entire hospital chase.

138

I was too scared of the undying monster to count that as a victory as I broke free of the tight hallway into the open area between the two campuses. I paused for half a second to figure out which way the sirens were coming from and headed that way. That half second was too long however, as a metal door came flying from the basement hallway and clipped my right leg, causing it crunch and pop as it broke beneath me and I fell to the ground, screaming in pain. I hazarded a look at my leg and saw the bone poking against my pants leg and blood rapidly matting against my leg. Adrenaline was numbing the pain, but not enough. I couldn't concentrate enough to move away or use my telekinesis to push the bone back into place to facilitate faster healing. I tried to muster my concentration, but that ended when I saw Voigt standing over me.

The brain has three responses to a situation given adrenaline: fight, flight, or freeze. I couldn't run and freezing had been largely trained out of me, which meant I went for my gun. Voigt just stood there as I pulled out my borrowed sidearm and emptied a full magazine into his chest. Every couple of shots the damage just faded away and the bullets fell to the ground. Some logical part of my brain concluded that I had killed him at least three times based on the regenerations, but it wasn't enough. He just stood there, confidently staring down at me.

When I clicked dry, I went for a reload. He stepped forward and grabbed my wrist. Without any visible effort, he crushed my wrist to powder and the gun to slag. Once again, I screamed in pain. Still holding onto my wrist, he looked me dead in the eye and smiled evilly, "Good thing you can heal."

Then Voigt's head exploded, followed by the sound of something breaking the sound barrier. I spared a glance to the side and saw a pair of Humvees each mounted with recoilless rifles pointed at Voigt. I managed to get through the pain well enough to state to his reformed head, "I could say the same to you."

At which point he staggered back two steps towards the maintenance doors before a second shot ripped his entire arm from his body, snapping him back to fully healed. The third shot took out his leg, sending him tumbling down the stairs into the bowels of the health center.

Safe from immediate threats, I let myself fall down. The blood pumping into my broken wrist gave it a faintly solid shape, which would speed the healing. The leg, however, was going to take far longer than I cared to think about if someone didn't push the bone back in. I started thinking of ways to do it myself when McCoy and Miles entered my vision. Miles was concerned and just this side of frantic, but McCoy looked bemused.

"This is twice I've pulled your hobbled ass out of a sticky situation in less than a day Tennant," she quipped.

Miles looked as if she had slapped the Pope. I, despite the crushing pain, laughed my ass off. It was perfectly irreverent and just what I needed to take my mind off the process of slowly healing and the pain that would come with it.

"And I'm very grateful. But, since you're making wise cracks, mind pushing my bone back into my body? Makes the healing go faster," I asked with the momentary clarity laughter brought.

McCoy cocked an eyebrow at me, then at Miles. I nodded, he bent over, and shoved the bone back into my body.[89] I think there was a crack, but I don't really recall since I passed out from the pain and stress.

141

Chapter 15: Back on the Hunt

When I came to again, I was at a different hospital and it was early morning. McCoy and Miles were keeping watch over me, though Miles looked like he was really fidgety and bored. McCoy handed me food, this time pasta from Rosati's. Once I started eating McCoy started talking.

"After you passed out, I pressed the Hoorah[90] boys into a posse[91] and we went hunting for Voigt."

I snorted around my garlic bread, "I bet that went well."

"Oh, it went swimmingly once I made it abundantly clear that the thing in there was likely to hurt people if they didn't get to work and this was the *legal* method of getting to work."

I shook my head but understood. There would be hell to pay on the legal and administrative side, but that was Slate's job. I didn't envy whoever tried to argue with Slate.

---

[90] That's the Marines. Hooyah would be the appropriate term for the Navy people, but your average civilian can't tell the difference. I wasn't about to correct McCoy though. She had brought me food twice. If she kept this up, I'd save her donuts until the end of time.
[91] This is a legal gray area. The Posse Comitatus Act formally prohibited the Army and the Air Force from acting in domestic disputes. The Navy and Marines are not explicitly named, but are generally expected to adhere to the rules, which gave the MCD enough wiggle room to work with. In theory, all it would require is to declare Voigt a terrorist (like Mary Morbid), natural disaster (like Harry the Hurricane), or something of the such and the Defense Authorization Bill allowed them to step in, but the U.S. Government generally didn't do that until the media and the public pressured them. I was personally grateful for that, since declaring metahumans natural disasters seemed like a highly dangerous slippery slope.

"Anyways," McCoy said, dragging us back to the retelling,
"We went in with the Navy and their ammunition and tracked
down Voigt." I cocked my eyebrow inquisitively as I slurped
pasta.

"Oh, tracking him is easy once I know he's in the area. He's
got a very distinct mental pattern. Just means I have to be
actively looking which is dangerous when there's more
people in the area. Also means that I can't do it and move"

I nodded and filed things away for later, while Miles jumped
in. "Which is how Voigt was able to ambush us. Came
through a wall and clubbed one of the seamen. McCoy was
able to keep him distracted by alternating between eyes and
groin."

"Immortal doesn't mean painless," McCoy chipped in.

"Right," Miles conceded, clearly flustered at having been
interrupted, "Which gave us enough time to fan out and start
opening fire. We focused on head shots, which seemed to
have worked."

I held my hand up, "Why headshots?"

Miles' eyes lit up and McCoy's rolled. Apparently, Miles had
been chewing on this for a while and using McCoy as a
sounding board.

"It was a guess based on observations. We had emptied
multiple rounds into Voigt previously, but he hadn't retreated.
It wasn't until he lost body parts to the recoilless rifles that he
stopped pursuing us. We theorized that doing large scale
trauma, such as removing body parts or cranial trauma
would push him to regenerate more frequently and actually
discourage him from pursuing us. Which begs all sorts of

143

interesting questions about his regenerative abilities and the conversion between flesh consumed and…."

I put my hand up to stop him, "Could you not? I'm trying to eat here."

He winced apologetically but bounced quickly back to smiling. Thankfully, McCoy jumped in while I resumed eating. "Anyways, apparently that did something. He got pissed, but really couldn't make a move. Looked me dead in the eye, declared," she paused and affected a John Kassir Tales of the Crypt Voice "I Will Enjoy Consuming You!"

I snorted at her impression, "Clearly you've practiced."

She flashed a rare smile, "Products of a wasted childhood," she quipped with a slight bow, "Anyways, that's when things got weird."

"Got weird? What's weirder than an immortal cannibal?" I asked, carefully not eating.

"He bugged out. Faded from existence."

I was grateful for my foresight which had stopped me from choking right now. "Like a werewolf?"

She and Miles nodded in unison, "Like a werewolf." The stereo sound was vaguely disturbing, but I had bigger issues. Issues such as, "How the fuck did our Wendigo get werewolf powers? I read Danver's research, nothing mentions bullshit like this."

McCoy chuckled at my outburst while Miles simply shrugged and offered, "No idea. However, Keitner's info turned up a lead. Apparently when Voigt went looking for the person who made him into a Wendigo, he got directions from the Menominee Indian Reservation. Once you're able to move, we're supposed to take you up there to see what we can't shake loose."

"Plus," Miles added a bit too cheerfully for my liking, "It means that you won't be in a hospital where it's likely Voigt might find you and rampage through it again trying to eat you."

I stared at him bug-eyed, "How and why are you so chipper about that?"

McCoy, equally repulsed, looked at me, "He was all gloomy and sad, so I sent him on a walk. Apparently, he found the animal therapy section which just infected him with a good mood."

I looked at the bouncing Miles. "Oh," I managed.

****

I slept through most of the three-hour drive to Menomonie, Wisconsin, which my leg and wrist thanked me for. When I came to, Miles was driving, and McCoy had passed out in the passenger's seat.

Blearily, I sat up and grunted at Miles. He had apparently calmed down and solemnly passed me a cup of coffee and a pair of folders.

"Now that we have a name, we were able to pull records on Curtis Malcolm Voigt. Thought you might want to read them over." He glanced over to the GPS, "We're about twenty minutes out."

145

I grunted affirmatively, set the folder down, and sipped my coffee. Twenty minutes gave me ten minutes to wake up, five minutes to read, and five minutes to be presentable to the Menominee. The midday sun scorched above us, but I was still grateful for the warmth of my coffee as it touched my insides and helped get me started. After a few sips, I started to peruse the smaller folder.

His history was relatively boring. Curtis Voigt was 47 years old. Graduated in 1992 from Georgia Institute of Technology with a degree in Electrical Engineering. Married in 1993, kid in 1995. Diagnosed with cancer in 1998, went missing from a hospital in 2004. Resurfaced in 2007 working for the World Wonder's Circus. Wife and kid have received no contact and are reportedly still living in Georgia.

The second folder was the far more interesting one. Attached were missing persons in towns and cities where World Wonder's Circus had visited since Voigt joined. There was a lot of guesswork on Danver's part, but he seemed to have identified each of the most likely candidates for Voigt to have snatched during that time and missing persons reports. You could almost see his hunger growing. A person here, a person there, until it was a regular stream of a person a month. Then two a month. Then three. The man couldn't control himself.

I said as much to Miles, but it was McCoy who responded, sounding as groggy as I felt.

"Well, hopefully," she said, "we can find something to control him here"

Miles shook his head, "Regardless, we're here."

****

Menominee Indian Reservation pretty much takes up the entire county of Menominee. No sooner had we passed the county limits, did we see the sign and lights for Menominee Casino Resort. Despite the mental amusement I had from the idea of shaking down the Casino owners for information, I had to agree with Miles that starting at the local Library and Job center would probably be better for looking into the community.

A quick visit had gotten us next to nothing. The Native Americans were always touchy about people coming asking them for help and since we were representatives of the Federal Government, we got shown even less love and support.[92] Thankfully, McCoy was able to talk her way into a deal and got us an address at the ass end of the park that might be a lead, but was just as likely to be a method of getting rid of us. Which is how we found ourselves on an old trail that couldn't even be generously called a road.

I poked my head into the front seat and spoke to McCoy, "Are you sure this is where we're supposed to be? This seems like a wonderful place for an ambush."

------

[92] After the Mayan Event, people realized that if other myths and legends had become true, then maybe the Native Americans had gotten some of the purported ancient magical powers that scared settlers and made for B-movies. This meant that people thought they could just flood to Indian Reservations and through some combination of spending money, time, favors, or badgering get their life sorted or helped by the spirits the Shamans could conjure or talk to, which brought up all sorts of angry complaints and legal friction. Between the Government pressing down on people to leave the poor Native Americans alone and the lack of magical remedies and cure-alls from both the Natives and the Metahumans in general, the tide eventually slowed down, but never stopped. I guarantee not a week goes by that someone drives into the town center like we did and try to buy their way free of cancer. All this has done is made the rather isolationist reservations far more stringent in their enforcement of their sovereign borders.

She turned my head into an armrest for my insolence and shook her head, "Not an ambush. Not a single thought has floated through my brain in the past twenty minutes. Unless they're all metahumans, we're good." I bit my tongue instead of pointing out how my 'good luck' had put me in the hospital twice in the past 48 hours. I pulled back and sat up to keep my eyes out while Miles drove us deeper into the woods.

A few minutes later the car twitched. I leaded forward again, and found Miles shuddering in the driver's seat. He had the face of someone who had just bitten into an apple and found half a worm. Instead of stating that, I asked, "What's the matter?"

He nodded solemnly, "Whatever's out here, it's got an air of malevolence about. No, that's not quite right," He quickly contradicted himself before pausing, searching for words, "It's more like the scene in a horror movie where the hero descends into the monster's lair and we cut to the monster watching the hero from a vantage point, ready to pounce." He looked at me plaintively, "You understand?"

McCoy and I nodded pretty much in unison. Now that he had mentioned it, I got the tickle at the back of my neck like someone was watching me. Carefully, I drew my Beretta and checked the ammo while McCoy did the same for the shotgun. Still, it didn't help our nerves when we came to a small clearing, barely big enough to turn the truck around in with the road in front of us blocked by an ancient and fallen tree.

I raised an eyebrow at McCoy in silent question, "Sure this isn't an ambush?"

She shushed me and pointed at a small column of smoke rising from beyond the log, previously obscured by the woods.

I nodded and made to leave the SUV. "Guess we're hoofing it then."

There was a small shuffle as we all stepped out of the car and grabbed weapons, armor, and other supplies. When we had locked, loaded, and otherwise prepared, we set out to follow the trail into the woods. Almost immediately past the log, the unease and feeling of watching intensified. Miles literally staggered and then fell to his knees, clutching his head. McCoy snapped her shotgun to the ready and I helped him back into the clearing. He was nearly catatonic, half words babbling through his mouth. I sat with him while he came back to himself. Eventually, he calmed down and was able to speak in complete words.

"Hunger. Pain. Malevolence. Death. So much death. The endless wailing. How? How?!" He rambled. I could only shake my head, not fully understanding. Miles had seen so many horrid things in his years, how could this be worse? McCoy, god bless her heart, stepped in. "I'm not sure, but you can stay here while we go investigate." He numbly nodded and we helped him into the car. There was the faint thunk of the locks engaging, before McCoy and I turned and headed back into the breach.

The oppressive fear wasn't quite as bad this time without Miles unconsciously radiating an amplified projection, but it didn't go away. We stepped carefully along the trail, eyes scanning and guns at the ready. Distantly, I noted that despite the distance from the public areas and roads, the trail was very well maintained and relatively straight. Hints of life. That was promising. Then the signs started to show up.

Each was adorned with an increasingly bewildering amount of black feathers hung at askew angles and issuing warnings about the inhabitant.

"Enter at your own risk." One sign proclaimed, while another asked, "What are you willing to pay for knowledge?" The most disturbing one to me, was painted with something so close to the color of dried blood[93] questions of malevolence and predation sprung the forefront of my mind and wouldn't leave. "The dead tell the truth of my claims. Ask yourself now, is what you seek worth this cost?"

But still, against my primal instincts kicking and pulling me to run, we continued forward. I tried to ignore the signs and found that made my journey easier. Still, it was slow moving through the horror. Eventually, McCoy and I found a small cabin, built on a weathered concrete bed and immaculately pristine in sharp defiance of the macabre woods and expectation.

Just in front of the house, sitting in front of an open campfire sat a man steeped in a cloak of the same black feathers that adorned the signs, skin the same color as rust, stirring a pot big enough to fit a person in with a seeming disregard for the heat or weather. He saw us and looked up, smiling wide. McCoy pulled up short and her gun started to rise, as she screamed in my ear.

I didn't need her to tell me. His teeth were too perfect and straight. The chair he sat in dented into the ground slightly, as if bearing a great weight. His voice was the same sickened honey that Voigt's was.

---

[93] I am, to this day, not entirely convinced those signs aren't painted with actual blood.

Wendigo.

The man's smile widened, "Oh good, I thought I smelled company."

Chapter 16: Crow Killer Joe

McCoy was screaming her head off, shotgun trained on the man, "U.S. Marshals. Put your hands up where we can see them! Do it!"

He simply smiled a tooth grin, slowly raising his hands, ladle still clutched in his right hand. On another day, I'd call that amusing. Today, it took all my restraint to not pull my weapon and join McCoy from the panic welling up deep in my heart. Wendigo, it had apparently decided, were scarier than any other thing on the planet. Still, this man hadn't broken any laws we could prove and strictly speaking, we didn't actually have jurisdiction here.[94]

As logic started to reassert itself, other things faded into my consciousness. There had been chairs pulled out for guests, making room for three additional people to sit around the fire. A tall pitcher of what looked like tea was nearby, as were glasses. And most tellingly, the man was complying with McCoy's slightly unreasonable request.

"Stand down, McCoy," I stated. When she didn't respond, I cranked up the volume, "Deputy McCoy! Stand. Down."

Her voice came out terse and seething, "Man's a killer."

"That's probably true. But we've got no proof and can't arrest based on his metahuman state. That would be discrimination."

---

[94] Native American tribes in Reservations are qualified as Domestic Dependent Nations, which grants them Tribal Sovereignty in the reservations, meaning the Tribal Councils are in charge of the laws and operations of these areas. No one from the U.S. Government has authority or Jurisdiction in those lands.

She hazarded a frustrated glance at me. In soothing tones, I continued. "Besides, we've got no jurisdiction nor court to try him in. Weapon down."

Slowly, McCoy's shotgun lowered. It never fully dropped, but I took the compromise as good as I was going to get and turned to the man, whose hands were still in the air. His smile seemed more genial than toothy now. I shook the fear a bit more and put on my diplomatic face.

"Sorry about that sir, clearly we're a bit high strung. Deputies McCoy and Tennant from the U.S. Marshals."

The man, hands still in the air, spoke. Much like Voigt, his voice was honied, but unlike Voigt, it lacked the extreme sachrineness that made Voigt's so sickening. "Oh, that's quite alright. I stopped getting flustered when people pointed weapons at me long ago. Side effect of what I am. Most of the good ones come to their senses before they shoot me." He tilted his hand towards the pitcher, "Would you like some tea?"

McCoy shook her head next to me, but I nodded. "Might I put my hands down in order to serve you?" the man politely asked.

I nodded and pointed to a chair, "Might I have a seat?"

He smiled and chuckled, "Of course, I got them out for you. Thought I smelled three of you though."

I shook my head, "No, just the two of us. Thank you, Mister?"

"Just call me 'Joe'" the man said, handing me a glass of tea. He had a bemused look on his face as he extended his arm.

Clearly, he caught the lie but wasn't pushing it. Interesting implications there. Based on my interactions with vampires, the implication there is that he was willing to be polite and was suggesting we should be honest with him, though I wasn't sure how that tracked with Native American creatures of myth.

Joe[95] smiled amicably at McCoy and I turned to see her still standing, shotgun as close to being pointed at Joe as it could be while still down, standing to the side so that if she snapped up, I wouldn't be anywhere near her line of fire. "Want some?" he offered. McCoy bit her lip and shook her head. Her fingers twitched and I saw the struggle to not bring the shotgun to bear.

Whatever was going on with this man's mind, I could tell it was troubling McCoy. I spoke for her to save her the miniscule amount of self-control it would take to respond verbally. "No, she'd rather not."

Carefully, I thought at her, "You can go back to the car if you need to," which caused her to face me and glare. So much for trying to be courteous. I turned back to Joe, and took the proffered glass of tea, sipping slowly. If it was poison, it was well brewed.

Joe smiled as I sipped and started talking, "What can I help you two fine folks out with?"

I took a sip, buying time to consider the best method probing Joe for the information we needed. Given the bemusement, I

---

[95] Normally, I would've fought against referring to anyone by their first name tooth and nail, but between his soothing voice, lack of other options, and desire to stay alive with a mass murderer ten feet away, I rolled with it. I mean, seriously, what else was I going to call him? Sparky? Killer?

decided to try and appeal to any sense of responsibility he might have.[96]
"A few days ago, a man was found murdered in a Chicago back alley." I left my comment hanging there. No need to mention the hearts yet.

Joe nodded solemnly, "And based on Deputy McCoy's reaction, you think it was a Wendigo."

"Spot on Joe," I motioned at him, "It would seem that not all Wendigo are so driven by their hunger that they attack people in back alleys. Any idea what's going on here?"

Joe smiled slightly, "Oh, you flatterer. Sounds like you've got a Revivalist on your hands." I cocked an eyebrow inquisitively and he continued on. "There's a process to becoming a Wendigo, one I'm not going to go into if you don't mind. Trade secret and all that." There was the barest of pauses after the sentence before he continued on, effectively bullying me into his terms.

"Normally, the person who's becoming a Wendigo is aware and ready for the process and is able to meet the new hunger head on. The driving force isn't the Hunger, but the man who made the choice to inflict this condition upon themselves. Because it was intentional and directed, the Hunger is manageable. Well, at least more manageable.

---

[96] This had a fifty-fifty shot of working. Some metahumans, such as vampires, were very big on the matter of appearances. If one of theirs had grossly fucked up and broken the laws to the extent we had to get involved, clearly they needed to be dealt with and we'd receive cooperation. For Vampires, who preferred the shadows and back alley dealings, it was generally a mark of shame to let things get so far that MCD had to step in. They wanted this black mark dealt with as quickly as we did. If Joe went the way of vampires, this would be a quick fix. If he went the way of werewolves, we'd have some trouble.

"But, when it's done on someone who's close to death, like it sounds like yours was, there's a chance the transition goes poorly. So poorly that the body dies, or near enough to cause issues. Call it system shock or what have you, but whatever intention or will was there is strained, broken even. And once whatever made the choice is shattered, the Hunger takes over. And once the Hunger has a body, it's got no intent of going unfed. The hunger drives the body forward and gets it back up. And the person who made that choice? Well, they're barely along for the ride."

I let out a low whistle and felt sorry for Voigt. Faced with bad circumstances and inevitable death, he took a risk, and it blew up in his face. Still, didn't excuse him from being a murderer now.

Joe nodded sadly, standing up to stir the pot a bit more. "That's not the worst of it though. Once the Hunger is fed, it starts waking up the person. Accessing their memories and such. Demanding more control and agency lest the Hunger go for someone important. Making demands such as 'Tell me how to blend in or I'll eat your child,' or some such. Most dumb bastards just give in, which is the issue. More power and information you give to the Hunger, the less in control you are, until eventually the Hunger has eaten all of your memories and you're just gone."

I gulped reflexively, disturbed by the and implications. Still, nothing exactly useful here. "And why might one of these start eating hearts?" I hazarded.

Joe shook his head sadly, "Well that's a morbid story right there, but I can't talk about it. Trade secrets and all that."

"Even when that Wendigo came here for directions?"

Apparently, that was the question of the hour. Joe stopped stirring so abruptly that the stew sloshed. The gentle breeze disappeared, and the air grew still. Despite the summer heat, I shivered. I tried to ask Joe a question, but the noise died in my throat, causing me to cough. I reached for the tea but knocked it over. That apparently broke Joe out of his silence. He started stirring the pot again and in hushed tones, murmured, "Curt. Poor boy. I knew he was going to be a problem."

McCoy found her voice first, "Define problem."

I wanted to shoot her a glare for her tone, but Joe was murmuring, in a reverent manner. I turned my attention back to him and listened carefully, "....I swear by those who gave me life and life again, I will not go down that road, but one of my line has. My name is Crow Killer Joe and I am to share information with outsiders to correct the mistake of a Craven One in our ranks."

As he finished, an endless number of crows burst from the silent trees and scattered to the four winds. The murders they formed into seemingly beating out Joe's fervent prayer with their wings. Leaves were rapidly shed from the trees, leaving them barren and hollow. Slowly, the crows started to swarm above us. I pried my eyes from the sky and spared a glance at McCoy, who seemed oddly calm despite all this and I took a small solace in that. I turned to Joe, who had quietly resumed stirring the pot. Immediately, Joe's voice spilled out. His voice had lost its honied tones and instead seemed to be full of the frantic infliction and pater of a man who is attempting to hurry through an exorcism[97].

---

[97] Ghosts, unfortunately, are real. And since the government only has two classifications for sentient beings, Human and

"What you're dealing with is one consumed, corrupted, by the Hunger. Curt was willing to die rather than consume flesh again and his Hunger took offense. Now, it is in control. The Hunger has eaten every memory or thought Curt once had and digested them. Without any meaningful soul to maintain it, the flesh of man alone is no longer enough to sustain it, it needs the heart's blood to satiate its cravings, since the Heart is the seat of all power and the soul. It contains all the power and vitality of life, a spark that will satiate the hunger for a while and make the growth they experience increase."

"Growth?" I asked.

Metahuman, dealing with them fell to us despite the fact they are not, in any way, considered alive. Most ghosts are anchored here by something that keeps them from moving on. The nice ghosts seek things like making sure their family is alright or that their kid graduates college. The nasty ones are those that want vengeance for their deaths or who attack any who might distract their child from graduating college. Standard Operating Procedure is to contract someone who can do exorcisms and send the ghost on. Unfortunately, most ghosts do not approve of being ripped from this world and sent to the next, which meant that people who could get through the rites and ceremonies quickly were in high demand. The Chicago MCD contracted a former thief by the name of Carter Biggs for most of our exorcisms, partially because he did the work as part of his parole and partially because he had a unique set of exorcism rites that meant he could banish most ghosts in under ten seconds. He was infuriating to work with so we tried to teach his rites to other people. Unsurprisingly, it doesn't work. Since Biggs had refused any testing or government assistance that would require him to register and be tested under the Metahuman Assistance and Research Act (MARA for short) there was no way to legally confirm he was a metahuman. Still, man did good work, even if he was a cagier than a pet store and more annoying than a yapping dog..

If he heard me, Joe didn't show it. His voice continued unbroken. "The flesh will harden as if bone against blows, the body will leave craters its wake, and the Hunger will grow with it, endlessly increasing and moving to higher levels. Inevitably, it'll find one that is strong with the spirits, and the Hunger will kill and eat them. And the gifts of the Spirited will become the Hunger's own, turning it from a Wendigo to a Craven One. We have seen this, and it brought us ruin. So, if you find a Craven One, it must be cast out and killed. Once for each it has eaten, and once more to be sure that the deed is done. Only then will you be safe."

HIs fervent prayer finished, Joe sagged, looking like he had just run the marathon. His skin hung from his body as if it was hanging directly on the bones, skeletal outlines on his weathered skin. Silence hung heavy in the air, oppressively cloying. In a voice as dry and raspy as the desert wind, he looked me in the eye and stated, "Begone."

Fear abated at his apparently weakened form and questions burning in my mind, I leaned forward. "Not so fast, we have questions. When you say those strong in the spirit, what exactly do you mean? Supernaturals? Metahumans? How does that work? And does he have any weaknesses? Things that would make him easier to kill?"

Joe's droopy cheek started inflating as the muscles and flesh beneath them asserted himself. The slow transition back to a human form was more disturbing than the corpse-like appearance. His voice still harsh and firm, he stared me down. "I've said all I can. Begone."

I went to lean forward again, but McCoy caught my arm and pointed upwards. Where there had once been lush and verdant trees sat the skeletons of a forest fire with every burnt branch so thickly packed with crows, I perplexedly stared, wondering how they didn't break. And the crows stared back at me with a visceral hunger in their eyes that Alfred Hitchcock wished he could have mimicked. Slowly, McCoy and I stood up and backed out of the clearing that held Joe's cottage, countless eyes watching our departure. It wasn't until we backed around the fallen tree did I realize that I was shivering. Wordlessly, we climbed into the truck and Miles drove us out of there just this side of unreasonably fast.

Chapter 17: Unraveling

It wasn't until we crossed out of Menominee county that we found our voices again. Miles broke the silence first, "Okay, so can we all agree that was more than a little creepy?"

"Yep."

"Oh, fuck yes."

"Right," Miles continued, "Now that we've handled that, let's move forward. What did we find out?"

McCoy was busy watching the power lines, presumably for crows, while I filled Miles in. It took a while since we would all stop and eye any cluster of black birds we passed apprehensively. Didn't matter how far we got away from the reservation, every cluster of black birds on a phone line looked like the murderous crows and seemed like they were staring back. There would be a collective shudder and then the recap would continue.

At the end of the summary, I asked "So, 'strong with the spirits'. Does that mean he's eating metahumans?"

McCoy shrugged and Miles shook his head. "I doubt it's just any type of metahuman," he posited. "Probably restricted to ones that fit within the Native American culture."

McCoy guffawed, "Right, cause we're that lucky."

Miles pulled around someone who was silly enough to be doing the speed limit while he explained. "Think about it. Wendigo's are old and powerful, but the O'Dells didn't mention them. If the O'Dell's had known, they would've pointed us in that direction right off the bat, which suggests limited interaction and mixing of the two cultures if any. Far more likely it has to do with shamanistic ideas. Things that are strong in the spirit or have a tie to the spiritual world in some shape way or form."

"That's assuming the O'Dell's shot straight with us." McCoy interjected.

Miles could only shrug.

I chimed in, "No, he's probably right and they probably did tell us the truth. Lot of their reputation is tied to their credibility as information brokers. Besides, what do they lose from talking to us? They probably don't need our power, but to a vampire every shred of legitimacy is important."

McCoy unhappily nodded her head, forced to cede the point, "So, what qualifies as something 'strong with the spirits'?

I turned to Miles, who was already tilting his head in thought as he geared up to pass another car.

"Native American shamans for sure, but also representations of their various mythological beings. A real life kee-wakw or someone who seems to be tightly tied to whatever trickster spirit they have. Any one of those would be viable. We'd need to do research for a full list"

"We can put Danvers on that," McCoy cut in, "Right now we know he ate Hotchkiss. Why?"

"So, a werewolf might be tightly tied to the wolf spirit. It would follow that the Alpha would be more tightly connected which gives them more powers. That connection would be why Voigt went after Hotchkiss," I stated.

Miles nodded, adding, "And if Hotchkiss could fade out, then his gifts would become Voigt's."

McCoy interjected, "Not really, that's a second gen ability. Near as we can tell Hotchkiss was a first gen."

I bit my lip before jumping in, "But we know that the pack has some second-generation members in it. The bouncer that jumped us tried to fade out." McCoy and I went silent, considering that, but Miles didn't let us stew for long.

"Integrated pack? That's really weird. The only thing werewolves tend to hate more than the police is each other. Second and first gens are at each other's throats more often than they are together."[98]

He was right. I couldn't think of a single listed or known example of an integrated pack on file. "I can only imagine how poorly that would've been received. Lots of angry werewolves trying to buck back against the decision." I said slowly

Miles shook his head, "So, there would've been a challenge. A formal contest of Hotchkiss' Alpha status and a ritualized duel."

---

[98] It's true. The Rockford pack used to claim Chicago proper as part of their domain. Then the Walkers got a furry ability as part of the Mayan event. There wasn't even an attempt at peace. Someone, we're not exactly sure who fired the first shot, tried to wipe the other group out and every so often a werewolf would turn up dead. Not sure what happened, but about three years ago the Rockford group retreated and left the Walkers in charge of Chicago proper, to Org Crimes' lament.

"What happens if they can't beat him in a duel?" McCoy asked.

Miles pursed his lips in thought, "I'm not sure, but if I had to guess they'd either shut up and accept it or leave and find another pack."

McCoy wasn't having it. "But that's difficult even at the best of times. This isn't a small decision that you can just ignore or walk away from. This is going against the five years of precedent and conflict. Taking their most hated rivals and suddenly embracing them? That would be unacceptable to some of the old guard werewolves."

"Screw unacceptable. To some of the werewolves who believed in the Hunting Shroud, allying with those who dragged werewolves into the light would be blasphemous," I added.[99]

McCoy nodded, "Might be enough to drive them to thinking about how to remove them in a non-dueling manner."

---

[99] One of the few bits of Werewolf lore the ARCHIVIST system had was about the Hunting Shroud. The "Hunting Shroud" is a first generation werewolf term for the mentality of isolationism from non-werewolves. To summarize the best explanation I've ever received: "Werewolves are hunters and survivalists and such, despite any superiority that may or may not exist, their pride as hunters first and foremost demands that they never give up any potential advantage. Which means that they do not let humans know they exist when possible, do not reveal the full extent of their abilities, and do not engage in knock down drag out brawls if they can avoid them." Many werewolves consider the Shroud broken by the Mayan event, but some still stick to it, out of reverence for the old ways. Those that do adhere tend to also be the most anti-establishment types and the biggest problems for the MCD.

"Especially if there was an alternative sitting around. Someone that was more traditional," I added, following the logic.

Miles looked incredulous, "You think a werewolf turned against their Alpha? And people call me crazy."

"Power corrupts," McCoy rebutted, "Tell me that there isn't a werewolf way to justify that."

Miles shook his head, but the gears were turning. His shake gave out and slowly he started talking, "Werewolves firmly believe that the strong lead and everyone else follows. Arranging a murder isn't strong. What could be acceptable is something like, 'I don't know if Hotchkiss is strong enough to lead. Let's arrange this challenge. If he succeeds, clearly, he's the boss. If not, then we'll find a stronger leader."

That sounded like the exact kind of screwy bullshit logic a werewolf would use to try and justify arranging a murder. I followed that thought for a second, "Explains the bouncer types tracking down Voigt too. Ipsen needs to consolidate his power base, prove he can best the thing that took the old Alpha too in order to show his strength."

McCoy jumped in, "And he's using the second gen types as fodder to do so since they're expendable and unliked."

"Probably using their tenuous status to push them into dangerous situations, "I agreed. "Which might mean that Ipsen is cleaning house. Any idea if other werewolves have been killed recently?"

"Or sent to their doom and not officially reported," McCoy added.

Miles pulled into the right turn lane, heading towards the west suburbs, "Don't know about you, but I'd rather ask in person."

McCoy and I nodded, and then, almost in unison, we both reached for our phones. We hazarded a glance at each other. She explained first.

"Delanch for silver ammunition and coordination."

"Slate to smooth things over and fill him in."

"We should work together more often. Covering bases like that is good."

I smirked, "What, you're actually willing to work with someone?"

She smiled and laughed good naturedly, "Well, not willing. But you suck less than everyone else."

"High praise coming from you!"

"Oh my god," Miles cut in, "Get a room!"

We chuckled and dialed our phones. Or at least, McCoy started to and then she got a look of dawning comprehension.

"Since Wendigo are mythological creatures of the Native Americans, would a Craven One try to hunt them down?" she asked.

The car fell silent again as we considered the implications. Suddenly, Crow Killer Joe's reluctance to deal with this thing made a lot more sense.

166

****

Our trip to the Rockford field office was a quick one. Delanch had already cleared the ammunition, so it was really more of a pitstop and polite conversation with the desk jockey who was manning the office nearly solo than anything else. We then headed to the Burpee Museum of Natural History, arriving at 1650.

I've always enjoyed Burpee. It's like a smaller, more intimate version of the Field Museum, complete with a smaller version of Sue called Jane, plus it is far less stringent with security. So, bringing in full magazines of silver ammunition is much easier. Which we took and went straight to Syd Larsson's office. A security guard tried to stop us, stating things about how where we wanted to go was off limits and that the museum was closing soon, but a quick flash of the badge, and he moved out of the way. I stepped up to the door and was just about to knock when the door ripped open and Larsson stood there glowering up at me.[100]

"Took you long enough. I heard you stomp in the front door."

That caused me to stop and appraise the situation. She was dressed appropriately for the job, dress pants and shirt, but she didn't seem unhappy to see us.[101] In fact, glancing over her face, she almost seemed pleased.

---

[100] Larsson is a shorter woman, somewhere around 5'2" and is built like someone who worked in a field for a living instead of being a museum curator. Most incongruous though is her face, which has a structure that looks far more at home in a renaissance painting than in the modern day. Her hair was black as it could possibly be, which made me think it was dyed. Those two combined with the fact that her left pinky was missing from the second joint down and I suspected that there was much more going on with her than met the eye.
[101] A first for any werewolf I've ever met.

167

"Come in, come in. We haven't got all day." she said, waving me into the small office.

I heard the faint click of McCoy's safety being switched on. Now I was really worried. Larsson stepped out of the door and then I was shoved in by McCoy. There was a shuffling of bodies as we all shuffled in. Then, there was a click as Larsson locked the door behind us.

I braced myself, expecting the worst. This was a trap. I was going to be stuck fighting a werewolf in close quarters. McCoy had actually been infected and was subject to some kind of previously unseen werewolf pack mindset bordering on mind control and she was about to shift and kill Miles and me.

I turned to see Larsson stooping behind the desk and picking up a small backpack. I didn't mean to, but my eyebrow cocked. What the hell was going on here? Sharply, she shouldered the bag and looked me dead in the eye, stating in a voice strained with a thousand cracks, "I'd like to surrender myself to Federal custody. I have evidence that numerous murders have been committed and fear for my life."

Clearly, my imagination was trying to be hopeful with the scenarios it had thrown at me previously. This was orders of magnitude more horrible than I had previously fathomed. I could pretty much hear Miles' jaw hit the floor. McCoy recovered first.

"Of course, ma'am. We'll be glad to assist. Let's get you to the local office and go from there."

I whipped a look at McCoy, propriety be damned. She was glaring at me. Then, clear as day there was a knock on my brain. Just like someone knocking on a door, but it was on the edge of my thoughts. I wasn't sure how to handle that, so I mentally brushed it away. McCoy's eye twitched and the knocking happened again. Okay, so it was McCoy. Taking a gamble, I thought about how to let someone into my mind and suddenly I received a flood of consciousness and my brain was suddenly host to two minds. McCoy's voice rang out, distinctively hers and frustrated.

"Look, we don't have a lot of time here. This is hard for me and difficult. Larsson thinks Ipsen's gonna try to kill her soon and is willing to turn State to stop him."

Questions like "How?" and "Why?" swirled in my brain and I felt McCoy's mental brain shoo them away like one might swat mayflies, *"Could you stop that please? This is already hard enough. It was all over her brain when we came in. Us showing up here saved her the hassle and possibility of the lost face from calling us. We need to keep her safe and the only place I know that can manage that in town is the Rockford Office."*

I imagined nodding to her and the second mind receded, letting my mental state spread out into the parts of my brain I didn't know I had lost. Not a second had passed in the real world, McCoy's communication apparently traveled at the speed of thought. Still, I could see a faint red in her eye, as if one of the small arteries had burst. She turned to the door and I turned the opposite way to Larsson, military mind settling in.

"How long do we have?"

Larsson cocked her head to the side, listening, "Maybe ten minutes. I can hear the hunting howls on the wind, but Ipsen never has liked doing things publicly. Too much concern for the Hunting Shroud." She spat the phrasing out like a curse word. I wisely kept my mouth shut, but Miles couldn't help but jump in.

"Take it you don't care for the old ways."

She glowered at Miles and I felt a primal panic well inside me, much like how I felt with Ipsen in the morgue. "No," she said, biting her words off, "It's always been stupid and now it's just plain suicidal. We're outed and pretending we aren't is just going to get us killed."

Miles, by some miracle, smiled. "Well then, I have an unconventional strategy that will get us out of this without having to go toe to toe with a rolling pack of murderous werewolves."

I smirked and Larsson seemed intrigued. Miles reached into the hallway and grabbed the fire alarm, "I'd imagine having the fire department here would make the hunt too risky."

Larsson's eyes widened in understanding and satisfaction, "Oh, you beautiful child."

Miles sheepishly shrugged and pulled the alarm. I hoped no one noticed that I was annoyed he had stolen my trick.

****

By the time the fire department arrived, we had made a small fire in the banquet room downstairs that had already been doused in order to maintain Larsson's reputation.[102] I

---

[102] Larsson explained that werewolves would know if there was no

had never worked a CI before, but the basics of maintaining their credibility while doing work weren't unknown to me. To help further the ruse, we took her out of the building in handcuffs, loading her into our SUV. I caught sight of Ipsen and a few others standing on a nearby rooftop looking down. I pretended not to see them and loaded up in the car, personally taking the wheel.[103] By the time we rounded the corner heading towards the office, they were gone.

After a few minutes and turns, Larsson seemed to calm down, "Coast is clear, they're not following us," and then turned to hand the cuffs to Miles. He gave a low whistle, before stating, "I'm impressed that you managed to get them off that quick without breaking them."

She smirked at him in a way that I'm not entirely sure wasn't flirting, "Oh, I've been around the block a few times. Picked up a few tricks too."

I cut in before this could get any more awkward, "So why does Ipsen want you dead?"

She smirked; her tone playful. "Oh, the case files at the MCD are clearly less sophisticated than I thought."

I felt McCoy start to glare next to me, but I shot her a quick glance to get her to back down before addressing Larsson, "Look, I'd like to help you but I can't do that if you're dancing around the bush with us."

---

smoke, even without entering the building, so we had to start a fire. Times like this is where I really wish Quinn was around, but we made due with heating elements and the small bar.
[103] Let me tell you this, the urge to wave was strong.

She smiled grimly, but nodded, conceding the point, "Fair enough. I do suppose I owe you that much." She paused, digging into her bag to pull out what looked to be jerky, took a bite, before continuing, "I'm the only person in the pack who could contest his claim to Alpha."

Chapter 18: Sydney Larsson

I was so shocked, I nearly slammed on the brakes so I could whip around to look her in the eye and go "What!" like a bad movie cliché. Instead of causing Miles another headache from angry drivers,[104] I busied myself on changing lanes to make the next turn and let everyone else have their chance to respond. McCoy just shook her head and chuckled bemusedly, seemingly unsurprised by the revelation. Miles, Lord bless his heart, delved right into a slew of questions.

"Oh, is that why you're separated from the rest of the pack? How come you didn't challenge Hotchkiss? What special abilities do you have as someone as powerful as an Alpha? How *does* a werewolf Alpha challenge work? Is it ritualized? What are the rites?"

"Miles," McCoy stated placidly. He didn't hear her and kept going. Apparently, McCoy didn't like being ignored as her calm manner quickly gave way to a death stare.

"Is it first blood or is it to the death? What happens in the event of a tie?"

"Miles!" McCoy shouted.

I hazarded a glance at the back seat. Miles looked slightly guilty, but Larsson just looked merry, like someone watching a puppy thrash around with a sock. It was tempting to laugh, but I didn't want to undermine McCoy's mom moment.[105]

---

[104] I felt awful. Twice on this case, I had the chance to do a movie moment, and moved past them. And sure, <u>Temple of Doom</u> would've been inappropriate, but when else in your life are you going to get a chance like that? I consoled myself with the fact that I had been able to slam on the brakes with Miles a few nights back.

[105] Also, shortly after this, thoughts of Brecht Halthore's manifesto

McCoy let out a deep exasperated sigh, "She can't answer questions if you don't give her time to answer."

Miles honest to God blushed so brightly I nearly got blinded. Larsson chuckled, before turning to Miles. "The function of leadership is to produce more leaders, not more followers," she formally stated. Miles nodded in understanding, seemingly satiated. I was confused, but busy trying to not be cut off by an asshole in a Camaro.

McCoy, on the other hand, was having none of that, "Great line. Who said it and what do you mean?"

"Ralph Nader," Larsson replied with a smile, "And what it means is this. I've been around the block enough times that I've seen how werewolf packs fail and how they succeed. Anyone in a leadership position for long enough gets stagnant and rigid, both in rule and mind. If they don't have someone like me on the outside keeping them in line and advising them, it goes to shit. As such, I don't really have my own pack really, but rather, I talk to the Alpha of many packs

---

came to mind, and Larsson treating Miles like something harmless and cute became slightly darker in my mind. Halthore had released The Fury and Fang shortly after the Event proclaiming that it was time for the werewolves to claim their place as the masters of the world as the clearly superior race on the planet. Comparisons had been made to Mein Kampf, and they weren't entirely wrong. Danvers would argue that it was something closer to Stephens' "Cornerstone" speech, drawing explicit comparisons to how much like Stephens' explicitly stated slavery was the "natural and normal condition" of Africans since they were lesser than white folks, Halthore was demanding that "homo sapiens accepted their place in the world as the lessers and servants of Lupus superior." I started to tune out after that as he devolved into talking about Latin and taxonomy, but I guess he had a point. Enslaving an entire race seems almost worse than killing them en masse.

174

and help them find their own way to guide that is for the betterment of each pack."

McCoy scoffed, "That's some vampire shit right there. Are you sure you're a wolf?"

The tension in the car ratcheted through the roof and Larsson's smile turned knife-like. I glared at McCoy, but she caught my eye and shook her head. Clearly, she thought she knew what she was doing. And Lord help me, I trusted her enough to let her take point. Maybe it was all the food she had brought me. I would've dwelled on the oddity of that sentiment if it wasn't for the very angry werewolf and very small Miles in the backseat.

Larsson sniffed the air twice and then started to restrain herself, apparently considering the situation. "I see. Not sure how I missed it before. Do your coworkers know who your contact is?"

McCoy gave an overly pronounced shrug, "No, but you apparently do. Understand my worries now?"

Larsson nodded, "And you can understand mine."

This time McCoy smiled dangerously, "Intimately. Would you care to share, or should I?"

Larsson shook her head, "If you revealed my secrets, I'd be compelled to share yours. I'll tell."

McCoy turned around and sat looking satisfied. Despite the newfound trust, I personally wanted to strangle her for being so secretive.[106] However, that might cause some

---

[106] The fact that McCoy had leverage over a supernatural was

complications, like presenting a disjointed front to the werewolf. Instead, I settled for thinking about sticking her full of daggers and asking questions. If it phased her, it didn't show.

Larsson sat back and relaxed, "What your illustrious Deputy McCoy is referring to is the fact that my unique 'Alpha' gifts all relate to survival. To start, I haven't visibly aged in nearly four hundred years."

Miles made an "Oooo," sound from the back seat but didn't go much farther.[107] Larsson continued unabated, "Which throws many werewolves through a loop. Most werewolves die in battle or get old. The fact I haven't is an anomaly that is interpreted so many different ways. Steven Hotchkiss saw it as a good thing and sought my advice often. Brecht Halthorne sees me as an aberration to his way of life and thinking but can't bring himself to have me killed. Katelyn Walker respects me enough to let the peace stand."

"And Ipsen?" I asked.

"I'm not sure," she said with an uncomfortable shrug, turning to look out the window, "If I had to guess, he's afraid and trying to kill that which he doesn't understand. Fortunately, or not, that also means that he is being cautious. He's not sure the full extent of my abilities so he's not going to push me or

---

perfectly acceptable. The possibility that anyone, especially a supernatural, had leverage over her was a potential major breach of protocol and was possibly a fireable offense. Though, maybe it wasn't a secret from Slate and he decided not to share with us. I didn't know and I was largely okay with that. Compartmentalization is a good thing as I learned from my time in the military. The fact that it was being talked about in such a brazenly obfuscated way was the real and extremely frustrating issue.

[107] McCoy glaring at him in the mirror might've been a factor too.

take risks." She chewed her cheek for a second, thinking. No one dared to interrupt her. "Although today indicates something changed. Showing up with several of his Knot[108] to a public location where I'd be isolated sounds like him trying to manufacture an excuse to eliminate me. Means I've gone from an anomaly to a threat."

Miles cut in, "If you have made a point to stay out of pack hierarchies, why are you a threat then? Why target you at all?"

She sighed, "Because Steven was my pup. I brought him into the pack, and I raised him up to be a good Alpha. By the Hunting Shroud, I'm expected to seek vengeance against those who made his death happen." There was a pause as her voice softened, "And Ipsen isn't wrong. I do want vengeance. But not for the damned Shroud. Stevie was one of the first people to be willing to try for an integrated pack between the generations and I helped.:

She shook her head angrily. "No, that's not right and unfair. I *pushed* to make it happen and Stevie was just the person to get it done. However, it wasn't a popular position. Ipsen, for instance, thought that integration was a sign of Stevie's weakness. He came to me to see if I'd support his bid for Alpha."

"Wait," I cut in, "How does that work? I can't imagine your relationship with Hotchkiss was private."

She rocked her head slightly, "No, Ipsen knew. He just couldn't conceive of someone as old as I am being okay with

---

[108] A subsection of a werewolf pack. If the pack is like the entire house of representatives, then a knot is one of the voting blocks or committees.

177

making peace with the New moon upstarts. He thought my support was because I couldn't bring myself to condemn Steven and I just needed to be coaxed into it."

She turned towards the front of the car, "Being snubbed by the person who helped raise you is a much larger deal for werewolves than it is humans. With humans, you can just leave and make something new. For werewolves, you don't leave a pack, so you're stuck with this black mark that someone revered left on you. You take your shame, fall, and spend the rest of your days trying to redeem yourself before your elder passes and you're stuck with that shame forever. No one does it casually or easily. If I spoke out against Stevie, it would destroy his credibility and support and he'd be compelled to step down as Alpha."

She turned her head again, "Of course, Ipsen was wrong. I pretty much laughed him out of the office and told him I wouldn't move against blood." She paused, "That was two months ago. And now Stevie's dead." There was a strangled sound that might've been a sob, but I made sure not to look. Woman was already dealing with enough, no need to make her moment of weakness public.

****

By the time we pulled into the Rockford office, Larsson didn't even look like she ever cried. She kept her hands down and together, as if they were cuffed and then we quickly moved her into the building and then into a small office.[109] Larsson took a seat at the table and clasped her hands, waiting expectantly.

---

[109] Procedure dictated we put her into an interrogation room or a holding cell. I personally believe that giving that large of an insult to a werewolf was a bad idea. Like something flimsy like a cell door or reinforced glass would really stop her if she wanted out.

I sat at the table opposite her and smiled warmly, "So, now that we're safe here, I'd love to get your testimony so we can move forward with getting a warrant for Ipsen's arrest." I pointedly reached over, grabbed the tape recorder from a nearby table, set it on the table, and then clicked it on so that there were no questions about what was going on.

"Please state your legal name for the record."

Larsson's hand shot out and jabbed the record button off. "I can't be recorded. The moment that reaches anyone's ears, I'm a dead woman."

I pinched the bridge of my nose, "You came to us for protection because you were afraid for your life. Ipsen wants to kill you." I managed to get out. Levelly even.

"And if it gets out that I gave on the record testimony to the police, he would be one of hundreds," she retorted.

I felt myself groan and slump. She wasn't wrong but it didn't mean I had to like it, "Then why?" I asked.

"Because you only need probable cause to arrest and hold him for 24 hours," she said. I could hear her smiling without looking up.[110]

---

[110] Sure, we could arrest him. All we needed was probable cause. But judges and largely the rest of the law enforcement world hated to do that without the evidence to press charges because it opened us up to harassment charges. Not that werewolves were likely to sue, but it was the principal of the matter and us being worried about opening the door to questions of corruption in the papers.

I winced. There was no way I wanted the answer to my next question, but I had to ask, "And what do you intend to do with that 24 hours?" I inquired, looking up to her face.

"Simple," she said, her voice dropping a few octaves into what I was going to start calling the 'werewolf register', "I claim Vengeance for my pup and make my claim to Alpha irrefutable."

I hate being right.

Chapter 19: Planning

"Okay, but how?" was my inevitable question.

She just kept her face in a smile that I'm sure was supposed to be confident but was just starting to be annoying. I rubbed my temples, trying to resist the growing urge to bang my head against the table. So much for new adventures and unity between law enforcement and werewolves.

McCoy stepped up, "Tennant, may I talk to you and Cross for a second in the hallway?"

I wanted to say no because I was slightly bitter over the vagaries of the car conversation but arguing in front of witnesses is bad form and I was at an impasse anyways. I nodded, and we shuffled out of the room.

McCoy then guided us down the hallway to the kitchenette, where she turned on the fan, started the microwave, and started playing music on her phone before even uttering a word. When she did, she explicitly faced Miles and asked, "So, what do you think her plan is?" while simultaneously knocking on my brain. I thought about letting her in and was immediately slammed by a solid block of thought. Not an individual thought or sentence, but an entire brick of thought that unfurled into a short paragraph of text. It gave me a headache, but what I eventually got was this, formatted something like the Star Wars opening crawl:

"I'm not sure if the sound barriers will actually work, so I'm sticking to mental communication. Sorry for intruding on your brain twice in one day. It's far worse for me than it is for you. Regardless, I think I know what her plan is and can get something workable for both us and the MCD, if you let me

talk to her one-on-one. The end result will be Voigt dead and we'll have a long-term ally in the werewolves, at no minimal risk to ourselves and others."

"Think you know? Weren't you reading her mind?" I responded.

I got the impression of her shaking her head, *"Once she figured out who my CI was, she's been actively thinking about pushing me out. I can break through it, but she might catch me. Alternatively, I can go ask in person."*

"And who exactly is your 'contact' and why does that make her think that she could talk to you one on one?" I fired back. There was a sense of caution and uncertainty as, I think, she considered telling me. In the actual world, I was vaguely aware of Miles responding.

"I'm not sure, but I'd guess something involving Voigt which would make Ipsen's shot to the top a lot less solid. Perhaps killing Voigt, herself?"

The aura of uncertainty dissipated and was replaced with a sense of reluctant determination. *"I can't say who it is exactly, but the fact I'm affiliated at all gives the impression that I'm walking more on their side of the world than the law."*

My immediate response that unfortunately went through was, *"Impression, not truth?"* I didn't know you could mentally project a snub before that moment.

I regretted it immediately, and then a hurt feeling flooded out from McCoy's mental projection. The connection faltered as the pain settled in. *"I can see why you think that, and I know I'm not exactly liked around the office, but I believe in the job and what we're doing. I just need you back me here so we can stop Voigt."*

I wobbled back to reality for a second due to the failing mental link. I wasn't sure if it was the prolonged conversation or my snub that damaged her mental communication to the point of degradation.

"…. well, then she must have a way to find …." Miles continued before I snapped back to the mental bridge. Fucking hell, what had I gotten myself into? I almost missed going door to door checking in on MARA recipients. Fuck, I was stalling. What was I supposed to do here?

Well, there was really only one thing to do. I had already said I trusted her, what was one more leap of faith?

"I don't like it, but you say it'll stop Voigt." I felt her mentally nod, *"The go cut the damn deal."*

A wave of gratefulness rushed from her and the connection failed out. Apparently, time had actually passed this time as Miles was clearly much farther along in the conversation.

"…. still, it might be a thing we could research," he ended with dedication.

I looked up at McCoy who was nodding along, tiredly though with a weariness in her eyes that hadn't been there minutes ago. "Well, that makes sense," she agreed, "The question comes down to how we can spin that to our advantage. I think I've got an idea for that though. Can I go talk to Larsson?" she asked, tilting her head at me.

I nodded and felt my vision swim slightly as my brain wasn't used to the sense of body parts actually moving.

183

She smiled and left the room, taking her phone with her.

I turned to Miles, "How long were you two talking for?"

"McCoy and I have been talking for five minutes," He responded automatically before looking at me, concern crossing his face. "You okay? You looked really spacy."

I rubbed my eyes, "Long ass day. Long. Ass. Day."

****

Forty-five minutes later McCoy yelled from down the hall interrupting my power nap. Miles put away his phone, I smoothed my hair, and we trudged back into the small office taking seats around the small table. There was an awkward silence as we all sat there, all of our eyes slowly moving to McCoy. She gave us all a nervous smile, clearly flustered with being the center of attention.

Hesitantly, she spoke. "So, we have a plan to deal with Voigt and we think it'll work. It's simple enough."

I raised my eyebrow, "Go on."

She nodded slightly, "Okay, so here's how it goes. Once we arrest Ipsen, we let it be known that Larsson is being held at a safe house on the lake and you're guarding her. Voigt's already shown that he's willing to do stupid things to get food sources, and both you and Larsson being a viable snatch for him will probably be enough to lure him in. Once he's there, we bait him over to the lake, anchor him to something heavy and drag him out into the lake. Once he's there, let the anchor hold him down while he drowns repeatedly. Problem solved."

Miles and I exchanged skeptical glances and I could feel pain building at my temples. Simple, but so many places this could and probably would go wrong. Still, it had potential. Drowning at the very least would weaken him, I said mentally running the numbers.[111] It wasn't a no, so the question became how do we make it a yes?

"Setting aside the fact that we're using people as bait for a second, let's just list all the ways this can go wrong and try to make those work. Maybe the four of us can come up with a better plan." I reached over and grabbed a pad of paper and pen, looking at the group contemplatively.

Miles chimed in, "Issue the first, fading out."

"Well, the first question I have," Larsson cut in, "Is how the fuck can he fade out? That's supposed to be a werewolf only thing. A second gen-werewolf thing."

Miles and McCoy looked at me. Great, my job to fill her in. With no way to do it tactfully, I gave the straight truth. "So, we think he gets the powers of those he eats. We're not sure what's all included in that. Best case scenario, only things in Native American mythos. Worst case, everything."

Immediately Larsson rebutted, "But Hotchkiss couldn't fade."

------

[111] My quick math, since showing your work is important. The average person walks a mile every twenty minutes, swims it in thirty. Additionally, you generally die from drowning after three minutes traditionally. If we assume that he'll regenerate when he passes out. That's around the one minute mark. Using the swimming speed for walking along the bottom of the lake, that would mean for every mile we drag him out into the lake, he'd die thirty times minimum assuming he could walk back to shore.

Well, that was as close to a confirmation as we would likely get that Hotchkiss was first-gen. McCoy leaned back and answered for me, bringing the questions we had originally came to Rockford for to the front. "But Hotchkiss isn't the only one missing, is he?"

A look of concern crossed Larsson's face. Her lips pursed before offering, "I know that Ipsen has been sending hunting parties after Voigt. Not all of those have come back." There was a moment of silence and then a collective shudder as we considered the implications of that particular revelation.

Miles was the first to broach the practical question, "Is there anything else we should be worried about?"

Larsson shook her head almost reflexively before pausing and tilting her head slightly, "Nothing exceptional, but I suppose that doesn't tell you what we're looking at. Standard second-generation werewolf abilities. Strength, speed, claws, minor regeneration, improved senses, and of course, fading out."

So, nothing I couldn't have found in the ARCHIVIST records. I wasn't sure if that was a statement of how good ARCHIVIST was or how little she was willing to share. Given her comments about MCD files, I was willing to bet the second. Still, accusing her of holding back on us wouldn't get us anywhere. Pushing the paranoia aside, I turned our concern into a question, "Right, so how do we stop him from fading?"

Larsson paused and then heavily sighed. After a few seconds, she started to talk. It was slow at first, her tone clearly reluctant. "Well, if he fades like a werewolf, stopping him from fading is an easy enough fix. There's an upper limit to what people can take with them while Fading and you have to take everything you're connected to. Anchor him with enough mass and he won't be able to fade without being pulled back."

I made a mental note to shackle any werewolf to a building in future arrests and moved forward before she lost her nerve and didn't tell us more werewolf secrets and weaknesses.

"Okay, but what about him just breaking the cord attaching him to the deadweight?" I retorted.

Miles chipped in, "Get a galvanized high carbon steel wire, woven if possible, to attach whatever we're sticking in him to the mass. Breaking through that, especially underwater, will be damn impossible. Get a high enough tensile rating and we could probably reel it up and use it again if need be."

"Right, so what about the actual spearing mechanism?"

McCoy shrugged, "Figured you could TK lob it through his body. Get a solid stick, and we're set."

That, that was surprisingly simple. I looked at the notepad again and ran through the plan in my mind. There weren't any issues I could find, but that didn't mean there weren't any issues. I did a second scan, just to be sure, before addressing the group. "Okay, this might actually work. I think we can sell Slate on this."

Miles shook his head, "There's still the issue of how we're going to lynch him out into the lake. We'd need a tugboat or something to provide enough pulling force to move him into deep enough water."

I smirked, "I've actually got a solution to that. We use the retired North Point Marina safe house.[112] Once Voigt's there we can just drive the boat out to the lake while Larsson keeps him distracted."

Miles' eyes lit up, "Ooo, that'll work. Plus, it's just a matter of tipping him then and letting his increased biomass and density follow nature's course."

Increased bio….? That explained so much about Voigt, I nearly hit myself for not figuring that out sooner. Given McCoy and Larsson's profoundly confused looks, I probably could've gotten away with a facepalm. Instead, I settled for a groan of comprehension. As I considered all the implications of that revelation. It probably was why he didn't run, that much mass falling over would be probably very dangerous for his well-being.[113]

"Huh?" McCoy asked, cutting off my thoughts.

Miles looked sheepish, "Oh, I thought everyone figured that out. When he eats people, it adds to his own biomass. That's why he's been denting floors and causing cracks in the concrete wherever he goes. I think that it also explains his abilities. Or at least the non-werewolf ones. Instantaneous regeneration, exceptional strength, resistance to bullets, and…."

------

[112] I hate that safe house and was happy to see it go. The actual safe house was a 1970's house boat that always smelled suspiciously of Spam. It was donated to us by someone who's father managed to live due to the witness security division. Somehow, I think we got the short end of that tax write off.
[113] Elephants, and it's theorized many dinosaurs, don't truly run due to the amount of mass they have. It's a combination of the increased momentum being harder to stop, the inherent risk of falling over, and simple physics of having that much mass airborne, which is required for a true run, being nearly impossible to balance.

I put my hand up towards Miles to stop him, before he went on all hour. "We get the picture."

"Do we think he acquires the weaknesses of what he eats?" Larsson cut in.

There was a collective look around the room while we all considered it. We had no precedent to work off of here and Joe's words were too cryptic to give us a clear direction. I didn't know what to say, and given Miles and McCoy's faces they didn't either.

"Put that down as a maybe then?" McCoy eventually suggested.

I made a note and then looked at the scratched and marked pad, "I think that's about everything I can think of, minus the fact that I'm not sure how to make sure Voigt hears about Larsson and me on a boat."

McCoy's smile turned so wolfish I thought that she had been infected and turned into a werewolf. "Actually, about that. I think I have an answer. Something's been bothering me for a while that might let us kill two birds with one stone."

I let out an exasperated sigh, "Oh? Don't we have enough on our plate?"

"Oh, shush," she playfully admonished me before turning serious. "So, when you were in the hospital, the only people that knew we were there originally were Cross and me. We told the MCD, but no one else."

The pain in my temples intensified as the paranoia came back in full force. As much as I wanted to dismiss this out of

189

hand, I couldn't. Just because it sounded crazy, didn't mean it was wrong. "Could've been one of the nurses or someone like that," I offered cautiously.

McCoy shook her head, "Maybe, but then I realized that there was also no real way for the werewolves to have found us at the fairgrounds."

I wanted to say they could've been following us, but there was no way I would've missed a car trailing behind us on 94 for the hours it took us to get to Racine and had to concede that point and the inevitable conclusion. "There's an information leak at the MCD?"

McCoy smiled wickedly, "And I think I know where it is too."

****

The conference room at the Chicago Office was in disarray. The table sat on its side and the chairs were all askew in the center of the chaos sat Jacob Danvers and a dismantled desk phone. He smiled widely at McCoy and me when we walked in, holding up a small wire and microchip.

"Found it!" he proclaimed looking very proud of himself.

McCoy scowled at him, "Weren't you supposed to do so that the person on the other end didn't know we had figured out there was a bug? Doesn't yelling defeat that purpose?"

Jacob waved dismissively at her,[114] "Once I figured out what frequency it was broadcasting on it was simple to set up another signal broadcasting on the same frequency. I've got

---

[114] A surprisingly brazen move on his part, what with him normally being scared of her since the door kicking incident. I chalked it up to a good mood or him being too absorbed in his success.

a loop of ambient office noises set up in my office to broadcast. There's no chance of getting caught until we're ready."

I focused on the more practical reality, "Any idea how this got here?"

Jacob shrugged and waved to his laptop, "I'm not sure. I've been through the entrance and exit cameras for the past three months, and no sign of anyone not expected entering or leaving. Still, based on where it was, they'd need a few minutes to get into the internal workings of the phone and enough know how to do that. And given we haven't gotten any false signals or static, they're pretty deft on the installation."

I sighed, "Which means that either it's someone with access who's on the take or someone that can bypass the cameras.[115] Hell, given that Voigt can fade, might even be him." I personally didn't think that one likely, due to Voigt's lack of restraint and general lack of subtlety, but I figured I should at least consider the possibility given his degree in Electrical Engineering.

McCoy shook her head, "Neither seem good, but one issue at a time."

I nodded solemnly, filling a potential mole away as a tomorrow problem. "Right, so what's the broadcast range?"

---

[115] Things on this list included, but wasn't limited to: Doppelgangers, mimics, werewolves, Carter Biggs, elementals, teleporters, phasers, cloakers, and people who move too fast to be picked up by a camera. I was far more concerned about the intrusion from within. Occam's razor indicated that it was easier to use the existent access than to try to steal some. Then again, I was a cynical bastard.

Jacob gave it a once over considering the object carefully, "Can't be more than twenty-two-hundred feet before there's a receiver or relay point. I'd guess a relay point where it's rebroadcasting in some manner for safety concerns. I'll work on something to locate that once I put the room back together."

I nodded again, "Fair enough. Now just to get Slate to approve the plan."

"What plan?" came Slate's voice behind me.

I jumped a bit, before slowly turning around. The thin wooden door was replaced by the wall of meat that was Slate, frowning at the mess that had replaced his conference room. I felt Jacob reposition himself so he was slightly behind me. I didn't blame him, but it certainly made the uncomfortable situation more pointed.

McCoy stepped forward, taking point. "Well, our plan to catch Voigt," she stated in what seemed to be a confident tone. How she managed that, I don't know.

Slate eyed the room carefully, "And that involved trashing the conference room."

McCoy turned and snatched the bug out of Jacob's hands presenting it to Slate, "Not quite sir. Sorry we didn't loop you in sooner, but we needed to make sure that in house matters were dealt with first. Seems we've been bugged."

Slate stared right through me at Jacob, "Danvers, are you sure the room is secure?"

"Uh, yes sir. As confident as I can be at least," Jacob haltingly replied.

Slate nodded, pulled the door shut, and locked it. With a low rumble he ordered more than asked, "Why don't you catch me up."

And so, we caught Slate up on everything that had happened since Monday. And while he knew most of it, this was less about filling the gaps and more about explaining the chains of logic that had brought us to dismantling the conference room phone. When we were done, Slate looked us over and asked a single question.

"And where is the werewolf Larsson now?"

"Secure in a holding cell downstairs," I responded, "She wouldn't come peacefully if we didn't at least put on the show of arresting her."

There was a solemn nod before Slate sighed and sat down in one of the swivel chairs. It was the closest thing to an emotion I had ever seen from the man. We waited for whatever was coming next, be it reprimanding or clearance to go on with our crazy plan.

Hands folded and resting on his leg, Slate began to talk, "I want you to understand that this is going to be a bureaucratic nightmare."

"Sir?" McCoy and I asked.

Undaunted he continued forward, "In a sane and rational world, we would call in backup from other departments in other states. People so far removed from the situation; they couldn't leak information in a meaningful way. We'd have an

IA investigation. You'd have back up, support, and I'd be pulling every favor and string I could to get you enough firepower that Voigt couldn't pose a credible threat to society or the people tasked with bringing him in.

Unfortunately for everyone involved, we do not live in a sane and rational world."

I wanted to comment, or make a joke, but there was too much solemnity to the moment.

He sighed again, "So, I'm going to do the insane thing and give you everything I can to make this plan work."

"Thank you, sir," I responded automatically, a smile starting to bloom.

He cast a meaningful glance at me which had that smile retreating faster than I care to admit.

"You'll be taking Carlson with you," he stated matter of factly.

I was too cowed to comment, but McCoy wasn't. "Sir?" she asked.

The glance shifted to her and she stepped back slightly. Satisfied, he explained his logic

"I wouldn't risk him trying to grapple Voigt, but he's got the strength to back him up if you can't do it telekinetically and can haul around the harpoon and wire you'll need. Plus, I'm positive he's not our mole."

There was a pause there, where he expected us to ask questions and neither of us had the confidence to do so.

194

Eventually, he tilted his head towards me, giving me permission to speak.

"And how do you know that sir?"

"Discounting my personal opinions," he stated raising his hand to start ticking off points, "He's routinely out of the office which makes him a poor choice for a mole, the mole would want to have as much access to information as possible. Given his tendency to only be in the office around other people makes it exceptionally difficult for him to have planted the bug. While Chalmers and Brooks have been reporting back in, Carlson hasn't been in the office at all since the team meeting and given the time frame didn't know about your hospitalization until after Voigt had already shown up. Need I go on?"

Truthfully, I trusted, or was afraid of, Slate enough to have let it go at he had personal opinions, but the list of reasons didn't hurt. It wasn't airtight, but good enough for me. I nodded, mollified.

"Good," he said before reaching into his pocket to produce a pad of paper and pen. He quickly scrawled on the paper before tearing it off and handing it to me. "Go to this address for your supplies. Carlson will meet you there."

With that, he stood and left us there.

"Well," McCoy said moving towards the door herself, "No time like the present."

Chapter 20: Best Laid Plans

The next evening found us holed up inside the safe house waiting to ambush Voigt. Well, waiting might be the wrong word. It had been seven hours since we had set up and five since Ipsen's arrest and the leaked information. We were starting to get restless and were killing time.

The boat gently rocked underneath me as I checked my phone for the twenty-third time, looking to see if Voigt or the werewolves had raided the Dirksen building or the Cook County Jail looking to grab Ipsen. It was unlikely, given that Voigt seemed to have some semblance of self-preservation and the werewolves would have to go through Walker territory to do so, but possible.

At the table sat McCoy who was cleaning her secondary shotgun and preparing for the coming battle. If it wasn't a spare weapon, I might've critiqued her choice of calming hobbies as leaving her unprepared for when shit actually hit the fan.

Nearby was Larsson, who was sitting in a meditative position, but fidgeting. She had spent the day alternating between meditating and eating. The small cooler she had brought had at one point been stocked with smoked fish, boiled eggs, and other high calorie food, but it was mostly gone at this point.

Over the radio, Trevor Carlson's raspy voice came in a low growl, "Minus the frat party five boats down, coast is clear. Tell me again why we aren't getting the Navy Boys to help like they did at Lovell? Over." He and Miles had drawn the short straws and were in an overwatch position, covering us with Miles' small armory and the harpoon gun that Slate had provided.[116] Thin as we were on people, I was grateful to have Miles above. He was a good enough shot that I trusted him to do his job, but curious enough that having him in the boathouse asking Larsson his gamut of questions would have worn my nerves far thinner than they already were.

McCoy got to the radio first, "Because Slate's ass is already in the fire for that stunt and we don't want to scare Voigt off. The Navy isn't subtle. Over."

There was a burst of static, and then a groan, presumably from Carlson. I fired back, angrier than I probably should have been, "Keep your opinions to yourself Carlson and maintain radio discipline. We know Voigt can mess with electronics and don't want to expose ourselves to that. Over."

They were probably just as bored as us, though at least they had a view to keep them entertained and were outside where the temperature was surprisingly reasonable for late August. The issue was that the houseboat didn't have an AC unit and the windows didn't open enough to allow air flow or heat exchange at a reasonable rate turning the safe house into a safe oven. Honestly, that was probably a notable contributing factor to my temper.

McCoy shook her head, "Why did we have to bring him again?"

---

[116] Harpoon cannon might've been more accurate. I'm not entirely sure where he got it, but the thing looked like it had actually been used to hunt whales at one point. The thing was easily as big as I was, but Carlson tossed it around like it was a football. I wasn't sure how we were supposed to use it ourselves. Then again, I wasn't sure if anything smaller would actually hold Voigt.

I avoided the bevy of logical reasons to commiserate with her for a moment, "Because Slate's a prick who said so." McCoy smiled at that as she moved from wiping to reassembling her shotgun.

Larsson chuckled from her lotus pose, "I should be filming this."

There was a pair of glares shot in her direction. "Oh?" I managed.

She nodded without opening her eyes, "Yes. Show it to the pack and humanize you all. Prove you aren't just mindless drones looking for excuses to kill us all."

That, that was almost a sweet sentiment.

"Seems San Antonio cut both ways," McCoy commented, calming down.

Without any real words to say, I grunted affirmatively and strolled over to the curtains, peeking outside for nominal security reasons. Really, it was to give me something to do that wasn't just sitting and waiting. Laughter and bad part music wafted towards me from the party. I wasn't sure if they were waiting for someone or were too sauced to leave the port, but the fact they were still here was a mite concerning. Part of me still wanted to clear them out so they wouldn't get caught in a crossfire, but McCoy had made a good point that an empty dock would be almost too suspicious. So, we left them be.

"It did," Larsson agreed, "Having a prominent member of your society killed over what was a miscommunication. SWAT had no reason to kick in his door, he had every reason to protest being arrested, and for that they shot him.

And when he defensively shifted, it was used to justify the entire act and sweep it away. There was no justice for Miguel Hosand. It's enough to make people scared. Make them angry." She opened her eyes, sorrow heavy in them, "Make them stupid. A bad combination for anyone, let alone a group with hardwired anger and impulse control issues."

"Never thought of it like that," I confessed, turning from the window. "It's… humanizing? Is that the right word?"

"Humanizing," Larsson said with a laugh, closing her eyes and returning to meditations "will work. At least around me. Some werewolves will find the word demeaning. I can see the point, but I don't have a better alternative." There was a pause where she shifted her legs before continuing dryly. "Personizing just sounds wrong and personified would probably just make people confused."

We all laughed at that. McCoy went to continue the conversation, but I ignored her, focusing on the radio which was buzzing with static again. Angrily, I clicked the coms on, "Could you please stay off the radio Carlson! Over."

There was a pregnant pause before Miles, who was sitting next to Carlson, squawked, "Uh, that wasn't him. Over."

There wasn't even a moment of consideration as I went from angry to gun in hand and moving towards the window. My animation got everyone else moving.

Larsson's eyes snapped open and McCoy dropped the pin she had been sliding into place. By the time Larsson was standing, I was back on coms, giving orders. "Interference on our comms probably meant we were hacked and that meant our ambush was about to get screwed. Which means

Voigt's probably nearby. Assume we're compromised and go to plan B. Combat stations people! Combat stations! Over!"[117]

Larsson started sniffing the air and listening while McCoy cocked her head to listen telepathically. I meanwhile made my way to the deck and started looking around. The dock approach points were free and clear. Even the party was keeping itself contained. "Clear. Over," I murmured into the radio. Shortly, everyone else chimed in,

"Overwatch indicates clear. Over."

"Not picking up any Wendigo thoughts. Clear. Over."

"Nor his scent. Clear," and then belatedly, "Over."

I paused before responding, "Overwatch keep position, assume that this is a ploy to lure us out. Over."

McCoy and Larsson joined me on the deck, armed and dangerous. In a staggered column, we prowled down the dock towards shore, eyeing every shadow skeptically.

Near the mainland, Larsson grabbed my shoulder and pointed towards the marina antenna atop the administrative office, "I smell something up there, but it's faint, like they

---

[117] As the person who was on the phone more often than not since I was the one who spoke the lingo, I became the effective comm officer. Learning to pay attention to communication irregularities was possibly the hardest part of the military but damn was it useful. Most of the time for me that meant that I was paying attention to odd tone shifts, phone calls that didn't have people on the other end, or a dozen or so other issues commonly associated with line tapping. Thankfully, the training covered issues such as extra static too. My guess was a signal jammer, which most infantry would tell you, generally meant a trap.

were here hours ago." She sniffed again, considering, "At least one hour, no more than three."

Her smell was starting to seem like the most bullshit power ever, "And you didn't smell it sooner because?"

She shrugged, "Wind wasn't blowing out towards us and the lake smells would've clouded it if it did."

Definitely bullshit with arbitrary restrictions. I sighed, "Let's check it out."

I found the access ladder bolted to the building and climbed up. Just before I made it up to the roof, there was a small "whumpf" sound and I came to see Larsson already standing on the roof.

She smiled wolfishly at me, "Jumping seemed quicker."

I shook my head, "Just point to the stinky thing."

There was a pause as she sniffed around, then pried open the electrical box attached to the antenna and sniffed some more. Eventually, she pointed, "There."

I reached in, grabbed a boxy looking device and ripped, wincing only slightly from the shock. Based on the solder and differing brand name parts, I could tell that this was a homemade job. Clearly, Voigt's engineering degree wasn't entirely for show. I didn't have much time to consider the device though, because my phone found a signal and immediately started buzzing a horde of notifications. Larsson's nose had served us well.

"Good job," I offered to Larsson. She smiled at me, and I wasn't sure if she was proud or patronizing. Rather than deal

201

with that confusion, I pulled out my phone and checked the notices.

There was a small pile of text messages. Chalmers was keeping us in the loop about the arrest and status of the station, Quinn wanted to schedule a winter conference, and Jacob was letting me know that the signal booster hadn't been found, but he had narrowed down the location. I was about to put away my phone when the voicemail notification buzzed. There were only three people in my life who left me voicemails, and the number wasn't any of them.[118] Hesitantly, I dialed it in, a small sense of dread building in my stomach.

"You have one message in your mailbox. New message." A small and panicked voice crept through the speaker, "Silas, I mean Deputy Tennant. This is, uh, Emily Fairbrooks. From the Circus. You said to call if I saw anything else weird. Well, I didn't see something exactly, but all the animals are unsettled like they were when Curt first joined up, and although I haven't seen him yet, it's really weird. You said to call if I saw anything weird, so I thought you should know. Uh, anyways, I've got a show. Um, bye."

"End of message. Received, TODAY, at ten, FORTY, two P.m."

I checked the clock on the phone, 11:01, and swore. Then, into the radio, I filled people in, "Apparently, Voigt's not coming. He's just been sighted at the Racine County Fairgrounds not twenty minutes ago. Over."

------

[118]Those three people are Telemarketers, Slate, and my mother. Every time I managed to dodge a call from one of them, I thanked Kazuo Hashimoto for inventing caller ID.

Carlson responded, "What the fuck is he doing there? We already hauled away the werewolf corpse."

"Right, there's nothing else that would be strong in spirit up there, there's only…." I paled as dawning realization hit me, "What if he wasn't just coming after me as a replenishing food source like he claimed. What if he was looking to add to his power set?"

Miles spoke up, "We don't have any indication that he's aware of the strong in Spirit requirement we know about do we?"

"No," I said, "but even if he does, we might be wrong about that. It could just be any metahuman. Hell, even if he just thinks that, there's a whole mess of metahumans at the fairgrounds." My mouth stopped, but my brain continued, 'Even if he's wrong, there's no way he's not going to kill and eat all those people.'

The lines went silent for a long second before McCoy cut in, "So, we need to get to the carnival asap."

I started thinking tactically. Clearly, this was a bust and we were in the wrong location. Driving would take at least 25 minutes. No helicopters possible to get to us in time. Boats don't go on land and are actually slower than cars.

I shook my head, "To the SUV's, it's our fastest travel method."

Carlson cut in, "They're too slow. By the time we'll get there Voigt will have had almost an hour to do whatever he wants. It would be better to get support and show up prepared. We need to get reinforcements. And maybe a helicopter."

I wanted to yell. He wasn't wrong, but I didn't like it. People were going to die and if we waited more would. I wanted to go save these people who had entrusted me to their care. I wanted to hurt Voigt horridly and make sure he could never hurt anyone again. I wanted to cause him to suffer like I had and would from being too late. I wanted to do things I couldn't put to words as raw angrish consumed my…

Larsson tapped me on the shoulder. "I can get us there in thirty seconds."

I blinked twice. "Come again?" I managed.

She shook her head in a slightly frustrated manner,[119] "If you trust me, I can get us there in thirty seconds. But you'll have to trust me."

I cocked my eyebrow, silently asking how. She started to shake her head but stopped mid shake. Her voice heavy with resignation, she confessed, "I can fade out with you all and we can take a shortcut that way."

I considered my options for all of no time at all and nodded, "I'm in, but you'll have to ask the others individually." I had gotten this far on faith, time to double down.

She shrugged and then nodded, "Fair enough."

We stood by the SUV's side by side and waited for people to arrive. McCoy was the first to show up having been searching in the nearby area. Barely a minute later, Carlson loped up carrying the harpoon gun casually over a shoulder and a sack of harpoons. Miles, with his duffle bag of doom,

---

[119] In a way that uncomfortably reminded me of what my mother would do when my father started telling military stories.

wasn't far behind. When they stopped short of the SUV's, Larsson stepped forward, "So, I want to kill Voigt for my reasons and you all want to help the people at the fairgrounds. I can get us there in thirty seconds if you're willing to Fade to do so. If not, I'll understand."

Before people could consider, I cut in. "I'm already planning on going, but I can't order you to follow. Anyone else coming with?"

Almost instantly, Miles said, "I'm in," and moved over towards us. I turned to Carlson and McCoy.

McCoy was palming silver rounds into the shotgun but shook her head. Carlson however simply swallowed and then asked, "We can bring the guns, right?"

Larsson tilted her head before nodding, "Yes, but I thought you didn't need them?"

He shrugged, casually bumping the harpoon gun as if it were a pillow, "I don't, but the harpoon was supposed to stop him from fading, wasn't it?"

I nodded slightly, but clearly my face was showing doubt, because he continued, "Look, I don't have a problem going to save people. I have a problem with recklessness. If we were driving there, we would've been late anyways, might as well have gotten help," he stepped forward, leaving McCoy alone, "I'm in to save people. This is the fastest way to do that."

I eyed McCoy, still shaking her head, "Nope. Nope nope nope. Nope," she muttered, "I'm not going with the anti-authority werewolves into a place where they'll be able to abandon us cause they asked nicely. Not a chance."

I couldn't blame her, each person had different definitions of what worth it was. "Okay, well then just the three of us will be taking the ride…."

Larsson cut in, talking at McCoy, "You know, if you stay here, you can't shoot me in the head if I backstab your friends?"

McCoy's hands shuddered for a second, nearly fumbling while loading another shell. We all waited for her to respond.[120] After a pregnant pause, "Okay, fine, I'm in. Fuck you all."

Larsson smiled pleased with herself and then whistled loudly into the night, "So, here's the trust moment. I can't fade, Full Moon[121] and all that. But I have friends who could. And they refused to let me act as bait with only cops as my support."[122]

Almost in unison five wolfman werewolves stepped into our reality ten feet away, and Carlson jumped in surprise. I somehow managed not to not show my shock and McCoy only twitched her trigger finger instead of shouldering the gun and firing. Miles however simply looked over at them and instead started asking questions, curious wonder

---

[120] I was guessing with a shotgun blast to Larsson's head.
[121] A werewolf euphemism for differentiating between the types of werewolves. 1st gens were "Full Moon" and 2nd gens were "New Moon" if people were being nice. "Broken moon" was a more disparaging slang for 2nd gen werewolves who responded by referring to the 1st gens as "Hollow mooners". And I thought name calling stopped in middle school.
[122] I made a note of this for later. Werewolves acting against their leader's words for their best interests? It was the first piece of evidence the marshal's had that the rule of the Alpha wasn't absolute. Then again, that might've been because Larsson wasn't the Alpha yet.

creeping into his voice, "So they followed us from wherever you fade to?"

"They fade to," she corrected with a shrug, "But pretty much. I don't fully understand it and they didn't give me much choice."

Miles' eyes lit up, "Think they'll be willing to answer questions as we travel?"

At this point, McCoy started muttering again. I couldn't hear her, so I leaned in, tuned out Miles, and she repeated herself, "This is such a fucking bad idea. You're lucky you're the only person in the MCD I can tolerate."

I decided not to mess with her,[123] and instead said, "Thank you, this means a lot."

She just shook her head, "This fucking sucks."

---

[123] "AWWWWWWWWWWW, someone's got a crush!"

Chapter 21: World Wonders

One of Larsson's werewolves looked me in the eye and they slowly grabbed my shoulder with a hand bearing claws that looked even nastier than the ones that had disemboweled me. Despite myself I swallowed. They,[124] met my eye, I nodded, and then I felt myself yanked sideways.

The world I found myself in was only tangentially related to the one I left. There was a covered cove, a large lake, and land, but the similarities ended there. Where there had been a smattering of boats in a small cove turned into large and gaudy palaces and skyscrapers built on stilts over the water, stretching high enough to block out the sky. Surrounding the decadent structures was a wall so high that Donald Trump would've been envious with a fortified gatehouse that looked vaguely like the administrative office I had just finished climbing. Turning, I saw the sky unmarred with light pollution, the moon somehow at the center of it all. Around it the constellations, instead of little blips of light, actual animals and figures, danced and moved in mesmerizing patterns. I took a second to witness a celestial dragon stop talking to the large bear that I think was Ursa Major, moving past a smaller bear, logically Ursa Minor, to start another conversation with a swan.

My wonder was interrupted by a throat clearing to my right. I managed to peel my eyes from the wonder above to see the wolfperson who had brought me here looking bemused. For a second I saw triple, with both their human face and their wolf face superimposed with the hybrid form, fading away too quickly to pick up on the details They pointed to Larsson.

---

[124] I wasn't about to do the awkward thing and look at the furry bits to figure out a gender. They would do as a pronoun.

Larsson was an intimidating person in reality, but here she towered over us and was wrapped in a pale white armor that covered her wolfman form and an inexplicable sword buckled to her hip. The seeing triple thing happened again, before reasserting into her human form.

"Why do you look human?" I asked and apparently Miles asked in unison. She smiled in a way that made me want to both shrink in fear and have her protect me from those who would make her frown. "Because I felt it would be more comfortable and appropriate for you. Welcome to what the New Moon call the Shade, where truth is laid bare and thought affects reality. Since the truth is, I am all my forms, so I express the one you are most comfortable with for ease."

I glanced at my hands but saw nothing different. Curiosity got to me as I turned to look at Miles, who stood there looking much as he normally does. His eyes were slightly wider and tinted with his curiosity. His entire face was expressive and full of emotion, from the tear stains and smile lines, projecting his emotions just as well as his abilities did in real life. He had a slight and darker than expected shadow, but it was fraying at the edges. As a whole, the Miles I saw was who I knew him to truly be; caring, inquisitive, and trying to move past a part of his life he didn't want anymore.

McCoy however floored me. What little of her skin I could see had a grey pallor that almost looked like stone or armor. I say what little, because she was clad in spiked armor that didn't have discernable gaps, almost as if it was welded on. It was black in such a way that sucked in the color from the air around it. The air around her was several degrees colder and her head was inside what looked like a fishbowl full of whiskey which made her eyes look bloodshot and red.

Through the cracks in her armor, I saw a dark shroud that obscured a bright core, frantically fighting to be seen. I tried to make sense of it all. Closed off, reserved, but with a good heart and willing to fight. She looked at me looking at her and the cracks in the armor closed even farther, smothering the light within. I choked on my words for a second before offering, "If I look half as good as you do, I'd be surprised."

There was a slight chuckle that rumbled from deep within her personal fortress and the cracks opened back up, not as much as they were before but some small amount. "I wonder why we can't see ourselves."

"Two reasons," Larsson interjected, "One, Because the truths about ourselves are always more apparent to those around us. And two, because you see yourself the way you see yourself in the mirror, not as the truth. Overcoming that is always difficult."

I didn't have the mental capacity to fully contemplate that right now, so instead I pushed to put us back on track., "As fun as this is, shouldn't we get going?"

She smiled, "Oh, that won't be an issue. While you all were talking, our friends were taking us there."

I turned sharply and felt myself completely thrown off balance as if I had a weight on my back that I hadn't accounted for. When I staggered back to my feet, I noticed the five werewolves we had come with were now dressed as knights too and had dug their swords into the ground. That had, apparently, lifted us and the ground we were standing on and propelled us across the alien landscape. A man in pristine military dress uniform turned to us and spoke in Carlson's voice, "Remind me to never go on missions with you again." His unmarked face was looking slightly green around the edges, "Motion sickness sucks."

I shrugged, "I'll keep that in mind," I said before motioning to the uniform, "I didn't know you served."

Carlson's face wrinkled in confusion, "What? No, I never served. Couldn't. Why I became a bounty hunter. Way to stop assholes without needing to sit the ASVAB."

I took a second look at the uniform and noticed that none of the medals were spelled correctly. Often the words were just jumbled messes. Man thought himself a servant of the country even though he couldn't actually serve due to a disability. Suddenly, my respect for the man shot up and sympathy went out to him.

"My apologies," I managed before we were lurched to a stop. This time I felt whatever it was on my back start moving to stabilize me. With a mighty "whump" I managed to stay on my feet even as the bubble lurched.

"We're here," Larsson proclaimed.

The carnival looked like a Wonder Ball, a thin layer of sugar, excitement, and happiness but on the inside the real truth was laid bare, and all those niceties were just false promises to a hollow and, in this case, trapped center full of predatory monsters. I shuddered, not knowing if the monsters this reflected were Voigt, the showrunners who hid him, or both. Still, there was work to do and I was sure we'd find that answer out soon enough. We partnered backup with our werewolf buddies who brought us sideways. Cautiously, I leaned over towards Miles, "Do I have wings?"

"And so much more."

211

I wanted to ask him to clarify, but we were then abruptly yanked sideways and into the Fairgrounds. The overwhelming sense of dread hit me first followed by the smell of the burning. I looked upward and found one of the concession stands collapsed into a flaming mess with the fire threatening to spread. Civilians were running haphazardly and faintly I heard a canned version of "The Stars and Stripes Forever," playing. The attempt at patriotic tones through bad speakers somehow making the scene turn from disturbing to outright macabre. I took a moment to orient myself, looking around frantically.

To my right, I found Miles collapsed on the ground, overwhelmed with the dread pumping through the Fairgrounds. Carlson was trying to help him but was completely at a loss of what to do. The werewolves seemed better off but were clearly awaiting orders. To my left, Larsson and McCoy were scanning, trying to bring this all in with panic stretched across their faces. My mind raced and it wasn't going anywhere fast. This was a shit show, we were screwed. We were all going to die.

This was not okay.

I paused and pushed the compounding dread to the side, recognizing it having the same artificial feel as the sorrow in the hospital. The environment and Miles were creating this horrid feedback loop, so to be able to work, we needed to start there. I pointed at the white furred and scarred werewolf who seemed least affected and said, "We need to get Miles out of here and deal with the crowd. Let's kill two birds with one stone. Could you take him and go over there," I said pointing towards the parking lot, "And get people out of here. This much panic, I imagine the police are on the way. If you can make it so they can get in, that'd be awesome, but right now my priority is getting potential victims away from Voigt."

"And potential power ups." McCoy added in.

"Not helping McCoy," I snapped. Miles really had to go before the panic got the best of us, but the werewolf was looking at Larsson for orders. I groaned, this was no time for 'you're not my boss' politics and questioning. "Larsson," I growled, "Can you tell your friend that my idea is okay for him to do."

I felt her laugh more than I heard it, "Go and help the small one Decapitates-the-Leech," she rumbled while pointing at a werewolf with matte black fur "And you can help him Lupus Noctis."

McCoy's mouth started to move to put the smirk on her lips to words, but I shot her inevitable snarky comment down with a glare. I glowered mentally at her, "We need these people right now, and insulting them is not conducive." To her credit and my astonishment, she actually backed down.[125]

---

[125] Later, I talked to Larsson about this, she told me that werewolves, particularly second gen ones, all have what were referred to as "Awakened Names" which are their individual tickets to and from the Shade. As part of the werewolves' coming of age ceremony they are walked into the Shade and stranded there to undergo a vision quest to find who they are.

However, even walking through the realm of truth presents it's difficulties when there are no mirrors and you can't see your full body. The idea is by interacting with the environment and its denizens you gain the truth of yourself. When you got enough of an idea of that, you try to encapsulate that idea in a short phrase, subject to your personal interpretations. The young pup tries to speak that phrase and if they're right, they come out of the Shade and are welcomed to the pack. If they're wrong they wander more until they figure out their Awakened Name.

When I looked back, the ying-yang twins had already taken Miles off towards the crowd, casually leaping over cars, and with him it was as if the smothering blanket of dread lifted. I shook my head trying to dislodge out the remnants, but a thin wrapping of unease still remained. I was about to try again when a thought struck me.

"Okay, that feeling we're feeling is one of the metahumans in the area by the name of Emily Fairbrooks. If we can figure out where she is, we'll probably find Voigt and be able to....," I trailed off considering my words for a second, "Secure Larsson's deserved spot as Alpha."

The remaining werewolves seemed to rally and cheer at that idea and Larsson took that as her cue to start giving orders, "Guide, take point, find the source of this unease so I might dine in vengeance for Lucien Vigilant,[126] Perilous Truth Seeker, cover our flanks, and Storm Before the Calm," she said motioning to brown furred with white spots werewolf who seemed just this side of boiling over with rage, "take vanguard position. I don't want anyone sneaking up on us."

Rapidly, they fell into position and we started moving towards the trailers at the back of the park. I'm not sure if Guide, a salt and pepper furred and shorter werewolf, was

---

So, 'Storm Before the Calm' was all about 'Earning peace through unfortunate violence.' 'Decapitates the Leech' was dedicated to "Removing the parasites and undeserving from society.' 'Lupus Noctis' was just as unimaginative, plain, and bad at Latin as his name implied. I then asked about those who never figure out their name and got a glare that stopped me from asking any other questions.

[126] Steven Hotchkiss' honorary Awakened Name. Even though he was a first gen, apparently he commanded that much respect. Larsson refused to tell me hers, but did confirm that she had received an honorary name too.

intentionally trying to make it easy for us, but we didn't run into any crowds or trouble along the way, ending up at the edge of the main thoroughfare where the metahuman tent still stood. Almost in waves, I felt the dread rushing out of there. Perilous Truth Seeker cut a hole in the side of the tent and dove in first, which was almost immediately met with a dull thunk and a growl. A voice brash male voice yelled from within, "You stay the fuck out of here you furred fucker. You're not disemboweling anyone today."

McCoy turned to me, "Is that Keitner?"

"I think so," I said, turning to yell back at the tent, "Mr. Kietner, this is Deputy Marshall Tennant. We're with the werewolves to try and help you all."

From the hole cut in the tent Keitner's massive head and only one of his shoulders popped out, "Holy shit, it is you. I thought you were dead?"

I smiled despite myself and patted my stomach, "Nope, still alive and all in one piece."

"Emily told me you were gifted like her. Didn't believe it until now." His brow furrowed in thought, "But did these furry types try and kill you? Why are you working with them?"

My smiling turned into laughter despite myself. From the outside this was certainly a confusing turn of events. "Different group who don't like the group who clawed me up. These ones are friendly."

He smiled in response, "Oh good!" There was a slight shuffle as he moved out of the doorway followed by Perilous Truth Seeker bounding out of the tent looking annoyed in a way I didn't know something with a wolf's muzzle could.

Suppressing another smile, I stepped into the tent, where Emily, Keitner, and a few other members of the circus were circled up, trying to ride out the storm in the one place they were comfortable enough to mount a defense.

Emily's face lifted in a wide smile when I walked in and the dread wave went away, "Silas!" she cried bounding across the room to bury me in a hug. "I was worried you wouldn't come."

I stood there with an assault rifle sitting awkwardly in my one hand as I patted her back and tried not to think about the crushing sensation on my ribs, "Uh, good to see you too Emily," I glanced around the room, "Where is everyone else?"

She pulled herself off of my chest, her voice valiantly trying to suppress a worried waver, "We're not sure. About ten minutes ago, the disaster march started playing and we all rushed to figure out what was going on. All I saw was the elephants starting to stampede out of the big top, and decided the best idea was to hide out in here. Charlie, Stan, Lilith, and Henry all had the same idea. We were really worried when we heard a wolf howl, thinking that the werewolves had come back, but then you all showed up."

I paused and looked at Larsson, who was in her human form and walking into the tent, "Did any of yours howl?" She just shook her head.

"Well, that's probably where Voigt is then," I said turning back to Emily, "Do you know which way the howl came from?"

She shook her head, but one of the carnival workers who had in what would be called humorously large ears in other situations, Stan, if my memory was correct, stepped forward, "It was by the animal cages," he said confidently, "We don't have any wolves in the circus, but it would explain the panic."

I nodded, "Thanks. Larsson, can you spare any one to help keep these people safe?" She glowered but nodded and whistled. I began to wonder if she had any other facial expressions. Before I could do something stupid, like ask, someone who was vaguely Native American in build and coloration walked in, "Come with me folks, I'll get you out of here." I made my way back through the hole to where McCoy stood with Storm Before the Calm[127]. As one they turned to me, SBtC spoke first, "You do well to protect your mate from the abomination. You're alright for an unawakened servant of our oppressors."

I stood there in shock trying to figure out if I should respond to the backhanded compliment or the implication, I was having sex with Emily first.

"I'm not dating, let alone mating, that woman," I eventually stammered out. Apparently, that was the more important thing to establish here. Great job brain.

Their eyebrows rose, "Truly? She seems very interested in the idea of mating with you. I could practically smell and hear her offer herself to you from here. Eagerness is a good quality in a mate."

McCoy spoke up, pent up sarcasm finally bursting free, "No, he's too busy trying to mate with someone far too pretty and

---

[127] I decided to mentally abbreviate that as SBtC. It was shorter and so much easier to keep a straight face when saying.

smart to fall for his dumbass." I wanted to shoot her but was still reeling from the implications of my sex life.

SBtC scoffed, "Don't go for an Alpha. You're not worthy. Consider someone more akin to you and your abilities, such as the Emily or the McCoy here, and you'll be much happier in life."

McCoy and I looked at each other and burst out laughing almost in unison. Through the laughs she managed to get out, "Oh no, not a chance. He's not even close to my type."

I was too relieved that she found it as preposterous as I did that, I didn't even add in. SBtC just looked at us confused, "Why not? You are clearly a fine battle pair. Your children would be great warriors."

I responded first, "Not exactly my first thought when seeking a, uh, mate."

SBtC shook their head, "Humans are truly weird," they said before walking away.

McCoy and I had a good laugh before Larsson joined us looking matronly, "What is so amusing about Voigt?"

I breathed deep and pulled myself up out of the laughter, "Oh, it has nothing to do with Voigt and everything to do with Storm Before the Calm's ideas about how human dating should work."

"Wolfborn," she responded with a finality that suggested that explained everything. Before I could ask questions, a howl went through the camp and we all stopped to contemplate it for a second. Larsson started moving towards what I suspected were the animal cages, "That wasn't one of mine, or even a werewolf as far as I could tell. There was a moment of consultation, a nod, and then we took off running.

Perilous Truth Seeker dashed out ahead of me, leading the path. After a few moments, I spotted Carlson and SBtC converging from wherever they had moved off to. We moved as a unit, covering each other's flanks and blind spots. We dodged tent lines and rounded corners without missing a beat. It was an exhilarating feeling moving as one, and for a moment I could almost see the appeal and mentality of a werewolf pack.

And then it all came crashing down.

Right as we rounded the final corner to the animal cages, we found the first bodies. Two stagehands, who looked like they had been sitting around a small fire, were splayed out over their bucket chairs. Hearts ripped out of their chests; bodies discarded like burger wrappers.

They were only the start of the trail of carnage. Slowly, we crept forward, delicately stepping over the remnants of stagehands, animals, and other workers alike. I paused to offer my respects to what looked like the remains of the man-anaconda[128] hybrid I had seen on my first visit. It disturbed me slightly to realize that my first thought was not about the loss of life but instead trying to figure out what, if anything, Voigt might have gained from that kill.

------

[128] Were I a clever man, I would've called him a Manaconda on the spot. Sadly, it wasn't until Leo Walters at the Tribune wrote the story about this entire shit show that I even heard it, and by then it was too late for my brain to contemplate taking credit. In fact, by then I was too frustrated that human life, especially metahuman life, had been reduced to pithy one liners.

219

Eventually, the trail of corpses led to a small clearing where a wolf thing stood in slightly dented ground from its impressive weight. It paid us no mind as it finished using its snout to eat the heart straight out of the chest instead of needing to pull it out first. I suppressed the urge to vomit and toggled my safety off. At the same time, McCoy raised her gun to shoot and Larsson started to shift into her wolfman form and Voigt dropped the body and spoke without turning to face us, "Oh good, I was wondering when my main course would arrive. These morsels barely whetted my appetite."

Chapter 22: The Challenge

Voigt straightened and smiled wickedly at us, the rotten honey of his voice pouring all over us, eyes focused on me, "I wasn't expecting you to show up so soon Deputy. I figured that you'd still be at the boathouse, waiting for me to walk into a trap I saw from a mile away." He paused, smiling his slasher smile. I wasn't about to give him the satisfaction of letting my frustration reach my face.

"Well, bully for you. Still, why come here?" I asked, fingering my safety off. "Why not just run?"

He shrugged and dropped what looked to be half a rib cage carelessly to his side, "Well, I still want you to be my mobile snack bag. I figured, If I just went after the pathetic little freaks you're charged with policing, you'd show up eventually. And now the advantage is mine."

I shouldered the rifle but didn't open fire quite yet. To my sides, Storm Before the Calm, McCoy, and Perilous Truth were all fanning out, looking for optimal angloo. Stalling for time, I carried on Voigt's conversation, "Ya know, the 'little freaks' I'm responsible for includes your cannibalistic ass. And policing in this case means putting you in the ground."

Voigt cast a careless eye at the attempt to surround him and actually started to walk forward, making the process easier. It might've been over confidence on his part, but I wasn't sure it was going to help us here. "Please, Deputy, cannibalism only refers to those who eat their own species. I can do things that humans, metahumans, even Gods could only dream of. And, I'm not even at the limits of my abilities. We're no longer the same species."

"I've heard a similar speech from a Vampire before, right before we dusted him. You can have your delusions of grandeur, we're still going to put you down," I declared far more confidently than I felt.

"You will try," he rebutted, "And you will fail. I'll capture you and kill each of your friends. And then, I'll take you with me as I go find more people to eat and absorb. You'll be my perpetual snack to keep me satiated between full courses."

I shuddered and went to retort, but McCoy was apparently not having any of that. She yelled, "Eat this mother…" and the shotgun blast blew the rest of the sentence away. The slug blew clean through Voigt's head. Instantaneously, the damage was gone, and he was back to square one, fully healed, leaving only some errant debris flying through the air as if spawned by bad movie special effects. His head swiveled to McCoy, "Right, you. I think I'll eat you first for all the annoyances you caused me at the hospital." McCoy responded by putting another slug through his head, presumably adding another death to whatever unfathomably large number we needed to reach. I followed suit, carefully putting the trigger into three round bursts all aimed at his head.

There was a faint thud as he took his first step towards McCoy. When he went for his second step, a body shaking whump filled the air and a harpoon filled Voigt's left kidney, causing him to grunt in pain. Before he could respond, McCoy put two more slugs into his head and then a mess of fur I hadn't seen yet tonight plowed him over.

Despite the standard extra mass, fur, fangs, and claws that all werewolves had[129], Larsson had enough unique features,

---

[129] The average werewolf, when shifting into their wolfman form,

I could immediately see that she was a cut above the average werewolf. First of all, she was just plain faster. The average werewolf had an animalistic fury and intensity that gave them extra speed over humans, but Larsson moved so fast that if I blinked, she appeared to teleport. Additionally, her fur had an almost metallic gleam to it, the purpose becoming apparent almost immediately when one of Voigt's pilfered werewolf claws tried to strike her arm and the fur matted and then blended together to form an armor like sheen. The claw struck solidly, but couldn't find purchase against the armored fur, turning what should've been a crippling blow into a glancing one.

However, her survival abilities were apparently more in line with Ali's thoughts on boxing, as she rolled with the strike, deflecting most of its momentum and reappearing twenty feet away, giving McCoy and myself enough time to open fire on Voigt, aiming for concentrated headshots. My shots weren't doing that much besides seemingly frustrating him. It seemed especially useless because every time a slug went through his brain, all the head wounds disappeared, and he reformed. I stopped, looking to save my ammo[130] and figure out what was going on here. Just shooting him wasn't getting us anywhere useful, we needed a way to end this for good.

The claw marks and tooth marks from Larsson's assault were gone as were all my bullet holes, but the harpoon was

---

gained between one and two feet in height, nearly 45 to 75 pounds of muscle, their teeth sharpened to a razor sharp point, and their nails extended into claws that were between two and three inches long. Larsson was on the upper end of all those ranges. Can you understand why I don't want to be on their business end?
[130] Also Silver ammo was expensive. Using it because it was the only option for the situation was unfortunate, but tolerable. Wasting it would've just added to the headache that was the situation and would've earned me a much deserved tongue lashing.

still logged in him. Okay, that could be useful. It suggests that when he heals, he has an upper limit on what his body auto-rejects.[131] I had the start of a plan forming when he started to stand up. Carlson yanked on the harpoon tether to unbalance him and then suddenly Larsson was on top of him, claws and fangs in tandem, not doing much damage, but working to distract him long enough for McCoy to reload. I started to feel hopeful, if we could keep this pattern up, we could just grind him down. Only issue is if McCoy ran out of ammo before Voigt ran out of lives, I didn't have a backup plan.

My contemplation was interrupted by a noise that would've been called a yip if it didn't come from a gravel voiced werewolf. I looked up to see Larsson suddenly flying through the air. I looked over to Voigt who was putting his foot back on the ground and trying to break the harpoon off. That struggle was compromised by Carlson pulling on the tethering line causing the harpoon hooks to dig into Voigt's abdomen. Voigt was unbalanced for a second before gaining purchase and pulling back on the line. Carlson's momentum was broken and then reversed, slowly sliding forward.

It bought enough time for McCoy to finish her reload, level, and put a slug through Voigt's head. Staggered, Voigt stopped fighting the pull and Carlson was able to stop his slide. Once he stopped, he started pulling again, knocking

---

[131] It was very similar to how my body healed, though from what I saw, my body had a much lower threshold. Needles and stitches were often easily shunted, but there was a time I had a bullet lodged in the arm and the flesh just healed around it. Worst part was that the body kept trying to heal into the bullet and couldn't. By the time I got to surgery, cutting the bullet out was buried deep under freshly healed skin and the anesthetic barely worked. In order to avoid that from happening again, I signed myself up for classes at this point to help me brush up on field medicine skills so I could cut them out by myself and save everyone the hassle.

Voigt to the ground. As McCoy sighted on the now prone Voigt, he twisted and grabbed the harpoon. One hand on the hook in front of his body and one on the tether loop on the back. Without hesitation, he shoved on the harpoon, pushing it through his left abdominal wall and taking several large chunks of flesh with it. Despite the confidence he had in destroying his own body, Voigt laid on the ground, his eyes clearly bleared in pain. Blood and bile poured from the gaping hole in his side.

Now that was a first. Hope started welling up again. Didn't matter how strong you were, missing muscles and blood loss would eventually get to you. The hole started to knit itself together, but even if his healing was three times faster than mine, he'd die of blood loss first.

McCoy wasn't about to give him that chance. She pumped a fresh shell into the shotgun, topped off with one final shell, squaring up to blow Voigt's head off again. The lightbulb went off in my head: he didn't reset until he reached a point of actually being dead. Killing him wouldn't stop him but maiming him would. But, before I could even start to say "No," and explain to McCoy, she squeezed the trigger, resulting in a very small amount of brain being splayed across the ground and fully healed Voigt smiling wickedly at us all.

"Well, fuck," is all I managed before Voigt rolled to his feet started the terminator walk towards McCoy. McCoy unloaded one, two, three slugs into Voigt's head, each of them resetting his body, but not slowing or staggering him the least. I tried to yell but being heard over the roar of a shotgun wasn't within my skill set. McCoy was slowly backing up, trying to maintain distance, but she was going to run into a tent soon and then be trapped.

I snapped my rifle to point and instead of going for headshots, I aimed for the ankle, looking to cripple him. If it worked on werewolves, why wouldn't it work here? I exhaled and let a full auto burst carry me up his left leg, tearing his muscles and almost causing him to stumble. Unfortunately, McCoy's next slug tore through his face and undid that progress. I went to swap magazines but fumbled the reload when McCoy tripped over a tent anchoring line and fell. She was scrambling, but not getting much of anywhere on the muddy ground as Voigt stooped low to grab her. I frantically dug for my telekinesis in a last-ditch attempt to save her, but knew I'd be too late. She was going to be dead and there was nothing I could do about it.

Then suddenly Carlson was there, running the harpoon through Voigt's back and lifting him off the ground. I had to mentally scold myself for forgetting the other people here. McCoy, relief in her eyes, managed to scramble under Voigt's flailing legs, grab her shotgun, and move to a safe distance. Before she could bring the gun back to bear, I yelled in the relatively quiet night, "Shoot to maim! Shoot to maim! He doesn't heal until when he's actually killed!"

McCoy didn't even hesitate, the gun stopped far short of the head and she squeezed the trigger, turning Voigt's left foot into a mushy pulp. Voigt cried out in pain, validating my insight and halting his flailing for a split second. Which is all Carlson needed to upend the harpoon and drive the point into the ground, pinning Voigt face down, before stepping back satisfied. I blinked, and Larsson was there again tearing at Voigt's tendons, severing most of his fine motor control. There was a whoosh of air and then she was standing next to me as we watched his flayed arms try to knit themselves back together while he screamed in pain, without any real direction or motion. Carlson stood a pace or two back watching him warily.

McCoy stepped to my side, "So, now what?" she plainly
asked.

I shrugged, "I'm not entirely sure. He's too crippled to do
much of anything right now. He's growing back, but we can
keep him pinned for the time being, tearing open what
heals." I said, pointing at the damage. "But, the drowning
plan won't work here," I said, stating the obvious.

Larsson appeared next to me, "Well, we still need to kill him
permanently. His death is the only way I can solidify my
power base and displace Ipsen."

My brain kicked on something, and I could feel the engine
that would ignite a light bulb starting up. "Power." I
murmured.

McCoy caught the spark too, "What did Crow Killer Joe say
about the heart?"

I nodded fervently, "That the heart is the source of all
power."

"And vitality" we said in unison.

Out of the corner of my eye, I saw panic replace the pain
and anger in Voigt's eyes. Jackpot. Without turning, I
proclaimed to Larsson, "Destroy the heart."

Her lupine features curled into a cruel grin, "With pleasure,"
she purred.[132]

---

[132] Odd word to describe a noise coming out of something canine,
but it's the only one I have that really does it justice. I don't know a
word for canine predatory pleasure, but the moment they come up

She slowly stalked forward, obviously relishing the torment stretched across her kinkiller's face. As foolish as it felt to take any time here, seeing the panic plain on his face was wonderfully cathartic. His flailing arms reaching forward, seemingly clawing for purchase on the dirt ground. Larsson stepped over the flailing arms and straddled his back, sinking her claws deep into his body, digging for his heart. Blood welled up and oozed out of Voigt's back as tears of pain streamed down his face. Frantically, his right arm flailed to what seemed to be an effort to hide his tears and shame. The entire thing was a horrifying distortion of the human body, but I couldn't help but watch in morbid fascination.[133]

A large chunk of flesh went flying and I saw Larsson reach for something, presumably the heart. Her grin widened into a full-blown slasher smile.

But then, the arm covering Voigt's face twitched, pulling his head sideways with it. A sickening crack rang out, his head lolling for but a moment before snapping into a natural position and then Voigt's other arm, fully healed, lashed out and grabbed Larsson's leg. The color drained from my face and my bladder nearly emptied.

"Oh fuck," I managed, too shocked by the not quite suicide to do much else.

"Oh, yes," responded Voigt.

---

with one, I'll use it.

[133] Out of the corner of my eye, I noticed Carlson looking away, but McCoy was still watching analytically. Filed that away as interesting information.

Chapter 23: How to Kill an Immortal

Larsson's leg crumpled and cracked under Voigt's pulverizing grasp, the armor like fur unable to deflect the raw crushing strength. McCoy snapped her shotgun back up, but Voigt tugged, causing Larsson to fall and provide him with cover. Unable to get a shot, McCoy pivoted and maneuvered looking for a clear shot. Meanwhile, Carlson ran in, looking to pin Voigt again. He got as far as grabbing the harpoon before Voigt grabbed Larsson like a club, rolled, snapping the harpoon haft in half, and clobbered Carlson with 500 pounds of fur. Carlson flew like a line drive, plowed off his feet and into a tent which promptly collapsed atop him, tangling him inside. McCoy took the clearing to put a slug through Voigt's leg, before Voigt pivoted and put Larsson back as a shield between us.

"Where the fuck did all this come from?" McCoy yelled out, strafing left to get a clear shot.

"Maybe he's desperate or he was trying to lull us into a false sense of security?" I responded, strafing to the right.

McCoy found another angle then and opened up, ending our banter. Her first shot tore into his upper leg and the second found an errant foot. However, by the time the third shot was in the air, Voigt had grabbed Larsson's arm, crushing it as he pulled her overhead like a riot shield. Her armor fur did its thing, but there was still a notable chunk of arm blown away by the slug. Thankfully, McCoy wasn't using silver rounds, probably due to running out, so the wound started stitching itself together and I didn't feel too bad about the unfriendly fire.[134]

There was another sickening crunch as Larsson's arm crumpled and she howled in pain again. Desperate to stop the damage on her, I dropped to the ground and emptied my entire magazine into his right arm. A few stray rounds deflected off Larsson, but apparently it was worth it as the grip loosened and Larsson was able to pull the pulp that was formerly her leg out from his grip. She pivoted and slashed her free hand across the wrist pinning her down. The claws went clean through, splitting flesh, arteries, and tendons as she went. Without grip strength, Voigt couldn't stop her from squirming free. I whooped in triumph when all of a sudden there was another snapping sound as Voigt put his hand to jaw again, resetting himself once more. Whole once more, he reached out towards Larsson. She moved to leap away, but was slowed due to having only one foot, Voigt still clipped her, which caused her planned leap to turn into a disoriented tumble. That tumble, naturally, sent her directly towards me, knocking us both to the ground.

"Ooof," I said as the air was driven out of my lungs.

"Oh, shut up," Larsson responded, starting to stand up, "I'm not that heavy." McCoy, meanwhile, opened up, trying to

---

[134] There's a common expression in the military, "Friendly Fire, isn't." Thankfully, I wasn't in an active combat region since my main duties were acting as a translator and Cultural Liaison for Captain Lee Winters, a Civil Affairs Officer. One of the guards around the camp however, was part of a friendly fire incident as the shooter, crippling an infantry man. The entire incident ruined him mentally, having hurt someone on his own side like that. And the Army sweeping that under the rug to save face only made it worse. In exchange for keeping quiet, he got transferred to a post of his choice, and decided to push for the most quiet job possible, intentionally wanting to be a fobbit. Anyways, long story short, I've seen what that guilt can do to a man, and I'm glad that McCoy wouldn't be crippled from it.

maim Voigt enough that we could reach his heart, but being hampered by Voigt's neck snapping solution to that problem. I remembered an odd trivia factoid from a bad romance movie that stated that a sane human couldn't bite through their own skin. I wondered how many more steps into insanity you had to be where snapping your own neck was okay. Larsson repositioned above me, which put most of her weight on my leg and dragged me back to the present.

"You aren't exactly light either," I said as I managed to help her up. I hazarded a glance at my gun and saw it bent like a boomerang. Slate wasn't going to be happy about replacing it.

She stood, clearly favoring her uncrushed left leg, but starting to put small amounts of weight on the rapidly healing right leg. Even with a good night's rest, I wouldn't consider walking on a crushed ankle. "Damn," I thought, "She really is built to survive." Annoyed, I motioned to Storm Before the Calm and Perilous Truth Seeker, still standing at the edges of the arena. "When are your boys going to tag in for you?"

She growled, flexing her crushed hand's claws experimentally, "They can't, or the kill can't be claimed by me alone, which will weaken my claim as Alpha. The hope is that if I die, they can finish him and *attempt* a contestation by deed."

I hazarded a glance at McCoy, who was darting around keeping Voigt distracted, using his unnatural slowness to her advantage. She wasn't doing much damage anymore, but she was certainly buying time for Larsson to heal. I made a mental note to buy her something nice when this was over.

"And what about us?"

231

Larsson shrugged, as if the response was obvious, "You're not pack. You don't count."

Ignoring the implicit condescension, wheels started turning in my brain again as a new plan started to form. Walking towards the dropped harpoon gun, I asked her curiously, "Does getting Carlson untangled count as helping?"

She paused her self-diagnostic and looked at me curiously, "It could be argued that it doesn't. Do you have a plan?"

I stooped to heft the massive thing, but nearly threw out my back, "A stupid one, but if you can distract Voigt long enough, I might be able to end this in one shot."

She eyed me critically, and I sheepishly shrugged before pointing my head at the frantically dodging and weaving McCoy, "She could do with some help." Larsson nodded and then whistled at SBtC, who lopped off towards the crumpled tent. With a delicate step, she sprinted off towards Voigt, still not quite at full speed, but getting closer by the second.

Meanwhile, I looked at the massive harpoon gun. My predictions about being unable to heft it proved correct. Out of the corner of my eye, I saw blood splay artfully as Larsson knicked Voigt and pulled his attention on to her. McCoy took the distraction to move over towards me, casting a curious eye at the harpoon gun.

"You out of ammo too?" she asked. Voigt was trying to grab Larsson again, but to no avail.

I shook my head, "Larsson bent my gun when she landed on me."

McCoy blew out a deep sigh, "That's rough. So, what's the plan?"

I tapped the cannon with my foot, "We've already established that this can go through his body. Spear the heart out."

She gave the harpoon gun another look, sizing it up. "Ballsy," she declared, "As plans go it's kinda stupid."

I nodded, "Well, it's this or running away and giving him time to rebuild and leaving Larsson out in the wind. Besides, the military is fond of saying. 'If it's stupid and it works, then it isn't stupid.'"

"Fair enough. Though, I don't think we can heft that thing."

Carlson rumbled behind us, "I can though."

I turned[135] to see more of SBtC than I had ever wanted to see. He had returned with Carlson and looked very pleased with himself. Pride in his voice as he declared, "I fetched your errant packmate and got him here without interrupting the Alpha's fight."

McCoy cut in, clearly tired and frustrated, "Good boy, do you want a treat?"

The mirth died and turned to righteous rage. Through bared fangs, he hissed, "I. am. NOT. a. pet."

Carlson stepped in before I could, arms out wide and holding the two of them at arm's length, "We can handle this later, right now we have a Wendigo to harpoon."

---

[135] And in no shape, way, or form, jumped. Nope, not at all.

SBtC bristled, and then leapt away, leaving us to wrangle the harpoon gun.

"Can you not piss off the 400-pound killing machine?" I hissed at McCoy. Out of the corner of my eye, I saw Larsson duck in long enough to score some bleeding wounds before bouncing out of the retaliatory range of Voigt's grasp.

"Oh, shut up," She retorted.

Carlson hefted the harpoon gun with ease, taking a wide stance "Both of you shut up and help me aim this thing. It's got a kick and I've never been the best shot."

"You hit him earlier though," I commented.

Carlson snorted, "I was aiming for between the shoulder blades."

Ah. That was not the kind of error that would be acceptable here. If Voigt caught on to us being clever, there was nothing stopping him from just leaving the next time he pried the harpoon free besides hubris and hunger. We both turned to McCoy who was already sighting Voigt in, "If you can hold it, I can aim it." She peeked up from the sights, "Tennant, can you help guide the harpoon in? Not sure what the ballistic path on a harpoon is like and I'd rather hope for a second chance."

I dug for my telekinesis, "On it."

I slowly visualized a corridor directly between the harpoon gun and Voigt's back, creating an idealized flight path for the harpoon to travel. Distantly, I was aware of Larsson baiting Voigt into walking a straight line away from us. I pushed that from my mind to concentrate on the telekinetic corridor, blocking all else from my mind. I breathed rhythmically and deeply, letting it reinforce my corridor turning a gentle thought into solid will. I had never done this before, but it was a far cry easier than lifting myself had been.

"Ready" I breathed out.

I think Carlson and McCoy said other things, but I was off in my own world of concentration. Faintly, I was aware of another whump, but that was also pushed from my mind as the harpoon entered my telekinetic corridor.

I had been bull riding once. Not the real thing, one of those mechanical numbers at some country bar in Keane County. McCoy had bet me twenty bucks that I couldn't stay on for five minutes. I had won by cheating and using my telekinesis to keep me leveraged on and to mitigate sudden force changes that would throw me off balance. Never hard pushes, which is where most people go wrong, just little adjustments that added up.[136]

This wasn't too different. The harpoon wanted to buck and heave out of the corridor, and I corrected by nudging it, not shoving it back onto course, with a delicate hand. Idly, I was aware of McCoy and Carlson seemingly panicking, but I just kept myself in the zone, free of errant thoughts and giving delicate pushes.[137]

It wasn't until the splatter of blood hit telekinetic barriers that I let the corridor collapse and the breath I had been holding out. The force of the harpoon combined with the sudden loss

---

[136] McCoy paid me back the 20 dollars in mixed drinks that were half alcohol. I might've won the bet, but I didn't win the night.
[137] The one errant thought I had was, "Use the Force Luke!"

of his heart had driven him to his hands and knees, harpoon point barely though his body. Skewered in a raged and oozing mess, his heart convulsed but didn't beat. We all breathed a sigh of relief. It was over. We had won.

And then his hands twitched and reached forward towards the skewered heart.

"Are you fucking shitting me? How can he live without his heart?" Carlson bewilderedly asked. My brain was trying to make the connection, but for now my jaw was just flapping in the wind.

Meanwhile, Voigt tucked his leg up and planted a foot, leveling the harpoon. Larsson, started slashing at him, trying to slow him down, but it seemed to have no effect. His hands grabbed the harpoon and began to push it backwards.

"Hotchkiss," I cursed.

McCoy glared at me, "What?"

"Hotchkiss could live without his heart. That's why the harpoon didn't kill him."

Voigt lashed out with an arm, stopping his motion but forcing Larsson to slide backward so she didn't get caught again.

"Well fuck me sideways. Now what?" McCoy asked incredulously.

I started talking, panic seeping in the form of an increasingly frantic pater. "That should've worked. We've destroyed the heart. There's no seat of vitality left. There's no power. That's why Voigt was eati……"

The logic slammed into me. I yelled at Larsson, "THE HEART! EAT IT! EAT THE HEART!"

I felt the air grow still around me as we all held our breath, waiting for Larsson to move. She stood still for but an instant and then in a blur of movement, she was on Voigt, right arm extended. Her claws clipped his heart before Voigt's right hand crossed and grabbed her wrist, crushing her wrist so thoroughly that her entire hand fell limp and drove her to the ground.

That, however, was just a sacrifice play. Larsson's left hand snaked under his crossed arm and plucked the pulp that was once his heart off. With a quick pounce, she planted her feet on Voigt's chest and pushed, launching herself away. Voigt's grasp didn't let up, which meant that as she flew backward, her entire right hand was left behind, ripping from her body in a sickening tear, blood spraying as she flew.

Still, she was fiercely triumphant as she stood up, battered and punctured heart in hand. Panic and then, for the first time, dread crossed Voigt's eyes as she raised the bits to her mouth. Helplessly, he reached for her, arms striving for something just out of his reach.

"No," was all Voigt managed in a voice that only came across as frightened instead of the sickenly honeyed tones it previously had. He continued as Larsson placed the entire heart in her mouth and started to chew, "I'm supposed to be immortal. I'm supposed to be better than you. This isn't how this is supposed to go."

Larsson just smiled and swallowed.

A shockwave radiated outward, knocking everyone but Voigt from their feet. As I managed to sit up, his frantic pleas turned into wordless screams as seemingly endless chunks of flesh and muscle peeled from his body, piling around him. They oozed ichor outwards, creating a veritable pond of blood. As the process went on, the pattern became apparent as the shedded flesh started to take forms. Numerous hearts, piled around him, coupled with arms, legs, hands, and no small amount of faces.

Disturbingly, some of the parts were too small to be adults.

I wanted to hurl. Carlson did.

And still the process went on. The body parts started to pile up, building underneath Voigt. The blood and bits blurred together, but I couldn't pull my eyes away from the bodily horror that I was certain would plague my nightmares for years to come.

The cascade lasted for several minutes, lifting an increasingly emaciated Voigt, still harpooned higher. Three, five, ten feet off the ground. At the peak, his once proudly tall frame was crumpled and curled, looking more like the cancer patient he had once been. The withered frame slumped, and with that final humiliation a death rattle crept forth. With it, his flesh fell away, revealing a macabre skeleton that the harpoon promptly crushed to dust. Only then I was able to look away.

Chapter 24: Debts Repaid

I closed my eyes and tried really hard not to listen to Carlson's second round of vomit, worried that it would cause me to vomit too. Stupid sympathetic responses. Still, it was filling my ears and flooding my brain and my stomach was lurching, when all sound flooded out by a cacophony of wings.

"Oh, fuck me sideways," McCoy said next to me, looking upwards and seemingly unphased by the entire contents of Carlson's stomach.

I pulled my brain out of the blood pools and saw the horde of crows perched on every available perch as far as the eye could see. Tents, trailers, and cages. All packed with black birds. I didn't trust myself to speak, but I certainly agreed with McCoy. A sweet honey voice spoke from our right, "I do hope we don't need to go through the entire gunpoint mess again."

Crow Killer Joe strode into the clearing, uncaring about the lake of ichor pooled around his bare feet.

I swallowed and moved forward before McCoy's trigger finger got the best of her[138], "Depends on why you're here Joe."

He smiled wide and motioned to the carnage he stood in as if it were simply a puddle, "Oh, I'm just here to thank some people for their help and settle up some debts."

"Oh?"

---

[138] Forgetting that she was out of ammo, if I was totally honest.

239

"Yep," he said, clearly not wanting to elaborate. "Am I free to go about my business?"

"Don't think I can stop you," I confessed.

"Smart boy," he said with a chuckle and smile before walking over to Larsson.

Now that I had a chance to look, Larsson was not looking so hot. Her body was twitching and shaking and there were small puddles of bile around her. Her arms were shaking as a new hand grew in spurts out of her right elbow. It was currently the size of a child's wrist with a baby's hand on the end. Joe tutted, "Oh, you did a good thing here. Stupid, but good. The Wendigo spirit is fighting with yours trying to take over. Take it you don't want that, do you?"

Defiance crossed her face, but vomit came out of her mouth.

"Figured as much," Joe continued, his tone paternal. "I would like to pay my debt to you, incurred from your assistance in killing a Craven One, by stopping you from becoming a Wendigo. Do you accept?" Between the spasms, Larsson weakly nodded.

There was a small chant and then Joe drove the palm of his hand into Larsson's head. She fell backward, rapidly shifting back into human form, leaving behind a ghostly visage of something that was all teeth and anger. Almost immediately it tried to bite at Joe, but he just batted it aside with the back of his hand, causing it to blow into wisps and disappear in the wind. With a ceremonial tone Joe decreed, "The deal is concluded." And then, with a satisfied smile, Joe trudged over to Storm Before the Calm, dragging stray body parts in his wake. Joe amusedly met SBtC's eyes and swung his arm wide, motioning back towards Larsson.

"I would like to pay my debt to you, incurred from your assistance in killing a Craven One, by ensuring that your Alpha is at her strongest for the challenge against her rival. She'll have no Wendigo spirit in her body and her arm will grow back at least as strong as it once was. Do you accept?" SBtC looked at Larsson's body, as whole and unmarred as we had ever seen it and nodded.

"The deal is concluded," Joe stated in a ceremonial tone, before turning to walk away.

"Wait a second, what about us!" McCoy yelled.

As one, the thousands of crow eyes turned to us and glared. I wanted to turn and run, but there was nowhere free from their eyes. Joe's body turned in parts to face us, before striding right up to us, his feet cracking the ground as he walked, his face grim. I gulped, but McCoy was standing her ground, so I did too.

When he inches away, she started speaking. "I would like to consider our debt to you paid, incurred from your assistance in killing a Craven One, by virtue of us also assisting in killing a Craven One. Do you accept?"

A slight smile of amusement cracked Joe's face. It might've been comforting to some, but all I could think about is that those teeth had been used to rip apart human flesh. "Someone's trained you properly," he commented, "You are wise to ask."

McCoy didn't blink, but simply reiterated, "Do you accept?"

Joe's smile widened even further, "Yes, I accept."

To which McCoy responded, face still blank but affecting a similar ceremonial tone, "The deal is concluded."

Joe tilted his head, clearly amused and then turned to Carlson who had found his feet despite the pile of vomit. There was an awkward moment of Joe staring at Carlson and Carlson trying not look at Joe and thus have to see the pile of gore behind him.

Carlson broke first, "Good evening, uh, sir."

Joe just shook his head, voice honied again, "Oh, just call me Joe."

Carlson took a look at the gore that Crow Killer Joe had walked through and his cheery smile and nodded, not willing to argue. Joe asked, "I would like to pay my debt to you, incurred from your assistance in killing a Craven one, by a token of favor. Do you accept?"

Carlson cast a wary eye over at us. I had no idea what to do here, but McCoy fiercely nodded. Carlson nodded, "Uh, yes, I accept."

Joe handed him a single black feather, voice slipping once again from honied to ceremonial "The deal is concluded."

Immediately, there was a storm of crows beating their wings as they took flight simultaneously, we all ducked, despite our best efforts, and when we looked back up, the crows and Joe were gone. I eyed McCoy, "How did you know that we owed him a debt at all?"

She shrugged, moving towards Larsson's unconscious body. "Same way I know how to talk to Vampires and decipher their doublespeak."

I considered that for half a second before realizing she had skirted the question. "That's not an answer," I yelled after her as the sirens started to approach in the distance.

I heard her laugh a little, "No, it is *an* answer. It's just not an answer that satisfies you." Before I could continue, she was offering her hand to a stirring Larsson, talking with her politely, "You best get out of here, lest it officially look like you were colluding with the police."

Larsson took her hand and was pulled up. "I suppose we should. Thank you all."

I waved, "No, thank you. Couldn't have done this without you."

She smiled, and motioned to two followers, "Well, perhaps we'll have to work together again in the future."

Storm Before the Calm nodded along, "Yes, that would be desirable. It is good to see unawakened who aren't complete morons."

I hung my head and pinched my nose. "It was meant as a compliment," I thought to myself, "He's just really bad at compliments." To my right, McCoy chuckled, before saying aloud, "Safe travels everyone."

The air hummed around the werewolves, causing them to blur around the edges, and then start being transparent. After a few seconds, they were gone, leaving us alone with the mountain of carnage and lake of blood.

"So, now what?" Carlson asked.

I motioned towards the flashing lights in the distance, "We sit around for the next few hours, alternating between giving orders, being debriefed, and waiting for someone to come collect the evidence."

"And then we drink," McCoy added, "To celebrate we're alive."

"And so, I can dream without remembering that," I added waving at the carnage.

Carlson hazarded a glance at the devastation again, "Yeah, I could go for a drink."

Epilogue: Movie Night

That night went much as we expected, but what I didn't expect was the horde of media attention that we got. Apparently, 'Morbid Mountains of Mutilated Corpses' was sensation worthy news. The MCD got a lot of credit for dealing with the menace, and several Chicago Aldermen, including Trevor Lockwood and Michelle Fererick[139], lauded us as heroes and advocated for more support for our program. Which led to us getting publicly recognized by the mayor. Slate did the talking for that event, thank god.

However, the popularity spike also led to a dramatic increase in workload. I spent my days traveling all over the city dealing with every single event that may or may not have been metahuman related and answering a few questions for reporters. Spare time was at a premium, but when the buzz died down, it was time for a proper celebration.

I managed to find McCoy late one Thursday afternoon. She had spent most of the day dealing with reports of what seemed to be tiny faeries causing trouble around the University of Chicago campus and was in a horrifically foul mood. Thankfully, I had thought ahead. I knocked on her office door and stuck a plate with a donut into the room before entering myself. There was a shuffle, a snatch, and I heard her say with a stuffed mouth, "What do you want?"

I poked my head in and saw that the donut had already disappeared in its entirety. "We're having a movie double

---

[139] Both major players on the City Council. Fererick was the first openly homosexual Alderman and was loud advocate for both LGBTQ and metahuman rights. Lockwood's rise to power is nothing short of meteoric and there were already rumors that he was planning on running for mayor when Old Man Westervelt went the way of Richard J. Daley.

feature Saturday night. Terminator 1 and 2 at Miles' place to celebrate living. You wanna come?"

She choked on her donut, probably in surprise, and I sat there mildly amused as she alternated between struggling to say yes and coughing up donut. After a few moments, she found the water on her desk, washed the donut down, and glared at me.

"Ass," she stated.

I smiled wider, but didn't argue. "Starts at 7 pm. I'll text you the address," I said, producing another donut from behind my back.

She took that one too and then slammed the door in my face.

"Bring something to share!" I yelled through the door.

****

I spent most of Saturday helping Miles out with some research. Apparently, there had been an incident in Prague where someone with gifts needed to be defibrillated and their powers automatically kicked on as a defense mechanism. Unfortunately for the doctors, their powers dealt with magnetism, and turning those powers on had fried the room as they produced enough magnetic force to burn out the electronic devices and send various medical supplies flying to all corners of the room. Miles had gotten the idea about somehow triggering Carla's own healing powers on herself through a similar process in the hopes of helping her wake up. I was the guinea pig.

"Son of a bitch," I said for at least the fiftieth time that day. Miles looked studious. The first time I had fallen over after getting shocked, he nearly had a heart attack and insisted we stop the entire thing off and stop out of concern for my health. I didn't have the heart at the time to tell him that it was half surprise that I had actually felt something, and had foolishly insisted we continue.[140] Now, even though my responses were getting more severe, Miles had been desensitized. He started setting up another run, ignoring the fact that my arm was still slightly spasming. Desperate for relief, I looked towards the oven. 6:45, people would be showing up soon.

"Hey, not that I don't love this entire thing, but should we wrap it up for the night?"

There was a methodical pause as he placed the paddles back in their recesses and checked his watch. "Didn't realize it was getting so late," he murmured.

"I guess time flies when you're frying people," I jested, trying to pull myself back onto the stool. For the first time in a few hours, concern crossed his face. I worked quickly to squash it, "What, I'm not allowed to make jokes about becoming a...." I sputtered, "I got nothing."

Miles smiled slightly, "Guess that electricity is really getting to you. Best we rest. Pick this up next week?"

I paused, before nodding, "Yeah, let's crack this thing."

---

[140] Miles had insisted we start at the lowest levels and build our way to the point of cardiac arrest level shocks, in the name of scientific rigor. Good idea, but considerate and rigorous did not make for engaging. After about an hour of sitting on a stool and feeling next to nothing as he worked through the lowest settings on the defibrillator, I was half asleep, which is the only reason I fell off the stool.

Miles nodded resolutely and went about packing away the defibrillator and other medical supplies. I managed to plant myself on the stool, and while I wasn't exactly thrilled at letting him do all the cleaning, my legs insisted. Still, it was painfully quiet, so I decided to fill the void with a question that had been nagging at me.

"Hey Miles," I asked shakingly.

"Hrmm?" he asked distractedly.
"When we were in the shade, you told me that I had wings and more. What did you mean by more?"

There was a pause as he stopped cleaning up the wires and looked at me, clearly weighing his words. For someone else, I might've been worried about them trying to spare my feelings, but I knew Miles. This was him trying to find the right words to paint an accurate picture of what he saw.

"They weren't really wings. At least not what we typically think of as wings. They were more a multitude of disparately sized ethereal arms and hands woven together in the semblance of wings?" he tried before shaking his head slightly, not entirely happy with his descriptor.

"Oh?" I managed, not entirely sure what to make of that and struggling to imagine.

He grimaced slightly, looking for clarifying words. "Like, if you weren't paying attention it was definitely wings without any notable features. But the closer you looked the more arms you could see until they didn't look like wings anymore, just entwined limbs coming from a central point. Kinda like one of those many armed Hindu gods?" There was a pause before he added, "Wearing a tactical vest and jeans, which if anything made the entire thing more surreal."

I shot him a disbelieving glance. "What?" he asked defensively, "It was a really odd juxtaposition. I was expecting robes."

I didn't know what to say after that, so we sat in silence trying to internalize the wildly incongruous image. Eventually, our reverie was broken by the doorbell. He took a look at the half-cleaned supplies. "Grab the door while I tidy up?" he asked, motioning towards the door with his head.

"Sure thing," I said, reluctantly standing up.

It wasn't an easy walk. My legs shook and it took far too much energy to make sure I moved in a straight line. I spent too much brain power focusing on each step and hoping a random spasm didn't send me to the floor. When I reached the door, I leaned against the wall, buzzed people in, and waited, not trusting myself to move. I took a few deep breaths and let my healing do its job. After a few seconds, I heard voices in the hallway, which meant that Jacob and McCoy had probably carpooled. I readied myself, so that right when they knocked, I swung the door open, putting me face to face with Lindsey Niccols. I, the embodiment of grace and poise, greeted them with a hearty, "Good Even-I wasn't expecting you."

McCoy laughed and pushed past us with three cases of beer piled high, "Good even-i to you too. I was at the morgue and we got to talking about how the case wrapped up and she mentioned she had Saturday night off, and I invited her. Hope no one minds." I turned to catch her face, and she just winked at me.

I wanted to hug and strangle her at the same time.

249

"I can leave if you want," Lindsey commented from the doorway.

My mind rebooted, "No, no, no, no, no, no. Just caught me by surprise is all."

"Six nos of surprise even," Lindsey quipped with a slight blush and smile, before asking "Bathroom?"

I blushed slightly and moved out of the way so she could come in and pointed her towards the bathroom.

McCoy sidled up to me as she walked out of the room. I looked her dead in the eye and declared, in the same tone she had with me Thursday morning, "Ass."

She chuckled, "Carlson dipped out at the last minute chasing a lead on the leak and I figured payback was in order. Although, she seemed reluctant to show up until I mentioned you'd be here."

"Oh?"

McCoy waggled her eyebrows at me.

I suddenly felt like a flea confronted with a human's shoe, insignificant and at great risk of something catastrophic happening. "Oh," I managed to whisper.

Thankfully, Jacob showed up with his girlfriend, Quinn Michaelis, and was promptly swarmed by people who wanted to meet her, saving me from everyone noticing my blush.[141]

---

[141] He had also apparently invited Jennings, but didn't get a response until three days later. The response was, and I quote,

Eventually, it came time for the movies to start. Jacob and Michaelis had claimed the loveseat very early on, by the din of being a couple, leaving the rest of us to fight over the remaining seats. McCoy had grabbed a stool so that she wouldn't have to maneuver around the lovebirds' tangle of booted feet and Miles grabbed the opposite end of the sofa, leaving just enough room for Lindsey and me to sit next to each other. I suspected Miles and McCoy were conspiring at this point, but I didn't mind. Miles brought out a giant bowl of popcorn, McCoy passed around booze, and we sat back and enjoyed the show.

****

Four and half glorious hours later[142], the credits rolled on Terminator 2 and we broke off into smaller groups. We were all slightly inebriated, McCoy and Jacob more than the rest of us. Lindsey and Michaelis[143] were discussing something. Apparently, Michaelis was getting her doctorate from UIUC where Lindsey had done her undergraduate work, which meant they had quickly bonded over something called 'Unofficial' and had then burrowed themselves in private talk for the majority of the post cinema evening. I wasn't sure what they were talking about since McCoy, who had polished off both the expensive beers I had bought her as a thank you and one of the cases she had brought on her own,

---

"Sorry, I was busy trying to communicate with one of my alternate selves via an entangled aetheric resonance. Long story short, it didn't work and I spent a week and a half talking with myself." And that's why I don't invite Jennings places.

[142] Well not entirely glorious. The bathroom break while we changed disks was decidedly average.

[143] Normally, when someone works their way into being a friend, I call them by their first name. I decided that Michaelis never could be my friend because I didn't want to be confused between her and Quinn Eckles. Coming up with a way to differentiate sounded hard.

was loudly arguing that Voigt would've handily beaten a T-800 in a fight.

"Just look at body count. Voigt killed more and tougher than the T-800. Plus, he isn't programmable, which means he isn't hackable," McCoy loudly advocated.

Miles chimed in, playing the part of devil's advocate and loving it immensely, "I think it depends on how many people Voigt had eaten."

Jacob was in the pro-Terminator camp and thus the brunt of McCoy's ire. The poor bastard. "The number would be irrelevant. The Arnoldator is coming from the future, where they'd have access to our full case files, including how we took down Voigt. Superior information and tactics beats raw power any day."

"Well you're just all kinds of fucking wrong. Firstly, if we're talking prep time, Voigt was an electrical engineer. We could've rigged an electromagnet or something. Secondly, without prep time, raw power will win," McCoy retorted.

"No, cleverness wins. Take a look at the Spartans and you…"

"PREP TIME," McCoy bellowed, cutting them off, "THE SPARTANS HAD PREP TIME WHERE THEY CHOSE THEIR BATTLEGROUND!"

Lindsey caught my eye, and I motioned for the door. She politely disengaged from the short co-ed and met up with me.

"Making friends?" I asked with a teasing tone.

"Maybe," she said, sliding into her coat. "She's slightly socially awkward."

"Aren't all computer people like that?" I asked, sliding my shoes on.

"Maybe, but she seems exceptionally off. Plus, she's really far away going to school in Champaign."

I snorted dismissively, "You're making excuses now."

She laughed slightly, warming the atmosphere and my heart several degrees, "I suppose I am. We exchanged phone numbers. Next time she comes up for a visit, we'll try and set something up."

We slid out the door, heading into the chilly autumn air. She leaned into me and without thought I put my arm around her. It felt right. I soaked in the moment as we walked through the Chicago night.

However, all good things must end. McCoy's insinuations started ringing through my head. I looked over at Lindsey and caught her smiling. Emboldened, I broke the silence.

"Hey Lindsey?" I asked cautiously.

"Mmmmm?" she responded throatily.

"Would you like to go out to dinner and show with me next weekend?"

She stopped, standing up, curiosity sprinkling her eyes, "Are you asking me out on a date?"

Crap. I screwed up. McCoy lied, abort, abort, "Yes." Fuck, why did I say that. Stupid mouth.

She shook her head, a smile growing on her face, "Well, so much for me asking you out."

My brain spun. So many questions and implications. "Huh?" I managed.

"I got tired of being old-fashioned and waiting for you to ask me on a date, so I was going to ask you out. You beat me to the punch by like five seconds."

I stood flabbergasted for the five seconds she would've needed. It wasn't supposed to be that easy. Eventually, I found my voice and asked, "So, that's a yes to next Saturday?"

Her smile fully blossomed as she almost tackled me, arms wrapping around, and squeezing me in my hug. Nuzzled in my chest, she spoke. Her voice was probably muffled, but I could hear every word, "Of course it's a yes."

No sarcasm, I could tell this relationship was off to an excellent start.

Bonus Chapter: Many Years Later

It started with a telltale crash in the other room. Between my children, nieces and nephews, and now grandchildren, I knew what that meant. Nora, my daughter, hung her head in frustration. "Sorry dad. That sounded expensive. I thought leaving Cara in charge would prevent that."

I laughed despite myself, talking as I stood up. "They're kids. They break things. I remember when you were a kid and you and your brother just had to get the boardgames down yourself. Never mind the fact that it was atop the bookshelf with all…"

"DAD!" she yelled at me, blushing slightly.

Marcus, her husband, reached over and put a hand on her arm, "Now, I could stand to hear a bit more. Put us on even footing for all the embarrassing stories my folks have told you."

I chuckled again, making my way towards the den where the noise had come from, "Let's deal with the young'uns first. And then I'll see if I can't find the old photo albums. I think we took pictures of the entire mess."

Behind me Nora groaned, and Marcus laughed, but they stood up to follow me.

The den, as expected was a slight mess. Three guilty grandchildren stood around a broken curio case. Before I could even ask the question, the blame game started.

"...Cara wasn't in the room, she was busy texting with...."
"...And then Timmy shoved me...."
"... Well you hit me!"
"Did not!"

I put a hand up and they all quickly fell silent. In my best grandfatherly tone, I asked, "Anyone hurt?"

"No."
"No."
"Just my ego."

I did my best not to glare at Sam for being a smart ass, and instead smiled as warmly as I could. "Well, then we'll just have to clean it up. Timmy, go grab a garbage bag. Sam, get the broom and dustpan. Cara," I paused fumbling for something for her to do, "Let your grandmother know that there's nothing to worry about. You probably woke her from your nap with your shenanigans."

There was a small chorus of "Yes Sir," as they went off to complete the tasks. Nora and Marcus looked in behind me. "Do you want us to help pay for the damages?" Marcus asked.

I chuckled, "No, no. There's no need for that. I've got money to spare at this point and you've got two leaving for college in the next three years. It's just wood and glass." Casually, I reached out with my mind and righted the cabinet, sliding it back into the corner. I glanced over my shoulder at the two of them, "Although, I wouldn't say no to having Sam and Cara help with setting the glass panels and fixing the damages they made once the replacements come in. Probably be in a week or two."

Nora smiled and nodded, "And I'd imagine you'll want them for the entire weekend too. Take Timmy just because."

I smiled back at her, "You know me so well. It's almost like you're related to me."

We laughed for a bit. Timmy made it back with the garbage bag first. He was the youngest and thus the most inclined to try his hardest to make up for his mistakes. No room for half measures in his five-year-old mind. "Thanks kiddo, good job. Now, can you very carefully pick up the big pieces and put them in there." He nodded rapidly and went to work.

Cara came back next and stood quietly in the corner. She was the oldest at 18 and thus the one who understood things the most. I was ninety percent certain she had pieced together what my metahuman abilities were but was respectful enough about my privacy not to bring it up. Probably why she had left the room on such a blatant distraction without question. I cast her a considerate eye.

"Grandma's awake and, once she checked after us, mildly annoyed." She confessed with a sigh, "She'll probably be down soon."

I nodded and went back to supervising Timmy. Nora and Marcus caught my eye and then stepped out, presumably to talk about the logistics of their child free weekend coming up. Good, they could do with the break.

Sam slid in behind them. Sam had taken to dressing in baggy black clothing and using they pronouns recently as puberty sunk its hormonal claws in deeper. They were fifteen and frustrated at everything, which included their uncertainty about what gender they were and how accepting their family was about the questioning process. Sullenly, they went to hand me the broom. I cocked an eyebrow at them, "You've got arms, don't you?"

"Cara didn't have to clean," they complained.

"Cara also wasn't in the room when the curio cabinet broke," I cut off the incredulous stares with a simple question, "Did you forget I did this for a living?"

Humbled, Sam went to work sweeping up the bits of glass too small for Timmy pick up safely. I leaned against the wall next to Cara supervising. After a few moments she spoke up, "Hey Grandpa?"

I recognized that tone. It was the same tone her mother had when she was going to ask a really uncomfortable question. Bracing myself, I spoke to her without turning my head, "What's up kiddo?"

"How come you never talk about your time with the Marshals?"

Timmy and Sam both stopped to look at me, curious. It wasn't an unfair question, especially since I was entirely willing to talk about my time in the military. I shrugged slightly, "Because your parents asked me not to."

"That's bullshit," Sam declared angrily. Timmy gasped and I gave Sam my best reproachful look.

"Rephrase please."

They grimaced slightly, but responded, "We're practically adults. I mean, aren't you the one who said once you can drive, you're all but an adult? Why can't we know?"

As much as I hated to concede the point, he wasn't wrong. "That's a fair point. Are you sure you want to know?"

I thought their necks would break given how hard they were nodding. "Well, I'll talk to you parents and we'll see what we can do about that."

****

Two weeks had flown by before I knew it. Nora made a point of walking the kids up to the door personally and ushering them into the house so she could have a private word with me. All it took was a word about Grandma having made fresh muffins and there was a series of quick goodbyes and a stampede away from the door.

Nora a fixed me with a firm stare that she clearly got from her mother, "Marcus and I discussed it and…." she pursed her lips, struggling to admit it, "You're right. They deserve to know. Can't keep treating them like kids."

I smiled magnanimously, "They were going to figure it out anyways. Hell, I bet Cara already has. Not exactly like it's not hard to find."

Nora shrugged noncommittally before responding, "Harder than most people know how to search these days."

I laughed a little but conceded the point. She continued, "But not Timmy. He's a bit young for how graphic those stories get."

I nodded, having already come to that conclusion myself. "So, after we tuck him in."

259

She nodded, "You don't have to do this you know. I know how hard it was for you to write it down in the first place as part of therapy."

I pursed my lips and nodded but didn't say anything. I didn't have to. She knew me well enough to know that I wasn't going to back down from my trauma. We Tennants liked to face it head on. It's how my father did it. It's how I did it. And, despite her reservations, it's how Nora did it too.

She pulled me in for a hug, "Don't let them keep you up too late."

I hugged her back and laughed, "That's never exactly been the issue with me."

She laughed into my chest, "Fair enough dad. Don't let them stay up too late. Love you, I'll see you Monday."

****

Timmy responded to being left out of story time as well as you'd expect a five-year-old to.

"But it's not fair!" he whined.

I smiled, "No, but neither is life. Your mother and I have agreed you can find out when you're older."

He pouted, but I was prepared. "Grandma made hot chocolate for you and gave you extra marshmallows as an apology."

He sniffled but moved out of the den and towards the kitchen. Cara and Sam looked after him and then looked to me.

"Well, then. Let's get started." I said, patting my leg and standing up. I made my way over to a covered shelf, unlocked the cabinet that had no key with a telekinetic lockpick, and pulled out an old and battered book.

I turned back to a smiling Cara and a confused Sam. "I knew it," Cara proclaimed.

Sam looked confused, "How did you do that?"

I smiled and waited for the comprehension to set in. "Oh," Sam managed very quietly.

I patted the book, "Back when I was still a Marshal, I saw some things and was recommended to therapy. As part of that process, my therapist recommended that I write down my stories to process through them. This is the first truly serious case I went through. Lots of explanations in it. I figure," I said, hefting the book, "We can take turns reading it aloud, so you all get the full picture. I'll fill in any bits and add color commentary as we go. Sound acceptable?"

There were some murmurs of discontent that I silenced with a meaningful look.

"Yes sir."
"Yes sir."

I sat back and smiled, "Well then, I guess I'll go first."